W9-ACY-062

SNAKE IN THE GLASS

This Large Print Book carries the
Seal of Approval of N.A.V.H.

Southington Library & Museum
255 MAIN ST
SOUTHINGTON, CT 06489

SNAKE IN THE GLASS

SARAH ATWELL

WHEELER PUBLISHING
A part of Gale, Cengage Learning

GALE
CENGAGE Learning

Detroit • New York • San Francisco • New Haven, Conn • Waterville, Maine • London

GALE
CENGAGE Learning

Copyright © 2009 by Penguin Group (USA) Inc.
A Glassblowing Mystery.
Wheeler Publishing, a part of Gale, Cengage Learning.

ALL RIGHTS RESERVED
This is a work of fiction. Names, characters, places, and incidents either are the product of the author's imagination or are used fictitiously, and any resemblance to actual persons, living or dead, business establishments, events, or locales is entirely coincidental. The publisher does not have any control over and does not assume any responsibility for author or third-party Web sites or their content.

Wheeler Publishing Large Print Cozy Mystery.
The text of this Large Print edition is unabridged.
Other aspects of the book may vary from the original edition.
Set in 16 pt. Plantin.
Printed on permanent paper.

LIBRARY OF CONGRESS CATALOGING-IN-PUBLICATION DATA

Atwell, Sarah.
   Snake in the glass / by Sarah Atwell. — Large print ed.
    p. cm. — (A glassblowing mystery)
    ISBN-13: 978-1-4104-2312-2 (softcover : alk. paper)
    ISBN-10: 1-4104-2312-3 (softcover : alk. paper)
    1. Glassworkers—Fiction. 2. Murder—Investigation—Fiction.
   3. Glass blowing and working—Fiction. 4. Large type books.
   I. Title.
   PS3601.T83S63 2009
   813'.6—dc22   2009047419

Published in 2010 by arrangement with The Berkley Publishing Group, a member of Penguin Group (USA) Inc.

Printed in the United States of America
1 2 3 4 5 6 7 14 13 12 11 10

For my grandmother,
Ruth Hamilton Floyd,
who gave me my first peridot.

ACKNOWLEDGMENTS

Gems have always fascinated people, so of course glassblower Em Dowell has to check them out when she's looking for glass ideas. Besides, she lives in Tucson, home of the annual Tucson Gem and Mineral Show, the largest in the world, so she couldn't ignore them completely.

Less well known is the fact that the San Carlos Indian Reservation not far from Tucson is the world's primary source for the gemstone peridot — a fact that Em learns quickly, but for the wrong reasons. However, the events and individuals associated with the reservation are purely my own invention.

Thanks as always go to my agent, Jacky Sach of BookEnds, and my tireless editor, Shannon Jamieson Vazquez of Berkley Prime Crime. The dealers at the International Gem and Jewelry Show in Marlborough, Massachusetts, taught me a lot about

7

displaying and selling stones, and Gail Clark served as another set of eyes and ears at the show. And once again, the faithful members of Writers Plot, Sisters in Crime, and the Guppies were behind me all the way.

My husband didn't complain when I kept bringing home more gems "just for research!" My daughter still prefers the glassblowers of Cape Cod, who continue to provide me with both inspiration and practical information.

Glass is more gentle, graceful, and noble than any metal and its use is more delightful, polite, and sightly than any other material at this day known to the world.
— Antonio Neri, *The Art of Glass*

PROLOGUE

If a glass article cools too quickly, internal stresses develop and can lead to spontaneous breakage.

Sunday

"Another one, huh?" The assistant at the Pima County Medical Examiner's Office slouched against the wall of the building, watching his colleague pull a body bag out of the back of the van. He tossed the half-smoked cigarette away and stepped forward to help wrestle the bag onto the waiting gurney. "Any details?"

"Nope. Adult male, doesn't look like he's been out there long. No ID, nothing on him except some pebbles in his pocket."

"Hey, kid, if he's been out in the desert, it's hard to tell how long he's been there. At least he's not a mummy like some of 'em. How'd they find him?"

"Border Patrol noticed the birds. He

wasn't on one of the usual routes. Looks like he didn't want to be identified."

"Or someone didn't want him to be. Most people who cross the border, they've got something on 'em — picture of family, religious medal maybe. Could be he was traveling with a pal who thought he had something worth taking."

"That's lousy. You make it this far. . . . You think somebody killed him? I didn't see any marks on the body."

"I'll take a look, when I get a chance. It's probably nothing to worry about. Maybe he got lost, or maybe someone gave him lousy directions. These guys who get 'em across the border — they don't care squat about what happens to 'em next, as long as they've got their money. You got the paperwork?"

"Sure do." The younger man pulled a folded piece of paper out of his shirt pocket and handed it to him. "All there, by the book. What happens to him now?"

"No ID? We tag him as John Doe number whatever — I think we're up to thirteen already this year. We hold him until we can do an autopsy. Then, if nobody claims him after a few months, we'll probably end up cremating him."

"Poor guy. Not a good way to go. Somebody ought to miss him."

"Yeah, somebody should, but they may be out of luck."

CHAPTER 1

Waterford glass is known for prismatic cutting to create multirayed stars and sharply cut diamonds in wide fields or bands.

The Previous Friday . . .

On a good day it takes eighteen hours to fly from Dublin to Tucson. Thanks to the vagaries of February weather and customer-unfriendly airlines, it turned out to be closer to twenty-four, and I was ecstatic to arrive at the Tucson airport on Friday. At least, I thought it was Friday, but then, I thought it had been Friday when I left Ireland. I could have kissed the cacti in the parking lot, I was so giddy. Jet-lagged or not, I figured I could handle the few miles to my downtown shop and the apartment I lived in above it. Luckily I remembered where I had left the car.

As I drove carefully home, relishing the intense sunshine and the sandy terrain dot-

15

ted with saguaros and ringed by mountains (Arizona brown! Not Irish green!), I tried to sort through what I had to do. My brother Cam's plans had been vague when I left.

My brother Cameron is a high-end computer geek. He's a sweet, somewhat shy man with a genius for manipulating code. No, he's not one of those nerdy guys who loves to talk gibberish and tinker with the wire guts of computers, and he doesn't create animated games for teenage boys where things blow up loudly and spatter the screen with body parts, thank goodness. Instead, before he'd committed himself to the cyberworld, he had taken some biology and ecology classes, and now he specialized in modeling environmental systems, calculating things like the long-term impact of increased housing on dwindling aquifers. At least, that's what I thought he did. If there is a computer gene, it missed me. And luckily in my line of work — creating artisanal glassware — computers don't figure much. But I was eight years older than he was, forty-something to his thirty-something, and the world had changed rapidly in those years, when we were younger. It was enough for me that he liked what he did and apparently he was good at it.

Normally I was thrilled when Cameron came to Tucson, but this time I had to admit I had mixed feelings. Only a couple of months earlier, Cam had fallen madly in love with my sales assistant Allison Mc-Bride, who had dropped into our lives as a woman on the run, immediately awakening a chivalrous side of Cam that I hadn't known he possessed — and I don't think he had either.

Falling in love with Allison had thrown a monkey wrench into Cam's neatly organized life, and now he was in the process of relocating to Tucson to be closer to Allison. Once the way was clear for Cam's romantic intentions, he'd acted with what for him amounted to lightning speed. For the past several years he had been living and working in San Diego, although he could probably count on the fingers of one hand the number of times he had actually spent time on a beach. It was near enough to Tucson that he could make the six-hour drive to visit me several times a year, and since he was the only close relative I had, that made a difference. We had been muddling along quite well for years now.

But the advent of Allison in his life had made him impatient, and suddenly San Diego seemed a lot farther away from

Tucson. So he had resigned from his job and found one here, at what he described to me as a start-up company supporting desert ecology and sustainable development. I think. It sounded right up his alley when he described it, and I applauded his effort to preserve the fragile deserts I had come to love.

In any case, he was in the midst of a move, leaving one job and packing up before starting his new one. He had allowed himself a couple of weeks between the end of his old job and the start of the other, and he had intended to use the time to find a place to live in Tucson — and to hang out with Allison.

The bottom line was I wasn't sure where Cam was at the moment: in San Diego, in Tucson, or somewhere in between. And much as I adored my brother, I really didn't want to see him right away — because while I had left for Ireland with Allison, I wasn't coming back with her. That should teach me to try to be nice to people: I'd made what I thought was a friendly offer to take Allison on an impromptu trip to Ireland, the country of her birth, which she hadn't seen since she'd eloped as a teenager over twenty years ago. Allison had decided she wanted to stay on for a bit (length of time unspecified), and could I please tell my lovelorn brother that she might not be coming back? Allison's decision to get to know the relatives she had left behind decades ago certainly muddied things. Not that I didn't understand her need to reconnect, but I did resent her asking me to do her dirty work rather than telling Cam herself.

But right now I just wanted to go home and get reacquainted with my pups Fred and Gloria (had I ever been separated from them for this long?), take a long shower, and sleep for a week. Maybe then I'd be ready to sit down and talk to him. Otherwise, in my befuddled, jet-lagged state, I was sure to say the wrong thing.

I pulled the car into the alley behind my glass shop, Shards. The building had formerly housed a small machine shop, and I had taken over the whole thing, fitting out a glass studio and sales area downstairs, and my living space upstairs. A tiny bit of guilt nagged at me: I really should check in with Nessa, my long-term shop assistant and friend, in the shop, to make sure I still had a business. But since the building was still standing and the windows were intact, I decided to assume the best, and instead I tiptoed up my exterior stairs and, inserting my key in the lock, braced myself for a rapturous welcome from Fred and Gloria.

I was not disappointed. Fred, a wire-haired dachshund with a Napoleon complex, made dashes at my feet, barking all the while. Gloria, a more substantial and dignified English bulldog, maintained a cool demeanor until Fred had worn himself out. Me, I dropped my bags and sat on the floor and wallowed in doggy love for several minutes. When we had all had our fill, at least temporarily, I struggled back to my feet and looked around. No sign of human occupation, which meant Cam was still somewhere else. I will admit to a small sigh of relief. But the dog's dishes had been filled recently, so someone — probably Nessa, in whose care I'd left the doggies — had been here recently.

I spotted not one but two notes on the table in the kitchen area, weighted down with jars of salsa, which immediately started my mouth watering. Irish food was bland, and airline food was not food at all. But first things first: I picked up the notes. One was from Cam:

Went back to SD to pick up the last of my stuff — the rest is in Bedroom #2. Back Friday for good. Love, C.
PS Can't wait to hear about your trip.

I sighed, relieved: I had a reprieve, even if it was only for twenty-four hours. I could gather my wits before I had to confront Cam. The second note was from Nessa:

Stop by when you get back. All is well, or at least quiet. Nessa.

I guessed I owed it to Nessa to tell her I was back, which put a damper on my plan to fall directly into bed. But food first. I couldn't remember the last time I had eaten, but it was definitely in some other time zone, or country, or both. The fridge held reasonably fresh bread and some non-moldy cheese, so I threw together a sandwich, adding a bit of salsa to give it flavor. The dogs stayed no more than a foot from my feet. Was it love or the cheese?

Buoyed by my gourmet feast, I headed for the door, reassuring the dogs that I would be back very soon and then I wouldn't leave them again for, oh, maybe twelve hours. They didn't look as though they believed me. I clattered down the stairs and went around to the corner of the building and into my shop.

Nessa looked up from the catalog she had been reading and pulled off her reading glasses, breaking into a smile. "Em, welcome home! How was your trip?"

"I can say with assurance that Ireland is indeed very green."

"So I've been told," Nessa said wryly. "Did Allison enjoy the trip?" Nessa had worked with me for years and knew me well, and she must have seen something in my face. "What is it?"

The kindness of her expression made me want to throw myself on her and bawl. Definitely not my usual style. I must have been more jet-lagged than I thought. "Oh, Nessa . . ." I said weakly.

Nessa looked around the empty shop and then back at me. "I think we can take this upstairs, if you want to talk about it."

"I guess." I wasn't sure if I really did, but I wanted an ally and a sounding board before I had to break the news to Cam. I watched as Nessa shut down the cash register, turned off the lights, and locked up. Then I led the way back up the stairs, and the dogs and I went through the whole welcome thing again, compounded now by Nessa's arrival.

Inside, Nessa made a beeline for the stove. "You look like you could use a cup of tea."

I'm not wild about tea, but I appreciated the gesture. What I really wanted was the mothering that Nessa so happily offered.

"Sure. Hey, thanks for taking care of the dogs. I hope it wasn't too inconvenient."

"Not at all. You know I love them." Nessa had filled the teakettle and set in on the stove, and was now rummaging around for mugs.

I tried to remember whether I even had tea bags. Apparently I did. I sat in a funk until Nessa had assembled the basics and set a mug of tea in front of me.

"All right. Tell me what's going on."

I decided I might as well jump straight into it. "Allison didn't come back with me."

"Ah."

"Yes. Ah." The bitterness of my tone surprised me. "And she didn't have the guts to tell Cam herself. She wants me to do it."

"Will she be coming back?"

"I don't know. I don't think *she* knows." I sipped at my tea, trying to calm myself. "Look, I know it's kind of a shock for her, going back to a place she hadn't been in twenty-odd years, seeing all her relatives, all grown up now. It's weird. It's a pretty small town, in the middle of nowhere, and the place itself has barely changed at all, so I can imagine that she might feel she's in some kind of time warp. I can certainly sympathize with that." Especially because I had so few relatives myself, apart from

Cam. "But I think she owes Cam something. Don't you? I guess the fact that she couldn't face him — even over the phone — makes me wonder just how committed to him she is."

Nessa looked down at her mug, swirling the tea round and round. "I think that she has some catching up to do, learning to deal with the real world, without her late husband's influence. But I also agree that that should involve facing up to her responsibilities and talking to Cam herself."

"That's what I thought. Oh, hell, Nessa, I know that Cam is kind of over the top about her. He's never really been in love before, so maybe he's been storing it up all these years. And if I were on the receiving end of that, I might run the other way too, even without Allison's baggage. He can be pretty intense. It's just that I don't want to hurt him, and I guess I'm pissed at Allison for putting me in this position. It's not fair."

"It isn't, but neither is life. Would you like some more tea?"

I looked at Nessa then and realized she was kidding me. "And sympathy? No, I'm good. And thank you for letting me vent. I must say I'm glad Cam won't be back until tomorrow — I need time to think, when my brain isn't quite so addled." I swallowed the last of my tea. "Oh, by the way, we saw Allison's Uncle Frank while we were in Ireland. He said he was coming to Tucson for the Gem Show, any day now."

"Really." Nessa's serene expression didn't change.

"Nessa! Did you know?"

Was that a blush? "He might have mentioned it."

"Nessa, you sly dog, you. Carrying on behind my back."

"I wouldn't call a few letters 'carrying on.' And a couple of e-mails."

I smiled at her. "Well, Nessa, old friend, you have my blessing. I like Frank, and I'm glad he's coming back. Although how you two can manage any sort of relationship with several thousand miles between you is beyond me."

"One step at a time. And I don't see that proximity has made your relationship with Matt any easier."

Matt Lundgren, Tucson's chief of police, and I had had an on-again, off-again relationship for years — the "off" part came when his wife had returned from a so-called trial separation. The "on-again" part was the positive result of some unpleasant business that had taken place in my glass studio a few months back. "True. I should call him and let him know I'm back. I told Frank we should all get together while he's here."

"I'm sure we will. So, tell me all about Ireland." A neat deflection on Nessa's part.

"Cold! Most of the time I was wearing about seven layers of clothes, and it still wasn't enough." Nobody had bothered to tell me that Ireland in February would be freezing. And that they really weren't into central heating over there. "Maybe cold alone I could have handled, but not the damp. Even the room at the B & B wasn't a whole lot warmer than the outside."

Em, you are now officially a Tucsonan. I had missed my adopted hometown's justly renowned "dry heat." I might've grown up on the East Coast, but ten years in Tucson had changed my metabolism, and I just didn't do cold and wet anymore.

"We put the stone on Allison's mother's grave — that's why Frank was there — and had a nice service, and there were all these relatives. I gave up trying to figure out who was related to whom. Allison was kind of overwhelmed, at least at the beginning, but after a couple of days she seemed to slip right back into it."

"Did you get to see anything else?"

"A bit. I went to Waterford to see how they handle glass — it's a very different technique, and it's not really my style, but it was interesting. And I spent a day or two in Dublin — some gorgeous collections in the museums there. That's about it." A wave of fatigue washed over me. "Listen, Nessa, I really have to crash. I'm sure there's business stuff we should go over, but my brain is fried right now. I'll be down bright and early in the morning, okay?"

"Not a problem, my dear. You catch up on your sleep. I'm sure things will look better in the morning."

Half an hour later, the dogs walked, fed, and watered; myself scrubbed and tucked in, I was ready for oblivion. But my last conscious thought was, *Poor Cam. . . .*

CHAPTER 2

Iron impurities in the sand and limestone used in glassmaking can discolor the glass.

I awakened before dawn — my internal time clock was still operating on Irish time, which was hours ahead of Tucson. I tried to calculate how many and gave up. But at least I felt ready to take on the day and whatever came with it. When I stumbled out of my bedroom, I noted that there were more boxes stacked in the living area, so apparently Cam must've arrived while I was dead to the world. His bedroom door was shut, so on tiptoe, I did the necessary stuff, fed and walked the dogs, and went down to the studio, grateful for a chance to take a fresh look at things without distractions.

There was one big issue at the top of my to-do list. When I had first opened my studio, I had plowed just about all my available capital into buying the building, which I had figured would provide everything I needed — a roomy studio, a corner shop with good visibility, and living quarters above. Of course, the so-called living quarters had consisted of a single open space with brick walls and a poured concrete floor, but since it was just me living there, I could build it out as time and money allowed. The main living areas were still pretty much a single space, but I had carved out two bedrooms and installed a spacious bathroom between them. It suited me, and Fred and Gloria when they had come along.

Since money had been tight, I'd made do with a lot of secondhand glassblowing equipment in the studio. Some items were essential: a midsize pot furnace that held a crucible to melt and hold the glass at the right temperature, a couple of glory holes to work the individual glass pieces, an annealer to cool the finished pieces. A number of blowpipes, a pipe warmer. Benches to work at could be improvised, as could some of the other bits and pieces, like water buckets for the wooden tools. Some of the bigger pieces I had bought used, including the furnace. I'd replaced the relatively fragile pot inside the furnace more than once, but then the outer portion — the insulating castable refractory, to use the precise term — had cracked, and that meant it was time to replace the whole piece before things got any worse.

I'd had my eye on a larger, freestanding furnace, which would cut my energy costs, but it had seemed beyond my modest means. Then a nice little windfall had fallen into my lap, so for once I had some money in the bank. The trip to Ireland had been my treat to myself (and Allison); the new furnace was a business investment — a five-figure one. I had ordered it and entrusted its installation to Nessa's oversight, but now it was up to me to break it in. Even if it worked perfectly, I would still have to get the feel of it, find out where its sweet spots were, and how quickly it heated glass. That was one of the reasons I had scheduled the installation for this particular time period: I knew that business would be slow — more like nonexistent — during the annual Tucson Gem Show, and I had planned to use that period as my break-in time.

The world-renowned Gem Show, or to give its full title, the Tucson Gem, Mineral and Fossil Showcase, is a wondrous event — if you are into gems, which I am not. The event, or rather, events, takes over the entire city for two weeks every year. There are hundreds of vendors and dealers who show up and occupy fifty or so venues, and snap up every hotel room for miles. And that doesn't even include the visitors, or as they are sometimes known, treasure hunters. One might think that a small business person such as myself would welcome this influx of potential customers, but alas, they were all focused on gems, and not easily diverted. The net result was that business for the rest of us Tucson artisans was pretty much flat during the first two weeks in February, which is why I felt I could leave for a week to take a vacation of sorts, and why I could install and test new equipment. And the added benefit this year was that Frank Kavanagh was coming to see the show. I really liked Frank, an Australian diamond dealer and a real charmer. So, apparently, did Nessa.

I stood in the midst of my studio and stared at the new furnace against the back wall. Glass furnaces are seldom pretty things, and this was no exception. But it was clean and whole and, I hoped, properly connected. There was only one way to find out, so I loaded up a new crucible with clear glass, set it in place, and studied the control panel, tweaking a few settings before turning it on. I looked at my watch — I needed to know how long it would take to come to the right temperature to melt the glass. But the interior was glowing nicely. So far, so good.

I could see through the window between the shop and the studio that Nessa had come in and was setting up for the day. I turned my back on the furnace to return to the shop.

"Morning, Nessa. Listen, if Allison is going to be gone for a while, we'll need to work out some sort of coverage for the shop, although things should be pretty slow while the Gem Show's on. I can cover some of the time, but I should do some work and build up my inventory of glass, or you won't have much to sell when business picks up again."

Before she had a chance to answer, I heard the front door open and close again, and turned to find Cam. *Oh no.* I wasn't ready to talk to Cam. Unfortunately I had no choice.

"Hi, Em, Nessa. Em, you were snoring away when I came in last night. What were you saying about Allison? She hasn't answered my phone calls."

Nope, no way around it. I took a deep breath. "Cam, it's great to see you. I can't wait to tell you about the trip, but first I have to talk to you about Allison." I glanced at Nessa, who was suddenly very busy dusting the glass shelves. "Let's go upstairs."

Cam gave me an odd look, then followed me wordlessly out of the shop, up the stairs, and into my home. He barely let me get through the door and shut it before he turned and confronted me. "Is she all right?"

"She's fine, Cam. It's just that . . . Why don't we sit down?"

He remained standing. "Em, you're waffling, and that's not like you. Where is she?"

I swallowed. "She's still in Ireland. She wanted to stay a little longer, since she hasn't been there since she got out of school, and there are so many relatives to catch up with. . . ."

Cam was staring at me, his eyes cold. "When is she coming back?" he said tightly. "Or maybe I should ask, *is* she coming back?"

Trust Cam to get right to the point. "Cam, I don't know. It all just came up, and she asked me to tell you —"

He interrupted me, and now I could see that he was angry. "She asked *you* to tell me? She didn't have the decency to pick up the phone and talk to me?"

"I think she wasn't sure how to tell you,

and she didn't want to hurt you, so . . ."

". . . so she took the coward's way out," he said, finishing the sentence for me. "And she let you do her dirty work, after all you've done for her." I'd never seen my brother so angry and so icy at the same time.

"Cam, listen to me! She just needs some time to figure things out. The last few months have been hard, and I thought we could use the vacation, go somewhere away from here and have some fun. I wish you could have come with us. . . ." I trailed off. Who was I making excuses for?

Cam's face changed: his anger faded into sadness. "I wish I had." I could almost see his pretty castles in the air crumbling before his eyes. The woman he loved had blown him off and hadn't even bothered to tell him face-to-face. This little scene was as bad as I had expected, and there was nothing I could do about it. I wanted to grab onto Cam and hold him until the pain passed, but it really wasn't my place to do that. He'd have to deal with it on his own.

"I see," he muttered, more to himself than to me. "That's how much I matter to her." He straightened his shoulders, and I could almost see him shaking off the pain, like a dog shaking water from its coat. "I'm sorry she put you in the middle of this, Em. I thought . . . I don't know what I thought. Listen, I've hauled most of my stuff in and stuck it in the second bedroom. But I've lined up a freelance project here. . . . I think I'll just take a few days, go somewhere else, and work on that, if you don't mind."

"Cam, why would I mind? I'm glad you've got something to work on. You don't have to start the new job for another week or two, right?" *If you still want that job, now that your reason for being in Tucson is on another continent.* Well, there was still me, but that wasn't quite the same thing. And maybe it was a good idea for Cam to be somewhere else while he digested Allison's betrayal. Or what must feel like a betrayal. I didn't even dare ask about his plans for apartment hunting. Of course, he was welcome to stay with me as long as he liked, and he knew that. "What's the company called?"

"SDE." When I looked blank, he went on. "Sustainable Desert Ecology."

"Right. Listen, you can hang around through dinner tonight, can't you? I'd love to tell you about . . ." I censored myself again: the last thing he would want to hear about right now was Ireland. "Hey, Frank's headed for Tucson. He should be here in a day or two."

That at least brought a spark of interest.

"Frank? What's he doing here?"

"He said he wanted to see the Gem Show — he's never been, and he's heard about it even in Australia. He's planned to meet up with some people who came for the show."

"You talked to him?"

"Of course. He was there in Ireland. Oh." So Cam hadn't known that either. "I think he came as a surprise for Allison. He even set up a wake of sorts for her mother, his sister."

"And a good time was had by all, no doubt," he said bitterly.

"Cam." I reached out a hand but dropped it again. I was pretty sure there was nothing I could say or do right now that would make him feel better, no matter how much I wanted to. "I've got to get some work done, but I'll be right downstairs. We can talk about this later, okay?"

He shrugged. "I think I'll take a rain check on dinner — I may be busy. But give me a call on my cell phone when Frank shows up."

I couldn't think of anything to say that would help, so I turned and fled.

Downstairs, Nessa looked up when I came in and cocked an eyebrow at me. "That didn't go well, I take it?"

"As well as you'd expect. Damn! How did

I get stuck in the middle of this?"

"Because you have a good heart, Em. And you never know how things will turn out. Besides, I wouldn't be so quick to write Allison off."

I leaned against the wall and stared at her. "What, you're defending her? After what she just did to Cam?" Then I processed what she had said. "You think she's coming back?"

"We'll see. Em, I think you have to look at Allison as though she never had a chance to grow up. Her husband kept her isolated from the world, from friends. So she has a lot of catching up to do, and that takes more than a week. I think she's come a long way since we first met her, but perhaps all our lives might have been easier if Cam hadn't fallen for her." When I started to protest, Nessa held up a hand. "What is, is. If she loves him, she'll be back. When she's ready."

"I know — I do understand. I just hope Cam hangs on that long. Right now he's not a happy camper." I pushed myself off from the wall. "Well, we've got work to do. How were sales while I was gone?"

"About what you'd expect. . . ."

And we were off, immersed in the normal day-to-day minutiae of running a business.

There was only one interruption: a call

37

from Matt, midafternoon. "Hey, lady, welcome back. How was it?"

"Interesting. Cold. Complicated. Boy, am I glad to be back!"

"Do you have time for dinner tonight?"

"That would be great, if I don't fall asleep first. My body seems to be stuck in another time zone. But for you I'll make a special effort."

He chuckled. "I'll try to make it early, then. I'll come by about six."

"You're on." I hung up with a warm feeling somewhere in my chest. I'd missed Matt more than I had expected, and I was curious to discover how it would feel to see him again after we'd been apart for over a week — the longest we'd gone without seeing each other since we'd been together this time around. Or something like that. I shook my head. Time for some business.

My time sense was definitely whacked out, and the day kept alternately stretching and shrinking. The furnace was humming along nicely, but the glass wouldn't be ready to work with for a while. I reviewed my inventory of pieces on the shelves, trying to figure out what I should fill in. The December holiday season had depleted my stock, and I made a mental note of what pieces had sold well. Another part of my mind reflected on what I had seen in Ireland. The Waterford approach had been interesting, and I had been lucky to grab a chance to talk to their only woman glassmaker, but there wasn't much about the Waterford technique that I could use in my own work. I didn't do anything like cutting. In a way, the cut crystal was closer to faceted gemstones than to the more sinuous forms of handblown glass, and that thought brought me back to thinking about the Gem Show.

When I had first moved to Tucson, I had done some of the obligatory touristy things, in what little free time I had. Everyone I met told me the Gem Show was a must-see, but I had been so wrapped up in starting up a business that I never managed to go. Besides, I really didn't care much about jewelry. But if an insider like Frank was willing to escort me, it might be fun.

I spent the balance of the day doing inventory, ordering supplies, and checking on the glass and the furnace temperature periodically. No problems yet. It was nice that something was working right. Nessa had gone for the day, and I was pottering around the studio, cleaning up, when Matt rapped on the back door. I let him in, and he folded me into his arms. There are times when the strong silent type is nice to have around, and this was one of them. I leaned into him — and realized how upset I was about Cam. I didn't usually do clingy. I gave the hug another ten seconds, then peeled myself away. "Hi."

"Hi to you. You look tired."

"Gee, thanks. But you're right. This jet lag hasn't worn off, and I've been trying to catch up here, and then there's this thing with Cam. . . ." I trailed off, uncertain how to start.

"Cam?"

"Let's talk about it over dinner. Did you want to go somewhere?"

He studied me a moment. "I'll order a pizza, and we can eat it upstairs. Is Cam here?"

"Yes and no. I think he's finished moving his stuff in upstairs, but he said he wanted some time alone, so I'm not sure he'll be back tonight."

"Right. Well, I'll call for dinner, and you can close up."

For once it was nice that somebody else was making the decisions. I didn't even have to tell him what kind of pizza to order.

I turned off the lights and locked up, and then we made our way up the stairs. When I opened the door, Matt went through the usual greet-the-dogs routine. I took the op-

40

portunity to grab a quick shower — after a day working with glass I always felt sticky, even in Tucson's dry air. By the time I was done, the pizza had arrived, and Matt had produced a six-pack of cold beer. All I had to do was sit and eat. Heaven.

Except I had to explain about Allison and Cam, but Matt was a good listener.

"So I don't know what to think right now," I said, finishing the sad tale while working on my third piece of pizza. "I mean, I'm mad at Allison for doing this to Cam, but I do understand. But that makes Cam mad at me. And I hate that Allison put me right in the middle of this instead of facing Cam herself, even long distance."

Matt cocked his head at me. "You know, you might just let them work it out for themselves. They are adults, right?"

Men. "Yes, but I feel kind of responsible. You know, Cam's pretty new at falling in love. And Nessa thinks that Allison's kind of" — I struggled to find the right word — "emotionally immature, thanks to her jerk of a husband. So they both need to grow up a bit, I guess. But I do think they're good together. Maybe." What did I know? My own romantic track record sucked.

At least, until now. After a rocky start, maybe Matt and I were headed in the right direction. And I didn't spend too much time gnawing on that, did I? Maybe he had a point: let Cam and Allison be, to find their own way.

I stood up to throw away my paper plate. Matt came up behind me and wrapped his arms around me, and it felt good. I turned within the circle of his arms, and it felt even better. After a while, I said, "You know, we could sit down."

"We could," he agreed gravely.

We did.

Unfortunately, once I sat down, I went to sleep. Damn jet lag.

CHAPTER 3

The name "peridot" is derived from the French word <u>peritot</u>, which means "unclear," due to the inclusions that often appear in the stones.

I woke up to find myself alone on the couch. Matt had vanished, but not before throwing a light blanket over me. Sweet of him: even in Tucson, nights can be cold in February. Fred and Gloria sat in front of the couch staring at me eagerly. "Yeah, yeah, I know — breakfast." I hauled myself to my feet and dished up for them. The sky was sort of light, so I guess I'd managed to sleep a little longer than I had the day before. Give me a week and I might get back to normal, whatever that was.

I peeked into Cam's room, but it was empty save for a bed, a few pieces of furniture, and his many mismatched boxes. Cam and I, we traveled light — although I did own a building (well, me and the bank), which was more than he could say. I deduced that he had taken himself off to parts unknown to lick his wounds, as promised. I had no idea where that might be, but I didn't think I was his favorite person right at this moment. Poor baby. But he'd survive, I was sure.

I reviewed my day as I munched on a stale English muffin. Obviously shopping for food was high on the list, if I wanted to eat. I knew the dogs wanted to eat. I wasn't sure when Cam would be back, but he would need feeding too. I leafed through the stack of newspapers that Nessa had left in a tidy pile for me. Nothing urgent: same old, same old Tucson politics. Yesterday's paper featured the periodic update on the body count for illegal immigrants found dead in the desert; still low, but sadly, only because the year was young. It seemed to get worse every year. People — men, women, and children — sneaked across the border and set off into the desert, blithely assuming that they would arrive at civilization quickly, or that some good Samaritan would have left water caches at intervals. The good news was most of them did make it somewhere, and melted into the local culture or just kept going to points beyond. The bad news was too many did not, and died of dehydration and exposure.

Sparse breakfast done, papers read and set aside for recycling, dogs fed and walked, I was ready to go down to the shop and see if there were any fires to put out there. Figuratively, I hoped. I made my way downstairs and greeted Nessa.

"You're in early. You aren't supposed to start until after lunch," I said — then noticed Frank Kavanagh behind her. I broke into a grin. "Hey, you got here fast! When did you arrive?"

"Last night, or more like early this morning. Damned hard to find a place to stay around here."

"Oh, sorry, I should have warned you. The Gem Show takes over everything for miles. Are you going to be around long? Because I could put you up here, at least until Cam comes back."

"Cam's not here?"

"No. When I told him about Allison, he decided to go off and sulk, but he should be back in a few days. He said to let him know when you got here. How is Allison, by the way?"

"Sorry, I should say. She told me to tell you she apologized — again. And again. And for the record, I don't think she did

45

right by your brother." Frank glanced at Nessa, who smiled her approval. He smiled back. I smiled at them. One big happy family.

"Unless, of course, you have another place to stay?" I said innocently. Nessa tore her eyes away from Frank and glared at me. I smiled back. "Just asking. So, Frank, you have plans? I assume you want to head over to the Gem Show?"

"Plenty of time for that. I need to check things out a bit, see which of my mates are around. Maybe you can tell me the best bits to see at the show."

"Me? I've never been. I was hoping *you* could tell me what to see."

Frank laughed. "Blind leading the blind, eh? If you can give me directions to get there, I'll tell you what you should look at."

"That's a tall order — the show isn't just one site, it's scattered all over town."

"All the more reason I need someone who knows the area. When are you free?"

Kind man, to remember that I had a business to run. "During the show, business is pretty dead, so I'm more or less at your disposal."

"Grand," Frank replied, his eyes twinkling at me. Twinkling? Frank appeared to be in a very good mood, despite having flown a third of the way around the world recently. Of course, since home was Australia, he was probably used to it. Or he was just one tough old buzzard. Probably both.

"I was wondering if I could borrow this lady for lunch today." He nodded toward Nessa. No surprise there.

I sketched a sign of blessing over them both. "Of course — we don't even open until one on Sunday. Go forth and prosper, my children. Take as long as you like."

"Right. I'll scope out the territory and come back in a bit. Will that suit, Nessa?"

"That's fine, Frank."

Frank left with a flourish, and I turned to Nessa. "I get the feeling you haven't been telling me everything."

"Em, I'm over twenty-one, and you're not my mother. Frank and I are enjoying . . . a flirtation. We'll see where it goes. And there is the small detail of the geographical distance between us."

"Piffle. No problem. Love conquers all."

"Aren't you in a cheery mood? Oh, did you see Matt last night?"

"I did, and get your mind out of the gutter, please. We had dinner and I promptly fell asleep on his broad and manly chest. Anyway, let me get some work done, and then I'll come up and cover the shop while you're at lunch. That okay with you?"

"Just fine.

I went back to the studio and stared at the clutter around me, trying to remember what I was supposed to be doing there. Making glass, right. The new furnace sat glowing, its molten glass waiting silently. I turned on a glory hole, filled up my pipe bath and my tool bucket, and was just about ready to make a first gather when there was a rapping at the back door.

Few people came to my back door, and most of them were tradesfolk. I'd recently had some bad experiences with some who weren't, so the lock was new, and there was a good peephole, which I used. On the other side stood a man, who looked harmless enough. It was broad daylight, Nessa was in the next room, and the streets were busy. I decided I could risk opening the door. "Hi. The shop entrance is at the front."

"Yes, I know. You're Em Dowell, right? And this is your studio?"

"Yes, to both. Why? You want to sign up for lessons?"

"No, not exactly. Can I come in?"

I looked him over. A couple of inches taller than me, he was wearing glasses and he needed a haircut. He looked kind of soft and pasty — definitely not threatening.

"Okay, come on in. And your name is?"

The man walked in and looked around eagerly. "Oh, Ryerson, Denis Ryerson. I'm a professor in English literature at the university."

"Okay, Denis, nice to meet you. What can I do for you?"

"You've got a glass furnace, right?"

"Yes, right over there." I pointed. It seemed kind of a silly question.

"What kind of temperatures does it reach?"

Now that was a question I didn't hear every day. "About 2,200 degrees Fahrenheit. Why?"

Denis appeared to come to some sort of internal decision. "Can I rent it, by the hour?"

This was getting odder and odder. "I do rent studio time by the hour. Are you a glassblower?"

"No, nothing like that. What do you know about treated gems?"

My expression must have told the story: I knew exactly nothing. "What do you mean 'treated'?"

"Oh, sorry. I mean heat-treated. The practice of heating gems has been used for millennia — even as early as the Egyptians."

"Why?" I still didn't see where he was go-

49

ing with this, or where I fit.

"Usually to enhance the color, make it deeper, richer. Sometimes you can actually repair stones, fuse cracks."

"Okay," I replied cautiously. "So why exactly are you in need of my furnace?"

He shook his head, more for himself than for me. "I'm sorry, I'm doing this all backwards. Okay, here's the deal. I'd like to rent the use of your furnace to attempt to treat some gems that I've acquired, to see if I can improve their quality. Is that possible?"

Well, this was certainly new to me. "Uh, I think I need to know more. For a start, is this legal?"

Denis nodded vigorously. "Oh, yes, yes, of course. As I said, people have been doing it for thousands of years. In fact, many of the gems you've seen in stores today have been treated. Sapphires in particular, but also aquamarines, amethysts, tanzanite."

"If you say so. So you're doing this because you think you can make your own stones more valuable?"

"Exactly. People haven't played around with peridot much, so it's kind of an unknown quantity."

Peridot. I wasn't sure I'd ever heard of it. "What kind of temperatures are you looking for?"

"Well, most gems are heated within a range from 450 to 1,850 Celsius. Based on what I've read, a lot of gems can go up to 2,000 Celsius."

He'd read about it in a book? Great. I did a quick mental calculation and was shaking my head before the words were out of his mouth. "No can do. That's over 3,600 degrees Fahrenheit. I can push this to 2,400 Fahrenheit, max. Higher than that could destroy it." No way was I going to risk my new baby on a stranger's chancy scheme.

"Understood. But that's the temperature most often used for stones like diamonds, rubies. There hasn't been anywhere near as much work done with peridot. And for that matter, there have been recent discoveries in Madagascar of sapphires that could be altered at as little as 300 Celsius. That's about the temperature your home oven reaches, if you have a self-cleaning one. So I'll be happy to work within your lower ranges. And I can vary time of exposure, which also makes a difference. What do you say?"

"I say slow down. I can't let the furnace get too cool because then I can't work the glass, so that limits the lower end of the range. But I have an alternate suggestion. See that small boxy thing?" I pointed.

"That's a color kiln. I use it to heat up small batches of colored glass, rather than doing a whole crucible's worth in the furnace. It's electric, and the heat is easy to control. It'll go up to about 2,000 Fahrenheit, and in fact the heat is more even and more consistent than the furnace's would be, and it's a lot easier to access. Sounds ideal for what you're suggesting."

Denis nodded vigorously. "Right, right. For a start. I'm kind of learning as I go. If that doesn't work, at least I've eliminated some of the possibilities."

Jet lag was still gumming up my mind. Another question percolated to the front. "You said you're a professor at the university, so why aren't you using the facilities there? Somebody must have some fancier equipment than this."

"Yes, they do, but they frown on people using university facilities and equipment for personal purposes."

Or else he wanted to keep his efforts off the radar. "So this is personal, not professional. I mean, you're not going to write some scholarly paper about it?"

"No, nothing like that. I'm in the English department, after all. But I have these stones, which aren't worth much in their current state, and I wanted to see if I could improve them. If it doesn't work, I haven't lost much. So, can I rent your kiln thing?"

I thought, or tried to. "How much time do you need?"

He shrugged. "I really don't know, yet. Several hours at a time, I'd guess, although I don't have to stay around for the whole time."

It seemed harmless enough. "Okay, I set the ground rules. I've got a couple of advanced students who rent studio time, but I can tell you what their schedules are. I'd prefer you work when I'm on the premises, but I live over the shop, so I'm usually available."

"Okay," he replied eagerly. "How much do you charge?"

"Fifty dollars an hour for use of the studio. Why don't we start with a fixed amount of time and see how it goes? Say, twenty hours? That would be an even thousand — with payment up front."

Denis Ryerson was doing a good imitation of a bobble-head doll, and I wondered if I should have charged more. "That's great. I'll give you a check. Can I start now?"

This man is obsessed, I thought. And I really needed time to think this through, without Denis in my face. "Listen, I just got back from a trip and I'm still a little jet-lagged. Can you wait a day or two?"

I'd always wondered what crestfallen looked like, and now I knew: Denis was the perfect image. "Okay, I guess I could wait a day. And we can compare calendars, decide what other times are good."

Why was Denis so eager? Did this have something to do with the Gem Show, which was in Tucson for only two weeks? Or did he just have a bee in his bonnet, and he wanted to see if his crazy idea worked? Did he have dreams of getting rich quick? I'd have to ask Frank how this treated gem thing worked, both in the execution and in the marketing of the stones. "Fine. Call me tomorrow and we can set up a schedule. And bring a check."

"Thanks. I'll be talking to you soon." Denis departed the way he had come, leaving me puzzled. What had just happened? Still, if Denis was good for the thousand, that would help pay off the new furnace. Even though I had a little money tucked in the bank now, it wouldn't hurt to replenish it.

I turned back to my glass. The day before I had devoted to letting the glass come up to temperature and watching the furnace to be sure everything was working correctly.

Today I would be making the first piece to emerge from this new furnace, and I wondered if it should be something special. I drifted around the studio, looking for inspiration. This Denis guy would be using the color kiln, at least part of the time — did I want to do something with color while I had the chance? Or combine clear and color?

My bread-and-butter pieces, the ones I sold most often to visitors, tended to be small and easily carried or shipped — sets of matching glassware, vases, molded sun catchers. The pieces I made for myself, the ones where I got to flex my artistic muscles, were generally larger — although working alone limited the size I could handle, simply due to the mechanics of handling a hot piece, adding the foot, and so on. But over the decade or so I'd been working in my studio, I had managed to perfect a strategy that worked for all but the most ambitious purposes.

So, a clear body — a vase. With some color — maybe green, in honor of my Irish trip? An idea bubbled up that made me smile: a green snake, coiled around the body of the vase. There were no snakes in Ireland, right? Arizona had its share of snakes, but I'd never gotten personal with them. I detoured to my office computer and did an online search for snakes, so I'd have a visual image to work from. Under snakes of Arizona, the green rat snake popped out. Perfect — green, smooth, and it combined "rat" and "snake." Apparently I was going to work out my anger toward Allison in this piece, wasn't I?

Mentally I ran through the steps I would have to take: a gather first, using the clear glass. More than one, if this was going to be a largish piece. Melt some green glass in the small kiln — not a true kelly green, but something more golden, as befit the Arizona scrub where this snake lived. I filled a small crucible with a mix of yellow and green and set that to melting while I visualized the form. Sinuous, yes, with the snake looping around, its head near the top of the vase. There would be some tricky spots, where I would have to rotate the body of the vase and wrap the molten snake around it, but I had a small turntable that I'd used before for this kind of work. Once again I thought briefly about taking on an apprentice — there were occasions like this when a second set of hands would be useful. But that wouldn't happen today, and besides, I needed to challenge myself, to get back into the rhythm of glassmaking.

There are times when all things come together, and this was one of them. The clear glass flowed like thick honey; the furnace was clearly up to its task. The shaping of the vase was easy, a voluptuous balance of curves, bellying out then sweeping in again at the top. I attached and flattened a disk to the foot, so the piece would stand level, then handled the transfer from the blowpipe to a punty without mishap, smoothing the top lip with a brief dip into the glory hole. Then I tapped off the punty and set the vase on the turntable, grasping it with my insulated glove. The shape looked perfect. I took a deep breath before dipping a punty into the viscous green glass from the kiln — I had only one shot to get this right, to drape the thick rope of glass around the exterior. At this point I wished I had three hands of my own — one to rotate the turntable and two to manage the snake glass. But it worked. Quickly I shaped the snake's head with pincers, tapering its snout just a little, and then stepped back before I could overwork it. Yes!

Nessa looked up when I came into the shop to relieve her for lunch. "You look pleased with yourself," she observed.

I grinned. "I am. Take a look."

She went over to the large window that

overlooked the studio work area — good advertising for customers, who loved to watch the process. "The vase with the snake? It's lovely — and an interesting use of glass."

"Yes. The furnace works just fine. Damn, that was fun! I thought I'd quit while I was ahead, if you want to primp a bit for your lunch date."

"No need. Frank will just have to take me the way I am."

Wise woman, Nessa. At that moment Frank appeared at the door, looking right with the world. "Ready to go, m'dear?"

Nessa glanced at me. "I am. Just let me get a sweater."

Frank turned to me. "Want to go check out the fun, when we get back?"

"You mean the Gem Show?" I thought for a moment. As I had told Nessa, I was superstitious enough to believe that I shouldn't push my luck. I had turned out one good (I hoped) glass piece, and no doubt jet lag would sandbag me later in the day, so I might as well get this gem thing over with. "Sounds good to me, Frank. But you don't need to hurry back from lunch. I think I can handle the crowds."

He grinned at my joke. "Right, then. Nessa?" He offered a courtly arm, and

Nessa took it gracefully. They made their way out of the building arm in arm. Nice.

CHAPTER 4

Ancient Egyptians called peridot "the gem of the sun" because they believed it could not be seen in the desert by daylight.

Nessa and Frank were back in under two hours, looking no less happy than when they had left. At least there was no trouble in their little paradise. Frank relinquished Nessa's hand grudgingly before turning to me. "Ready to go?"

"I guess." I had mixed feelings about our planned excursion, although that had nothing to do with Frank. "What do you want to see? There's a lot going on, both big and small events. You have friends here?"

"Friends might be a bit strong. Plenty of colleagues, acquaintances."

"Are you selling this time around?"

He shook his head. "Thought I'd get my feet wet first, although if the right deal came along . . . I'll introduce you to some of my pals, but maybe you should see the biggest gathering first — at the convention center, isn't it?"

"There and about a million other places. But if you want big, that's the place to start. You want to walk?" I asked. "It's only a few blocks."

"Sure. Clear the head, stretch the legs." Frank looked ready to take on tigers. Didn't anything slow him down? I wasn't so sure about my own stamina, but a brisk walk sounded like a good idea.

One of the plusses of having a shop in the Warehouse District was that it was downtown, which made many things easy to get to, including the convention center. I liked to walk, and I drove only when I had to. With the seemingly endless reconstruction of the major highway through the center of town, which had shut down not a select few but *all* of the exits, there were far too many lost and/or frustrated drivers on the streets. Walking was much simpler and often faster.

We had covered a few blocks before we spoke. "Not quite like Ireland, is it, Frank? How does Arizona compare to Australia?"

"Not too far different, although we don't have the cactus — at least, not the tall ones. We've got succulents, and there's a lot of prickly pear, but that was introduced, not

61

native. We call it a weed." I could hear the grin in his voice. "Depends on where you are. It's a big place."

"But you do have kangaroos, right? That's not just an advertising gimmick?"

"That we do, more than enough. And the same goes for koalas. Come visit."

"I'd love to, but I've got a business to run." And I didn't want to guess what a plane ticket to Australia might cost. We walked another block.

"Heard from Cam?" Frank said, his eyes on the streetscape.

"Not since he stalked off in a huff. He knows you were coming, and he said he wants to see you. I hope it will work out. I left him a message on his cell phone that you were here."

"No worries. He's tough."

"I hope you're right."

I took us maybe fifteen minutes to make our way to the sprawling Tucson Convention Center, the biggest venue for the many gem-related events. Frank looked like a kid waiting in line to see Santa Claus, bouncing on his feet, his eyes lit up. Me, I was less enthusiastic: I don't like crowds, and I don't particularly care for expensive, useless things. From all that I'd heard, the Gem Show contained the worst of each. But

Frank was eager, and I tried to keep an open mind. "You ready?"

"I am. Let's do the public stuff first, eh? Then you can decide if you want to try the dealers-only part."

"Why would I want to do that?"

"Less crowded, and maybe better quality bits. I can get you in."

"Let's see if I survive the first round, okay?"

Frank chivalrously sprang for a couple of visitor passes, and we hovered for a moment near the entrance. I took a deep breath: the noise coming from the huge exhibition hall was daunting — and it got worse once we walked in.

The bare-bones room was the size of a football field — at least it looked that big to me — and the entire floor was taken up with row upon row of booths with giant banners and bright lights, all shining on boxes and baskets and bins of gems. Rough gems; cut gems, mounted and unmounted; beads, strung and unstrung. Shoehorned in between was the occasional booth selling fittings and findings and supplies. The place was packed with people, most of whom appeared to be conducting family reunions in the middle of the aisles, making it hard to move in any direction. Maybe that was the point: the vendors figured if you had to stand in front of one booth for any length of time, you'd eventually end up buying something. All credit cards accepted. I shut my eyes for a moment to listen to the din. Lots of voices, with a mix of accents. When I opened my eyes again, I noted signs for vendors from all over the world, but particularly Asia — Hong Kong, Shanghai, Burma, Thailand.

"Wow," I said, stunned.

"Too right," Frank replied, clearly eager to get started. "What do you want to see?"

"I have no idea. You pick."

Frank studied me. "You're not the pearl type, and there's no point in looking at the diamonds in this lot — I can show you better in the dealers' section. And you don't do beady things. So let's take a look at the colored gems — plenty of interesting stuff there. And if you want to ask questions, go right ahead."

"Yeah, sure," I muttered. I followed him meekly as he plunged into the throng. It wasn't easy to keep up with him as he wove his way along. He wasn't hurrying, but he wasn't dawdling. He stopped at a double-wide display, where the table was covered with small closed boxes holding cut stones, the boxes arranged by color to form a rainbow spectrum across the table. Even I had to admit it was impressive. And it reminded me of frit, the ground or powdered glass I use to add color to pieces. Maybe there was something I could use here after all. "Okay, Frank, tell me what we're looking at."

Frank launched into an analysis of the stones spread out before us, while the vendor behind the table watched with an amused smile. Finally he said, "Can I show you something? Looking for anything special?"

Frank looked at me and winked. "What've you got in peridot?"

Peridot? I bent forward for a closer look. So this was the stone that guy Denis had been talking about this morning.

"You want Afghan, Burmese, local?" the vendor replied.

"Show us what you've got," Frank countered.

The man directed us over to a counter area where there was a black velvet pad under a bright light. He collected several small plastic zip bags holding light green stones, then opened them one at a time, spreading the stones out on the velvet. They ranged from rough crystals through cabochon and faceted stones, and the colors

65

varied from a pale yellow green to a more intense grass green. Most of the stones were fairly small, no larger than a half inch. I poked idly among them, listening with half an ear while Frank asked what I supposed were knowledgeable and pointed questions. The dealer replied glibly, but I had no idea whether he was shooting bull or knew his stuff. Frank seemed to be enjoying the process at any rate, and in the end I was surprised that he ended up buying a stone, for a price that seemed quite reasonable even to me.

When the transaction had been completed, Frank guided me back into the traffic stream. "What was that all about?" I asked. "You need stones? And why peridot?"

"Just testing the waters — wanted to hear his patter. He was fairly honest, and he knew his stones. After that I thought I ought to buy something. And you should know a bit about peridot."

"Why?"

"Because most of the peridot in the world comes from your backyard."

"What, you mean from the U.S.? Frank, I told you I don't know anything about gems."

"Closer still — Arizona, maybe fifty miles from here. Hang on, let me look at something." Frank leafed through the vendors' guide he had picked up at the entrance. "Right — two aisles over, at the other end. The Stone Trade Exchange guys control most of the sales of local stones. Let's check them out."

"Lead on," I said. Much as I hated to admit it, I was beginning to get interested — not so much in the idea of buying or owning gems, but in the amazing range of colors that surrounded me. I could feel glass ideas bubbling into my head, and I was visualizing new combinations and effects. Heck, I could even see how changing the display lighting in my shop might make my glass pieces stand out better, based on what I was seeing here.

Frank led the way unerringly to a modest but tasteful booth, with a simple dark color scheme and some striking images of what I thought I recognized as Arizona hills. An array of gems on the table battled with assorted flyers and brochures, equally well designed. Behind the table two men in sober shirts and pants appeared to be in a heated discussion with a third, more casually dressed man. The Apache origins of all three were evident. Theirs was one of the less crowded booths in that corner, and when they saw Frank and me approach they quickly wrapped up whatever they had been talking about. The third man hovered uncertainly, but the other two — apparently the ones responsible for the booth — turned their attention to us, ignoring their companion, who finally turned and left.

"Welcome. What can we help you with?"

A nice nonpushy opening. I approved. I let Frank do the talking again.

"Frank Kavanagh — Kavanagh Mines in Australia. Been hearing about Arizona stones for years now but never saw many. Mind giving me a quick see?"

I could tell that the vendors recognized a colleague, and also that they were more than happy to talk about their wares and their organization, if the enthusiasm of their response was any indication. "Happy to, Mr. . . . Kavanagh, was it?"

"Call me Frank."

"You know of the San Carlos Reservation? We — my brother and I, and members of some other families who live on the reservation — created the Stone Trade Exchange some twenty years ago to handle the marketing of the stones mined at the reservation. Our business is international, and we've added finishing centers and branched into handling some other gems and producing jewelry."

"Sounds like you've got a pretty good deal

going. Exclusive handling of the reservation's stones?"

"Yes. We have long believed that our individual miners are better served if they are represented in world markets by a single organization. I believe we've all done well through this arrangement. Are you interested in some stones?"

"Love to look. Em, here — she's local, and I guess your advertising hasn't reached her. What can you tell us about your stones?"

I smiled and tried to look as though I cared, embarrassed by my total ignorance of this local industry. The spokesman didn't seem to notice, but pulled out a selection of stones and laid them on the now-familiar black velvet surface, describing the virtues and flaws of each. Several other strollers were attracted by his obvious expertise, and in the end Frank and I slipped away, leaving the field clear to the more likely buyers. I snagged a brochure before we moved on.

When we were a discreet distance away, I said to Frank, "I never knew about the whole peridot thing. Or that the local Indians were marketing them. Is it a good business?"

"It can be. Depends on world markets and

what the overall supply is. Some good finds have been made in places like Afghanistan and Burma, but politics there sometimes makes it hard to get quality stones shipped out. I'd guess the local supply is more dependable."

"Are they good-quality stones?"

"Some, sure. It's an attractive stone, don't you think? And affordable, which is a plus these days. Looks good with gold or silver mounts, not as fragile as some like opal." Frank scanned the huge room again. "What else do you want to see?"

"I have no idea, but I'm learning fast."

We wandered up and down the jammed aisles, stopping now and then to poke at piles of stones or strings of beads. Frank chatted with quite a few people, some of whom he obviously knew. He picked up a few more small purchases, but even I could tell he wasn't in serious dealer mode. Maybe that all went on in the exclusive dealer section. Still, most of the people here seemed to be having a good time agonizing over their decisions and haggling over prices. After a while I realized I was reaching some sort of saturation point: everything was beginning to run together, especially after I'd seen the same kind of stones on seventeen different tables.

"Frank, how much more do you want to see?"

He tore himself away from yet another display and took a look at me. "Had enough? I'm happy to call it a day."

"Thank you. I'd really like a chance to digest what I've seen, and right now I'm feeling kind of overwhelmed."

"Anything that strikes your fancy?"

"Come to think of it, yes — that multicolored tourmaline, that shades from green to pink. I've never seen anything like it, and I wonder if I could translate that into glass somehow."

"Right, the watermelons. Pretty things. Let me make you a gift of one, like a souvenir of your first gem show."

"Frank, that's sweet. But don't spend too much, please — I just want one as an example, not a quality stone."

"Trust me." He scanned the booths of the aisle we were in, then led me to one a few stops down and entered into dickering mode. Five minutes later he gallantly handed me a midsize stone.

I took it and held it up to the light. "Lovely. Thank you, Frank — it'll bring back nice memories of today. You ready to go now?"

"Sure. I'll be coming back, for sure — you

can come if you like."

"Let me think about it. Are you staying at my place?"

"If you'll have me. I don't want to be a bother."

"Frank, you're one of the least bothersome people I know. You may have to scrounge for food, but you're welcome to a bed."

"Deal."

CHAPTER 5

The ancient Romans nicknamed peridot "emerald of the evening," because its green color could be seen by lamplight.

At the end of the day, I still felt awake and in an expansive mood, so I called Matt. "Hey, sorry about last night. Do you want a do-over tonight? I still haven't told you about Ireland."

"Think you can stay awake?"

"I'll do my best. And Frank's here, if you need an added attraction."

"Frank? He here for the Gem Show?"

"Yup. So you coming?"

"Well, since it's Frank . . ."

"Jerk," I said. "See you sixish." I hung up before he could say no.

After Nessa and I closed up the shop, I made a dash to the market and stocked up on food and drink — plenty for myself and two hungry men, or even three, if Cam decided to come out of his sulk and put in an appearance.

Frank had gone to retrieve his baggage from wherever he had stashed it, and he arrived first, looking both tired and pleased with himself. The dogs greeted him with uncontrolled glee, and he responded with appropriate head rubs and back scratches.

"Looks like they remember you, Frank," I said, watching the lovefest.

"Too right they do. They've got good taste." Frank finally managed to stand up. "No sign of Cam?"

"Nope. This must be a major sulk, not that I blame him. But I'd rather talk about you right now. Let me get you something to drink, and you can tell me all about what we saw today. And maybe what else you'd like to see while you're here. You didn't get to do much sightseeing on your last visit." Namely because he'd been busy rescuing Allison from some nasty thugs and playing backup to Matt. I'm sure it had been lots of fun for him, especially since everything had turned out well, but that certainly wasn't on the usual list of tourist activities.

He accepted a cold beer from me, downed half of it, then threw himself down on my shabby couch, the dogs at his feet watching him adoringly. I scrounged up some chips and guacamole (fresh from the market) and sat down in an armchair next to the couch. "Was the Gem Show what you expected?"

"More or less. Lots of people looking, eh? Lots of stock, some good, some bad. Lots of wheeling and dealing going on in corners."

"Did you say you know some people here?"

"I do. This business is small enough that a lot of us know each other, do business now and then. I'll catch up with a few of them. You're welcome to tag along, if you're interested."

"I might. Ask me in the morning." I was curious about the whole process, which I knew little about, although sometimes I wondered if all aspects of Frank's business dealings would stand close scrutiny. Of course, for all I knew everyone in the business had a shady side, or maybe just pretended to in order to enhance the glamour of their trade. And Matt had accepted Frank at face value, so I had nothing to worry about, right?

Matt arrived shortly after six and presented the dogs with a dilemma: stay with Frank or rush Matt? I could see the frustration in their eyes. Gloria contented herself with grinning at Matt from her position next to Frank's feet, tongue hanging out, while Fred ran in circles halfway between the men, barking. I turned my attention to cooking, such as it was, and ten minutes later everything was ready. "Hey, guys! Food." They trooped over and sat down at the table, where I had set three places. "We're not expecting Cam?" Matt asked.

"Doesn't look like it."

"What's up with him? You didn't get a chance to say much last night." When Frank grinned and cocked an eyebrow, Matt said, "No, it's nothing like that. She fell asleep on me, literally."

"I was jet-lagged!" I protested. "Frank, how do you deal with jet lag all the time, when you travel?"

"I sleep whenever I can — you never know when your next chance'll be. Same with eating — and this looks great."

"Help yourselves, guys — I don't stand on formality." Heck, they were lucky they had plates. "Anyone need more beer?"

There followed a respectful interlude where most of the food on the table disappeared. When the pace finally slowed, Matt asked, "So, how was Ireland? I hear the two of you were there together?"

"Green, cold, and wet," I said. "And here I thought they were tinting all those pretty tourist pictures. Except I think the green extended to the mold on my socks."

"That bad, eh?" Matt grinned; Frank pretended to be offended.

"Oh, not really. I just hadn't realized how acclimated I've become to Tucson, so it was kind of a shock to my system. It *is* pretty, and the people there were very nice. Friendly. Frank, how'd it seem to you, after so many years?"

Frank sat back in his chair and finished off his beer. "The same and different, I guess. A few new faces, a few less of the old ones. Thing that struck me was some of them were talking about the same things as when I left. Costs going up, bloody foreigners moving in. Like no time had passed."

"I kind of got that feeling too," I said. "Like I'd wandered into a time warp. You and Allison certainly have a lot of family in the neighborhood. No way I could keep them all straight. I didn't even know she had brothers!"

"I think she'd learned to keep her mouth shut when she was with Jack. It's a hard habit to break."

I saw an opening and seized it. "I don't know much more about you, Frank. You don't have a wife or two tucked away somewhere, do you? I don't want you to break Nessa's heart."

While Matt looked bewildered, Frank said, "No fear of that. She's a grand lady. Besides, she'd see right through me."

"Have I missed something?" Matt asked.

"I'll fill you in later," I said, focusing on Frank. "You think Allison will be back?"

Frank nodded. "I do. Ireland's her past, and she knows it. She's got some catching up to do is all. You can tell your brother that, whenever you see him."

" 'Whenever' is about right."

"Em?" Matt again, still confused.

"I explained last night, didn't I? When I told Cam that Allison said she was staying on in Ireland, he said he was working on a project for someone before his job starts next week, and then he went off in a snit. He'll probably immerse himself in writing code as a way to clear his head. When he gets into it, he forgets what time it is or sometimes what day — I'm the same way when I'm working with glass. I hope he makes it back before you leave, Frank — he'd be sorry to miss seeing you."

"I suspect I'll be around — I'm in no hurry."

"Speaking of folks in a hurry, I forgot to tell you about this kind of interesting conversation I had with a very eager guy in the shop this morning. He came in and asked me what I knew about heat-treating gems. He said he wanted to rent some time in my studio to try enhancing peridot." I wondered if any of the stones we had seen today had been treated. It hadn't occurred to me to ask. "I wanted to run it by you, Frank — do you know what he's talking about? And could it work, with the equipment I've got?"

Frank shrugged. "Maybe. Depends on a lot of things. You know anything about treating gems?"

"Anything I know about gems, I learned today, thanks to you."

Frank sat back in his chair and stretched. "It's done a lot, even to diamonds. Sometimes it works, sometimes it doesn't. What'd he want?"

"Furnace time," I said. "At least that's what he asked for, but he seemed kind of clueless. After he told me a little more, I suggested that the color kiln might work better, because it's smaller and more controllable. And I told him he could have a fixed number of hours with it, as long as he didn't interfere with my business."

"He a gem dealer?"

"He said he was a professor at the university, in literature or something."

"Ah," Frank replied. "Probably one of those eggheads who thinks he knows more than anyone else. Well, no harm in letting him play around, as long as you get paid. Not in stones, I hope?"

I smiled at him. "No, I told him cash up front."

"Good girl!" He yawned, then stood and walked over to the door to pick up his battered satchel. "Looks like the day is catching up with me. You two mind if I make myself scarce?"

"Not at all. Let me dig you out some clean sheets. You know where everything else is."

"That I do. I'll get out of your hair now. Thanks for giving me a bed." He looked at Matt. "Em offered to put me up, since rooms are so hard to come by."

"Frank, you're practically family," I assured him. "Take Cam's room, and if he happens to come back tonight he can darn well take the couch."

Frank headed toward the bedroom, and I looked at Matt. Matt looked at me. "Seems like your place is getting kind of crowded," he said.

"Seems like," I agreed.

"You know, Em, we can always go to my place, if we want some privacy," Matt said quietly.

I didn't answer immediately, trying to figure out how I wanted to respond. When he and I had first been together, I had never visited his house, preferring to keep things on my turf. Then Lorena had reappeared on the scene and I had backed off, I had thought for good. I don't believe in messing around with married men, so I hadn't seen Matt for a couple of years after that. Now he and Lorena were finally, officially divorced. Since then we had trodden carefully — and I still hadn't seen his house.

As a city employee, Matt thought it wise to live in the city, although I had no trouble picturing him on a ranch somewhere, mountains and sky behind, his cowboy hat tilted back. . . . *Em, get a grip! Matt's a police officer, not a cowboy.*

Anyway, when he'd been married to Lorena, she had done her real estate homework and identified the most prestigious neighborhood — the Sam Hughes Historic District — and found a house there, all the time whining about how small and tacky it was. Or so Matt had told me, long after the fact. He'd said that after the divorce, Lorena couldn't wait to shake off the dust of Tucson. So he got the house.

At last, I said, "I'll think about it."

Matt stood up. "I should be going. You

81

want me to run a background check on this professor of yours, make sure he's on the up-and-up?"

I stood up too. "I don't think so. I'd guess he's pretty much what Frank describes — a guy who thinks he's got a good idea and wants to play around with it. It's easy money for me, as long as he doesn't get in my way, and if it doesn't work out I can send him packing. Don't waste your time."

We made our leisurely way toward the door and made our good-byes, undisturbed by Frank. Tactful man, Frank.

CHAPTER 6

The Egyptians also believed that peridot glowed at night, and mined for it after dark.

When I stumbled out of my bedroom the next morning, Frank was already dressed. He had even made breakfast and fed the dogs.

"My, you're chipper. Do I need to walk them?" I said.

"No, we're good. Even followed the letter of your local laws and cleaned up after them."

"Frank, you are a marvel. If the diamond business doesn't pan out, can I hire you as a housekeeper?"

He threw himself into a chair opposite me. "You couldn't afford me, love."

I swallowed a lot of very good coffee and leafed through the newspaper he had brought in after his dog walk. I noticed one of the more bleeding-heart columnists had a longer-than-usual article about a body found in the desert over the weekend. He really pulled out all the stops, ending with a bleak statement that the unknown man had died "with nothing more than the pebbles in his pocket."

Frank had wisely let me absorb my quota of caffeine without attempting conversation, but I thought I should make an effort. I'm not used to having people around first thing in the morning. "Frank, you've got a lot of desert in Australia, right?"

"That we do — the Outback. A lot of the middle of the country. Dry as a bone."

"Do people get lost there and die?"

"Cheery talk for the morning. But yes, they do. We try to warn tourists that they should carry water with them if they're headed toward the Outback, because if they break down, might be days before anyone comes by. Why do you want to know?"

"We're near the border with Mexico here, and we get a lot of people who cross and then get lost in the desert. Too many of them die, I'm afraid." I gestured toward the paper in front of me. "Here's another one. No ID, no way to track him unless his fingerprints are in the system somewhere. All he had on him was the pebbles in his pocket, according to this article."

"Not as odd as you might think. Some people believe that sucking on a pebble helps get the juices going so you don't feel so thirsty. Doesn't work for long, though. Heck, sometimes they even drink sand, thinking it's water. Not a nice way to go."

"No, it's not." I folded the paper. "What're your plans for the day?"

"Places to go, people to see. How about you?"

"What day is today? Monday, right? Yes, it's Monday. That means the shop's closed, so I'll try to get some work done, I guess. You and Nessa have plans?"

"Dinner maybe. I was going to go back to the show, see some of my mates, if you want to come."

"You know, I think I'd like that. Feels kind of like playing hooky, but business is so slow during the show weeks that I'm not going to miss much. But I can't take the whole day, because I think this professor guy is coming back — with a check, I hope. So, uh, not to change the subject, but . . . do you think Allison will get in touch with you? I mean, you did tell her you'd be in Tucson, right?"

He shook his head. "I did, but I'm not sure she'd contact me, not from over there.

But listen, she'll come round, in her own time."

"I thought she had signed up for a class at the university this term, but I don't know that she's taking anything for credit. What do you think she should think about doing, long term?"

Frank leaned back in his chair, coffee in his hand. "I'm not the one to ask. She's a bright enough girl, no question. If things with Jack had turned out, she'd have had a brood of kids. . . ."

"Who'd pretty much be grown by now. You a throwback, Frank? You want to keep women in the kitchen?"

He grinned. "See, I told you not to ask me. And for the record, I like my women independent. Still, I think Allison wanted kids."

Damn. Another thing I hadn't considered. Cam and I had never discussed offspring; for most of our adult lives it had been a moot question, since there was nobody in our lives to have children with. Our own parents, who had died more than a decade ago, hadn't been the greatest of role models. But I could see Cam as a father. He'd be offhand, sheepish, and adorable. I could even see the children that he and Allison might produce — with red-gold hair and plenty of brains. I shook myself: what was I thinking?

"Well," I said crisply, "that doesn't mean she shouldn't have a job, or something else in her life. And any woman should be able to support herself."

"You'll get no argument from me, Em. Are you headed downstairs?"

"I am, as soon as I finish my coffee. You?"

"I've a meeting or two lined up. You want me to stop by later, see if you want to go back to the show?"

"Sounds good. And maybe Cam will have touched base and we can all have dinner together."

"Grand. See you later, then." Frank said good-bye to the dogs and headed out the door. I had no idea how he was getting around a city he didn't know well, but I had faith that Frank would be able to manage just about anything, with a minimum of fuss.

After I'd finished my coffee and tidied up a bit, I walked the dogs again, more for my own exercise than because they needed it, and then I meandered downstairs to the studio, running through what I wanted to work on. I figured I'd better use my time wisely, because once the gem folk moved on, business would return to normal, and the classes I taught would resume — I'd put them on hiatus while I went on vacation — eating again into my precious free time. I sighed and started gathering my tools.

I hadn't had a chance to start a gather — I was still waiting for the glory hole to heat up — when I heard a tentative rapping on my back door. It was Denis Ryerson, and this time he'd brought a woman with him. Blast! So much for my getting anything done. I opened the door to him and said, "I thought you were going to call first? All right, come in."

He sidled in, uncertain. "I hope I haven't come at a bad time? I took a chance you'd be here. I was hoping to get started today. Oh, sorry — this is my wife, Elizabeth."

"Nice to meet you," I said with minimal courtesy. Elizabeth looked too brittle to me, and it was clear she didn't want to be here. In any case, I really was itching to get started on my own work and I had no patience for social chat. "It's okay, Denis."

"Great! Oh, I brought that check along."

"Good." I took the check from his outstretched hand, folded it, and slipped it into the pocket of my jeans.

Denis turned to his wife, who looked as though she was afraid a glass piece would jump out and bite her. "Why don't you go look at the items in the shop? I won't be long."

"All right," she said. She paid no attention to me.

When Elizabeth had taken herself to the shop, I asked, "Have you told her what you're doing?"

"No. I said I was investing in your business, and I'd promised you a check today. Can we speed this up? She wants to get to the office — she's in insurance — and I told her I'd drop her off." He glanced nervously at his wife.

"Fine." I led him over to the space between my furnace and my annealer, where the glass kiln sat. It was a top loader, maybe three feet high, with controls on the front. "I told you about the kiln here. What you see is what you get. The temperature control is here on the front, and you'll have to give it time to heat up." I opened the top lid. "You just place your material on the floor inside, here. Do you have a strategy for temperatures for your stones?"

"I thought I'd start by trying a range of temperatures and a range of times, then narrow it down. This is just preliminary. It might not even work."

"What kind of volume are you talking

about? I mean, a couple of stones at a time, or a couple of pounds?" I wondered how many stones he was willing to sacrifice to his experimenting.

"Oh, not much at once. A handful maybe. The unpolished stones — the rough — are not very valuable at this point — heck, you can buy them by the pound. So it's no great loss if this doesn't work. I just look at it as a business investment. How do you recommend I put them in the kiln?"

"I've got some small crucibles that should work, and I'll show you how to get them in and out of the kiln. You have to remember everything is hot, even though you can't tell by looking at it." An awful thought occurred to me. "Is this process dangerous? Because I'm not sure my insurance covers activities outside of normal glassblowing."

He shrugged. "Sometimes stones have been known to blow up."

"Then you're wearing safety goggles, at a minimum. Not negotiable. And maybe you'd better sign a standard liability waiver." I made my students sign something, but I wasn't sure if that would apply here. Still, it would be better than nothing. I was beginning to wonder what I had let myself in for.

"No problem. I understand your concerns, and I certainly don't want to put myself at risk, or anyone else. Not for a bunch of stones."

Elizabeth stuck her head in the door. "Are you about done, Denis?"

"Just another minute or two," he replied. He turned so that his back blocked his wife's view of us. "Would you like to see what I'm talking about?" he whispered.

"I guess." I watched as he reached into his pocket and fished out a bag filled with what looked like gravel.

Denis opened it and poured a portion of the contents onto his hand, where they glinted with a dull green light. "Arizona rough. Not very impressive, I'll admit, but they look a bit better when they've been cut and polished. I'm hoping to make them even better than that."

"What're you aiming for?"

"If I'm lucky, they'll come out a darker, richer green, closer to emerald, although they'll probably always have a yellowish cast, as opposed to emerald's rather bluish tone. Something to shoot for, isn't it? In any case, darker is better — and more valuable. Is there anything else I should know about the kiln?"

I thought for a moment. "No, I think we're good."

"Terrific! I think I can fit in the twenty

hours during the next week."

A week? This guy really was in a hurry. Still, I had no reason to say no, as long as he stuck to the rules I had laid out. "Let's get that paperwork out of the way. I'll show you the crucibles and the tongs, and how to turn the kiln on and off, and you'll be all set to start later today. Remember to leave time for it to heat up."

"Great!"

Denis certainly was enthusiastic. I tracked down some standard boilerplate forms for studio rental and liability, and we duly signed and copied them. I collected five or six crucibles from wherever they had wandered to in the studio, and showed him how to manipulate them with the tongs. When I glanced at the clock, I realized that it was after ten. "You'll be back later? I should be back here by four, maybe five."

"That's good for me. I'll be here."

"Denis!" Elizabeth stood in the doorway, looking annoyed.

"All done here. Thanks, Em," he said in a falsely hearty voice.

"Later," I said, and politely hurried Denis and his petulant wife out the door so I could actually work.

The furnace seemed to be functioning just the way it should, and I had a nice batch of clear glass waiting for me. I still felt a little rusty, so I started working on a series of tumblers, which always sold well, matched in size but varied in color, thanks to the different color frits I added. I was stowing the last of an even dozen in the annealer to cool when I realized it was noon and Frank should be back soon. I shut down the glory hole I had been using, checked the settings on the annealer, tidied up, and went into the shop.

I was startled when the phone rang. "Shards," I said crisply.

"Your cell's off." Matt.

"Hello to you too. I wasn't expecting any calls, and I was working. Anyway, I'm in the shop at the moment. Did you want something in particular?"

"To invite you to dinner. At my place."

Oh. Dinner at Lorena's — no, at Matt's house. I guess I was ready to handle that. "Tonight?"

Matt laughed. "Yes, tonight, if that works."

I took a breath. "Sure, sounds good. Shall I meet you there?"

"If you don't mind. You know the way?"

"I can find it." I didn't admit I had driven by the house once, a long time ago, when I had thought . . . "Seven?" I figured I'd have to babysit Denis for a while, make sure he

93

didn't blow himself up.

"Seven would be fine." He hung up before I could change my mind.

Frank arrived as I was hanging up the phone. "Are we on for another go?" he asked me.

"I am indeed, Frank. I had fun yesterday, and now you tell me there's more?"

I locked up, and we set off along the same path as the day before.

"I need to be back by four, if that's okay. My peridot guy really wants to get started, so I said I'd give him a few hours today. Tell me, can just changing the color of some stones make them that much more valuable?"

"Ah, that's a tricky question. Maybe, at least at first, until the market catches up. There's often a stampede to a new thing, and then the interest fades."

"Well, he said he was working with Arizona stones and they hadn't cost him much, so he didn't have a lot to lose if things didn't work out. Would he have gotten the stones from those people we talked to yesterday?"

"Most likely — they've got a pretty good grip on local output, I hear."

This time when we arrived at the convention center, Frank had a word with the person at the entrance, and once we were inside, he headed for a section we hadn't seen before, down a long hall away from the main hullabaloo. There was a sign over the door at the end of the hall: "Dealers Only." Frank presented the man at the door with a ticket of some sort, then nodded toward me. "She's with me." We were ushered through with no trouble.

Inside I took a moment to get my bearings. There were similarities to the main space: rows of booths filled the room. But the booths were both larger and less crowded with merchandise, and there were far fewer people, not many of whom were tourists or browsers. Most looked intent and serious.

I turned to Frank. "Are you doing business today?"

"Maybe. It's always good to talk to some of these guys, find out what's going on in the markets — as much as they'll tell me, anyway."

"You mean they don't always tell the truth?"

Frank flashed me a smile. "Not all of it. Come on, let me introduce you to one of my old pals."

He led me to a booth across the room, with a man and a woman behind it. Both greeted Frank warmly. "You old crank, what got you out of Oz and all the way to Tucson?" the woman asked. She was a striking woman whose age fell somewhere between mine and Frank's, although it was hard to pin down since her skin showed evidence of time spent in the sun. A lot of time. I wondered if she and Frank had had . . . something, sometime.

"Ah, Miranda. It was your siren call, of course."

"Go on! And don't make Stewart here defend my honor."

"Bosh — I could take him one-handed. How are you, then?"

"Couldn't be better, Frank," Stewart boomed. "Wish the economy would improve, but we're holding our own. You buying or selling?"

"Neither right now, although if the right deal came along . . . Let me introduce you to Em Dowell — she's a glassblower here in Tucson."

"And how do you know this lovely lady, so far from home? Has he been telling you he's a millionaire ten times over?"

I laughed. "Does Frank have money? Actually we met because his niece took a class from me." That was an oversimplified explanation, but true.

Stewart turned back to Frank. "You have

relatives, man? I thought you were a lone wolf."

"That would be your sister's daughter, Frank?" Miranda said more softly. I'd guessed right — they must have been close at one point, if she knew about Frank's family.

"She is, all grown up now. Back in Ireland for the moment. So, tell me . . ." Frank and Stewart leapt into an arcane discussion of international gem markets that left me baffled.

Miranda was kind enough to notice. "Are you interested in stones?"

"Until yesterday I would have said no — I've got my own business here, and any spare cash I have goes right back into that. But there's some lovely stuff here. Have you been doing this long?"

"Most of my adult life. It kinds of gets into your blood, always hunting for something new or better. The diamond industry has changed quite a bit over the past decade or two, so it's exciting to try to stay on top of things."

"I think it's great to find a woman here. Are there a lot of women in the gemstone business? Do you find it makes your work more difficult?"

"Sometimes yes, sometimes no. But I

can't imagine doing anything else. And you? I don't recall hearing of many female glass-blowers."

"There aren't," I admitted. "Maybe twenty percent. But I love what I'm doing, and I love being my own boss."

"There is that. Were you looking for any-thing?"

"Not at all. Just following Frank around. I'm learning a lot from him."

"He is one of a kind, isn't he?" Miranda smiled fondly at the two men, who were deep in discussion, and I noticed a few small packets of gems had emerged from pockets.

"He is that."

"Are you two . . . ?"

It took me a moment to figure out what she was asking, then I laughed. "No, not at all. Although he and my, uh, friend seem to be leaning that way."

"I'm glad. Frank's a good man at heart, although he's hard to pin down."

"Do you travel to a lot of shows?" My question set us off on a long dialogue about the gem trade and the places it had taken her, and I had to admit I was fascinated. It sounded like a romantic lifestyle — but also a dirty, uncertain, wearing one. I preferred my own, I decided, although it was delightful to learn about something so different.

It must have been an hour later when Frank extricated himself from conversation with Stewart, and it occurred to me that I hadn't noticed any customers approach in that time.

"Shall we tour out the rest?" Frank asked.

"Fine with me. Miranda, Stewart, it was great to meet you. I hope you have a chance to enjoy a bit of Tucson while you're here."

Miranda laughed. "Oh, you mean the world doesn't end at the doors of this place? Thanks for the thought, Em. I'm glad we met too. It was good to see you again, Frank."

As Frank and I meandered off toward another cluster of booths, I said, "I didn't see much business going on."

"It's not all done by daylight. But Stewart and Miranda have done well for themselves."

"So, are you friends? Colleagues? Competitors?"

"A bit of each. It's a complicated business. Ah, here's Virender!" And we were off again.

We made it back to the shop in good time, and Frank went on his way when Denis appeared again at four, ready to go. I got him started, then retreated to the shop where I could keep an eye on him. He spread out little piles of rough stones on the metal surface of a marver and then laid a notebook out. As I watched unobtrusively, he would measure out a group of stones into a crucible, stick it in the kiln, set a small electronic timer he had brought with him, and make a notation in his notebook. While I didn't spend all my time watching, I had the impression that he was starting with short periods of exposure to the heat and gradually increasing it. Two hours later Denis was still in the studio, and he looked depressed. When I opened the door from the shop, he must have jumped a foot.

"How's it going?" I asked.

He sighed. "Nothing yet. I've read up on most techniques, but I guess each type of stone is different. So far I've been trying out a fairly low temperature for different intervals. Next time I'll have to crank it up and see if that makes a difference. Oh, did you want me to leave now?"

"Yes, I need to close up." So I could get ready for my "date" with Matt.

"Oh." He looked disappointed. "Okay. Can I come back tomorrow?"

"Sure. We're open all day. But this time call me first, okay?"

"Right," he said in a distracted voice as he

gathered his materials up.

I escorted him out the back door and locked it behind him. Before I shut down the studio, I made sure the little kiln was turned off. At least Denis was neat: he hadn't left any mess behind him. Odd duck, he was, but maybe a lot of professors were lacking in social graces. Unpolished, as it were. Smiling at my own pathetic joke, I finished closing up and went upstairs to prepare myself for dinner with Matt.

CHAPTER 7

Peridot has been assigned many mystical powers throughout history, including warding off anxiety, enhancing speech, inspiring happiness, and strengthening both the body and the mind.

Three dinners in a row with Matt — it was a record. Maybe he really *had* missed me, although I'd been gone only ten days or so. Although maybe that first night home didn't really count, considering that I had fallen asleep.

I had to admit I was uneasy about going to Matt's house, but I told myself to get over it. I realized that it was stupid of me to insist that Matt and I get together only at my place. Matt deserved equal time, and he had been patient. After all, I believed in relationships of equals, didn't I? So I'd suck it up and go. I hoped he was a better cook than I was. Or that his neighborhood had better takeout than mine.

Still, in some corner of my mind it was still Lorena's house. Maybe I was projecting, based on my own experience: I had chosen and shaped my living space. It was *Mine,* with a capital M. My kingdom, my lair, my sanctuary. I had no reason to think that Lorena had looked at her house in that light; from what little Matt had said, she had seen it as a status symbol, albeit an inadequate one.

The Sam Hughes neighborhood was the kind of area that Tucson real estate agents love to gush over: "Most Desired Central Historic Neighborhood," "A charming neighborhood of mature homes" with tree-lined streets — closed to through traffic, so they were quiet. First laid out in the 1920s, now it was on the National Register of Historic Places. It was convenient to downtown and the university. Some of the homes were pricey, others less so because they needed some serious work. I wasn't sure how Matt fit in there.

I pulled up and parked, then studied the house. It was a relatively small bungalow, a few steps higher than the street, with a sloping graveled front yard. I couldn't see the back because of the high wooden fence, although there were clearly some substantial trees there. The building was typical adobe with smallish windows; the entry porch had a terra-cotta tile roof. The house would have looked boxy and plain, but the whole was softened by the brilliant bougainvillea that screened the entry. I took a deep breath and got out of the car. Why should I be nervous?

Matt had apparently been waiting for me, because he opened the door before I could knock. "Em," he said gravely.

"Matt," I replied. Great — we knew each other's names.

"Please, come in." Matt stepped back to let me in.

I stepped into the small vestibule, with a niche in the wall straight ahead. If I knew my architecture, the living room would be on one side, the dining room opposite. It was surprisingly dark. Was Matt frugal about electricity?

Once I stepped into the living room on the left, I saw the reason: the place was filled with flickering light from more candles than I could count. And where there weren't candles there were flowers. I turned to Matt and silently raised an eyebrow.

"I wanted this to be special," he said, his expression anxious.

Oh, my. This was a side of Matt I had never seen. Romantic. Of course, I hadn't precisely encouraged it either.

My prolonged silence must have disturbed him. "I didn't mean to make you uncomfortable, Em. I know you're not into sentimental stuff, but I wanted to make this . . . memorable, I guess."

I rallied my scattered wits and turned to him. "It's lovely, Matt. Really. I just didn't expect . . ." I swallowed. *Em, move on before you get mushy.* "Can I see the rest of the house?"

"Of course." Matt smiled tentatively. "This is the living room. The dining room's over there."

"Show me," I said, leading the way. More surprises in the small, square dining room: a beautifully set table, with more candles and flowers. "Oh, Matt . . ." I began helplessly. I really was touched at the effort he had put into this.

"Hey," he said gently, "I didn't mean to upset you."

I shook my head vehemently. "No, I'm fine. It's wonderful. I'm just kind of overwhelmed." There were good smells issuing from the adjoining room. "Kitchen?"

"This way, what there is of it. Lorena . . ." He stopped abruptly.

"It's okay, Matt. She lived here, she was part of your life. I can handle that. What did she think?"

"She thought the kitchen was too small and too old-fashioned. She was going to take out that back wall there and double the size."

I looked around the admittedly tiny galley kitchen, its aging appliances lined up along the walls, its window overlooking the verdant backyard, half hidden in the dusk. "Looks good to me. It has all its working parts, right?"

"It does." Matt led the way out the opposite end of the kitchen. "Bathroom's here — just the one."

I peered in: lots of Mexican tile, a skylight in the high ceiling, and a huge, glass-enclosed shower. "Nice."

"And two bedrooms — I use one as an office. But I saved the best for last." He put a hand on the small of my back and guided me to the double glass doors leading out to a small deck nestled in the L between the kitchen and the bedroom hallway.

I stepped out and heard the unexpected sound of running water. "What the heck?"

He pointed toward the back of the small lot. "There's a small pond there, with a little waterfall." He looked as pleased as a kid about it.

I made my way to the end of the deck and

stepped onto the tiny lawn — real grass was a luxury in Tucson, but this patch could have taken up no more than twenty square feet. "It's wonderful." The trickling water drowned out what little sound of traffic drifted this far into the neighborhood. What a delightful kind of white noise.

"It came with the place — that was one of the reasons I really wanted this house. I'm glad you like it."

Dangerous ground, Em. In another universe, an ordinary female would be sketching out an entire future based on a comment like that. *Would you like to live here, my darling?* But Matt and I didn't do anything by the book, and I wasn't ready to go in that direction.

"I can see why you like it. It fits you — efficient but with some unexpected surprises. How about that dinner you promised?" Nothing like changing the subject.

"All set. Would you care for wine or a beer?"

Somehow beer didn't seem to fit the mood. "Wine sounds nice."

He disappeared into the kitchen and emerged a minute later with a chilled glass of white wine. "Here. Give me five and I'll have everything on the table."

I took my wine and drifted through the

living room and dining room. The furniture was plain and sturdy, but I caught a hint of designer lines. What decoration there was, was spare and clean — masculine without being pathetic. It looked a whole lot better than my place, no question. And, I was happy to note, I didn't see anything that could be remotely construed as a feminine touch. Unless the bedroom was filled with white ruffles. Somehow I doubted that.

Matt escorted me to my seat, held out the chair for me. I half-expected him to unfold my napkin (cloth, not paper!) and lay it on my lap. I looked at the plate in front of me. "This looks great. Did you make it?"

"Are you worried? Yes, I made it all with my own hands, and I've survived on my own cooking for a while. Just taste it, will you?"

I did. I tasted again, just in case I'd been wrong the first time. Damn, the man could cook! "It's great. Remind me to come up with some more adjectives, will you? And you are full of surprises, Matt Lundgren."

I smiled. He smiled. We ate. We finished a bottle of wine, and another one miraculously appeared. "I'm not sure I should drive home," I said, after I'd lost count of glasses.

"Did you expect to?"

Well, no, I hadn't. Not really. If I had

found the house full of tasteful designer touches — in other words, still reeking of Lorena — maybe I would have turned tail and run. But the house was so Matt, I had to admit I felt at ease. "I wasn't sure. But I am now."

"So you're staying?"

"I'd like that. Although I kind of feel like we should have some sort of ceremony, like an exorcism."

"To banish Lorena forever?"

"That's what I was thinking."

"I think I have an idea about that," he said. He stood up and held out a hand, and I accepted it and followed him to the bedroom.

Sometime later, I lay in the unfamiliar dark, listening to the trickle of water outside the screened window, and Matt's steady breathing. I liked this house, I decided. It was Matt's house, and Lorena had done no more than pass through it. The exorcism had been a resounding success, and, wonder of wonders, we hadn't even been interrupted by some police crisis. Maybe this would all work out just fine, I thought as I drifted off to sleep.

I woke again about three in the morning and remembered the dogs. I sat up quietly.

Good — there were no lingering effects of the wine. I could be home in ten minutes, through the deserted streets.

Matt reared his head. "Wha? Em?"

"Shh . . . Go back to sleep. I forgot about the dogs, and I don't know that there's anyone there to deal with them. I mean, maybe Frank is, but I'm not sure. . . ." I was dithering and I knew it, but I just couldn't bring myself to stay all night. "But I'll talk to you in the morning, okay?"

For a moment I thought he was going to protest or even pull me back into bed. But he didn't, and I wasn't sure if I was glad or disappointed. I thought for a moment of the effort he had put into the evening, to make it special. For me. In a way the idea scared me. I had worked hard to be independent, and I liked where I was in my life. I wasn't sure where Matt fit in it, and I wasn't sure what changes I was willing to make. This night had signaled some sort of shift in our relationship. I needed to think that over — alone.

I slipped on my clothes, tiptoed silently out of the room, and let myself out. When I got home, the dogs looked up once and went back to sleep, and I discovered that Frank had left a note. "Fed and walked dogs. See you in morning." I heard the

sound of light snoring from the guest bedroom.

Still no sign of Cam.

CHAPTER 8

In the past, peridot was considered more precious than diamonds.

The next morning dawned fair and clear. Of course, it's almost always fair and clear in Tucson, except during the summer monsoon season, which was still a ways off. I lay in bed listening for sounds and heard Frank's voice. No one answered, so I had to assume he was talking to the dogs. Ergo, no Cam. He'd now been gone almost three full days without even a phone call, and I was beginning to worry.

I made the necessary ablutions and stumbled out to where Frank was busy frying eggs. I could smell coffee, so I made a beeline for it. Once I had a mug filled, I sat down and prepared to be sociable. "Morning." I swallowed more coffee.

"Morning, Em. Thought I'd get me an early start today."

"More gem stuff?" I said intelligently.

"Right. I've still got some people I want to catch up with. Don't think you'd enjoy it."

"Hey, I'm happy with everything you've showed me, but I have a business to run." I thought a moment before posing the question, "Frank, how tight is this gem community of yours? How many of them do you know?"

Frank slid filled plates on the table and joined me with his own coffee. "Diamonds are a funny business. Everybody knows about the big guys like De Beers, but over the last decade or two a lot of new players have come into the game."

"Like you?" I smiled at him.

"Ah, I'm small potatoes. But Australia's in the mix. So's Canada now, and new stuff's popping up in Africa all the time these days. Lots of changes, lots of shifting alliances."

"You're right — I didn't know. But then, I'm not a diamond kind of gal."

I stood up abruptly and went to the phone. Cam's cell number was on my speed-dial, and I hit that number. The call went straight to voice mail again, so I left a message. "Hey, baby brother, you're going to miss Frank if you don't come back soon.

Call me, will you?"

Frank had watched this exchange. "No hurry. I'll be around for a few days. But what's up with that brother of yours?"

I sighed. "I wish I knew. He's made a lot of changes in his life lately — new job, moving here." And he had believed that Allison was going to be part of that. "Maybe he's just trying to clear his head. But it is unusual that I haven't heard from him."

"When's his new job start?"

"Next Monday, so he's got some time yet. Well, I've done what I can do. Oh, by the way, that professor guy stopped by yesterday and put in some time. What're the odds that he finds something worthwhile in his twenty hours?"

"Hard to say," Frank replied thoughtfully. "Small, probably, but he could get lucky. If he's done his research, he's probably narrowed down the possibilities, so he'll focus on particular temperatures or combinations of heat and other factors. But no guarantees. The stones are just as likely to blow up in his face as not, particularly if they're flawed. And it's a low-end stone, although that might work in his favor, since it'll be cheap to experiment with."

"Was there an answer in there?"

Frank grinned. "Sure: maybe."

"Thanks a lot. Well, it's no skin off my nose, and he paid up front. Speaking of which, I'd better make sure that check gets to the bank." I made a mental note to take it downstairs and give it to Nessa. Speaking of whom . . . "You and Nessa have any plans?"

"Not yet. I've been keeping my options open."

"Don't worry, I owe her time since she covered for me and Allison when we were in Ireland. This is a slow season for me anyway, so it's no problem." I stood up and carried our plates over to the sink. "Well, I think I'll take the pups for a walk and then head downstairs. I gave you a key, right?"

"That you did. Thanks again for putting me up here, Em."

"My pleasure, Frank."

As I gathered up dogs and leashes, I reflected that I had meant what I said. Frank wasn't like anyone I had ever known, and while he kept his cards close to his vest, I trusted him. Of course, if he decided to sweep Nessa off her feet and haul her back to Australia, I'd be up a creek, but I wasn't going to worry about that until it happened. I had a suspicion that her grandkids would be a powerful tie to the Tucson area.

Fred, Gloria, and I made the circuit of the neighborhood. This was one of my favorite times of day. It was fun to watch the streets come alive as artisans trickled in, shop lights came on, doors opened. I nodded and smiled to those I knew, which was most of them since I was a relative old-timer, and dutifully picked up my dogs' deposits. It was still early, so I took my time, and it must have been a half hour later when I finally came back to my place — to find Denis waiting at the back door.

"My, you're early," I greeted him, fighting annoyance. "Haven't we talked about you calling before coming over, please? And don't you have classes to teach or something?"

"I'm sorry, I forgot. And no classes 'til afternoon. I thought I could get a couple of hours in, if that's not a problem."

"That's okay, I guess. You've picked a good time to do this, since there aren't a lot of tourists around, except the ones who come for the Gem Show. Are you hoping to have something to sell there?"

"Oh, no, no. You have to get that set up like a year in advance, and even if everything worked out here, I wouldn't have time to get ready."

"You have any luck yesterday?"

He shrugged. "Maybe. It's still too early to tell."

So much for small talk. "I'll let you in, but then I've got to get these two back upstairs," I said, holding up the leashes. The pups had held their ground at my feet: they hadn't made up their minds about Denis. Friend or foe? I unlocked the back door and held it open for Denis, who made a beeline for the kiln, turned it on, then went to my big table and started unloading his backpack. I closed the door behind him and went around to the side and carried the dogs up the stairs.

Once inside I was greeted with silence. Frank was gone. I checked my phone, but there were no messages. Cam hadn't said where he was going, and his phone was either off, out of power, or out of range of any cell tower — not unusual around Tucson. Well, there wasn't a lot I could do if I couldn't even talk to him. If Cam didn't answer his phone, I had no idea how to reach him. I just had to trust that he would show up sooner or later. I knew that Cam was definitely a responsible person and took his obligations seriously, so I could figure on seeing him in time for him to start his new job.

Dogs safely settled, I realized I had promised to call Matt. He was probably still at home. I dialed.

He answered quickly. "Hey."

"Hey. Sorry I ducked out on you this morning."

"That's okay. I know the dogs are more important than I am."

"Well, they haven't learned to feed themselves yet," I said more tartly than I intended. "Sorry. Last night was . . ." I fumbled for a word and finally gave up. "It meant something to me."

"Does that mean we can do it again?"

"As long as you cook. Unless that wasn't the part of the evening that you were referring to?"

He chuckled. "I'm happy to cook for you any time."

We said our good-byes and I went back downstairs to keep an eye on Denis. I kept myself busy dusting (an endless chore in dry Tucson), straightening the articles on the glass display shelves, figuring out where the holes were, and adding some new pieces from inventory. Denis looked like a chef waiting for his bread to rise. It would be a fine balancing act for him working with the kiln: he was eager to see results, but he had to give the heat time to do its work, and he couldn't peek without losing heat. I watched long enough to be sure he wasn't doing anything stupid but otherwise let him go on about his business.

His presence reminded me about the check I'd stuffed in my pocket after breakfast. In the shop, I greeted Nessa, then said, "Nessa, before I forget — can you make sure his check goes to the bank?" I fished it out of my pocket and handed it to her.

"The bank is on my list for today. There hasn't been much to deposit lately. Why don't I go now, before things get busy?"

I knew she was joking. "Things should pick up once the gem people leave town," I said. "We've weathered this before."

"We have. So he's back again?"

"As you can see. I'll keep an eye on the shop while you go to the bank."

Nessa left after gathering up our meager take from the last few days, and I pottered around until she came back. Then I did some bookkeeping and filing, but by lunchtime I was anxious to get to my own work. Denis would just have to make do. He was so engrossed in making notes in a notebook that he didn't even notice me approaching. He jumped when I spoke. "How's it going?"

"Oh, fine, fine. Or at least, I'm eliminating some of the range." He looked quickly at his watch. "Shoot, I've got a class in an hour — I've got to go. And I'm sure you need to use the studio."

"Yes, I do." I shouldn't feel like I was apologizing: this was *my* studio.

"Will the studio be available tonight?"

Boy, he really was pushy. "You want to come in when I close up? I guess that's okay."

"And I had another idea. Can I leave some stones in the kiln overnight and come back in the morning to look at them?"

"I guess." I wasn't all that comfortable having him around, alone, at night, but I couldn't think of a good reason to say no. And, after all, he was paying me for the time he spent here, and even the additional electricity wouldn't be that much extra. But why the hurry?

Denis was waiting outside my shop door at six fifty-three, shifting from foot to foot to keep warm in the chilly evening air. I let him in, locking the door behind me, then followed him into the studio. Even after he had taken his coat off, in the warmth of the studio, he still seemed nervous, so I decided to hang around and watch him for a bit. If I had had a stash of valuables on the premises, I might have worried that he was setting me up for a heist, but there was little worth taking. Maybe he was just a naturally nervous person — but that didn't make me feel any more confident.

"Progress?"

He was immersed in his research notebook and looked up blankly for a moment. "Oh, well, you know . . ."

I perched on one of my high stools. If he was using my space, he owed me a little polite conversation. "Have you gotten any results?"

He shrugged. "A little shift in color. Not enough to make a difference, really. But hotter seems to work better."

"How did you get interested in stones? That's kind of far from your professional field, isn't it?"

Denis pulled open the kiln lid and with long tongs carefully positioned a small crucible in the interior, rearranging a few others. He stepped back, considered, then moved it an infinitesimal amount, then shut the lid again. Returning to the table, he made a note in his notebook. Finally my question registered and he looked up at me.

"What? Oh, you were asking how I got interested. Well, it's hard not to be, living in Tucson."

I did not point out that I lived here too and yet I'd avoided it so far.

"My wife likes jewelry, but I'm afraid her tastes are a bit beyond my salary. I thought maybe I could create something unique, maybe even name it after her, and it would make her happy."

"That's a nice idea. What's her name again?"

"Elizabeth. I was thinking maybe 'bethite.' "

"That's sweet." Poor Elizabeth. "Can you patent this process?"

"Not really. It's kind of dog-eat-dog in the gem business, from what I've seen. You just hope to get in ahead of the curve, but other people are going to catch up. You haven't told anyone about what I'm doing, have you?" Suddenly he looked furtive.

"Why would I?" I replied. Technically evasive, but not an outright lie. I wasn't going to mention Frank, who knew all about treated stones anyway, and who I trusted not to steal Denis's process. And Matt knew too, but he was completely trustworthy. "How many more trials do you need to do? Because you're at least halfway through your twenty hours."

"I'll pay you for more," he said quickly. Almost too quickly. "Maybe another twenty, over the next week? That should do it."

I reviewed the rest of the week in my head

and couldn't see why that would be a problem. "That's fine. Paid in advance again."

"Sure, fine." He turned his attention back to his notes, shutting me out.

I wasn't sure what more I hoped to accomplish, so I stood up. "You said you're going to leave some stuff inside the kiln overnight? Okay, then shut the door and turn out the lights when you go. You can let yourself out the back — that's on a dead bolt. Just pull it closed after you."

He looked up at me then and manufactured a smile. "I'll do that. Thanks a lot, Em. See you tomorrow."

As I made my own way back upstairs, I tried to analyze why I felt troubled. Denis was paying me for the studio time, no problem. Sure he seemed nervous, but I didn't know him well enough to judge whether that was his general demeanor or whether he actually was nervous about something, and I certainly had no clue what that might be. He'd told me a sweet story about creating something for his wife — which I found unconvincing — but what difference did it make? I resolved to ask Frank a bit more about the commercial aspects of treated stones the next time I saw him.

CHAPTER 9

Peridot has been thought to give the bearer the ability to overcome adversity.

I was still trying to finish the book I'd started on the airplane when Frank came back that evening. He looked pleased with himself, but then, he usually did. "Good day?"

He grinned. "You saying g'day?"

I smiled. "No, just asking if you had a good day."

"That I did. No word from our boy?"

I shook my head. "How about our girl?"

"Not word one. Fine pair we make, misplacing our relatives like that."

They had misplaced themselves, deliberately, but I didn't see any point in mentioning that. "You have time to talk, Frank?"

"If you've got a beer handy."

I went to my fridge and came back with two cold beers, handing him one. He took a long swallow, then turned to me. "Worries?"

I settled myself in a chair and took a long swallow too. "Denis — the professor guy renting my kiln — has asked for more time this week."

"That a problem?"

"No, not really. I mean, he's paying me, and I don't need the color kiln very often, and there are plenty of times when the studio's available, when I'm not using it. I'm wondering why this is so important to him. I mean, is it just the mystery of stones, or something deeper?"

"Can't tell you. The stones aren't worth all that much, unless he makes them turn pink or something, and they still wouldn't be much more than a novelty then. So no way he's going to get rich fast with peridot."

"He said he didn't have anything to do with the Gem Show this year. But maybe he's got a buyer lined up, someone who's in town for the show? Does that fit?"

"Could be. There are plenty of dealers here, and some of them aren't too careful about their sources. Hard to track gems, sometimes."

"I hadn't even considered that aspect. Are you thinking that maybe Denis stole them and he's trying to disguise them?"

"Ah, Em, don't be seeing criminals under every rock. Chances are he's just what he appears to be: an ordinary guy who's playing around with an idea and has a little time and money to put into it. Wouldn't be the first to be seduced by pretty stones."

"I'm still embarrassed that I didn't know about the local mines. I guess I've been so busy in the years since starting up the studio and shop that I've never really had time to explore things around here. Heck, I haven't even seen Tombstone, and that's just down the road."

"You know the phrase, 'All work and no play . . .?'"

"I hear you. Maybe when things settle down again, and I get my staffing sorted out, I can take a little time to play." I wondered when, if ever, that would happen. Nessa was wonderful, and she knew my wares and she was an excellent salesperson, but she wasn't getting any younger. Allison had kind of fallen into my lap and luckily had worked out well as a part-timer in the shop, relieving Nessa, but I had never assumed that I could count on her for the long term, and that was before she had pulled this stunt on me in Ireland. I wanted her to build a life of her own, and I wanted her to have options beyond working in a small craft shop. All of which suggested that I should start thinking about finding some long-term prospects for staff. Maybe I could offer an internship. . . .

I think my eyelids must have drifted down. When I opened them again, I could hear Frank in the shower, whistling, and Fred and Gloria were stationed at my feet, looking at me expectantly.

In short order I was making the rounds of the neighborhood with the dogs, and I paused in front of the street-side windows to my studio. Denis was hunched on the stool, rocking slightly back and forth, staring at his notebook as though it held the secrets of the universe. He didn't look happy. What was so urgent about fiddling with a pile of stones? Something was definitely wrong, but what? And was it any of my business?

The dogs pulled me away then, in search of good smells. When I got back, there was still no word from Cam.

Wednesday Nessa was in the shop when I came downstairs. "Do you expect that man Denis back again?"

"Looks like it — he said he wants more hours, and he's burned through a lot already. He's really in a hurry, although I have no idea why. He was here last night late."

I immersed myself in my work and gave no more thought to Denis until after lunch, when I found Nessa hanging up the phone in the shop. "What's wrong?" I asked.

"Denis's check bounced."

"The bank called?" I had made of a point of using a local bank, and Nessa and I were on a first-name basis with most of the tellers.

"They did. Will you talk to him, or shall I?"

"I'll do it. I'm the one who gave him the go-ahead, and there's no reason why you should do my dirty work."

Frankly, I was pissed at Denis for taking advantage of me — and it served me right for taking his check and letting him go ahead. I didn't like being used.

The guilty party chose that moment to walk in the shop door, looking harried and disheveled. He stopped dead at the sight of the two of us glaring at him. "What?"

"Denis, there's a little problem with that check you gave me. It bounced."

He grew a shade paler, something that wasn't easy to do when you spend any time in the Arizona sun. "Oh, shit. I'm sorry. Look, I'll make it up to you, I swear."

I tried to feel sorry for him but failed. I

was running a business here. "I expect you to. We had an agreement. And I can't give you any more time until you pay me — cash."

"I'll be back, I promise." With that he turned on his heel and left abruptly.

I turned to Nessa, who said, "That man seems very upset."

"You're right. Embarrassed maybe? I suppose if his bank account's empty he may have good reason to be, but that's not something I'm supposed to worry about. Maybe this whole gem thing was nothing more than a get-rich-quick scheme. And as far as I know he hasn't come up with any useful results. Think we'll see him again, or should we just write him off?"

Nessa smiled. "Maybe he's gone off to rob a bank, so he can pay you."

"Heaven forbid! Well, I've got work to do. Let me know if you hear from anyone."

"Like Cam? Still no word from him?"

"Not a peep. I know he's a big boy, but it's not like him not to get in touch with me."

"I'm sure he's fine," Nessa said re-assuringly. "I'll let you know if he calls." She hesitated before adding, "Nothing new from Allison?"

"Nope. Frank hasn't heard either?"

"No. Well, there's not much to be done about it, is there?"

"Sad to say, no. Let me know if things get busy." I could hope.

I went off to the studio and immersed myself in hot glass — well, not literally. But each time I opened the furnace for a gather, I found myself looking at the little kiln, which still held Denis's crucibles. I wasn't about to mess with it. If he really wanted his stones back, I could hold them hostage until he paid me what he owed.

I was still in the studio when Denis reappeared. The man was crumbling fast: now he looked both pasty and sweaty. Without preamble he thrust a handful of crumpled bills at me. "Here. There's more than $800 there, and I can get you the rest by tomorrow. But I really need to use the kiln. Just a couple more runs. Please?"

I was torn. It seemed so important to him, and it didn't mean that much to me. I stuck out my hand and took his money. "Okay, but no additional studio time until you pay up. Got that?"

He bobbed his head. "Thank you, thank you. Oh, can I get last night's batch out now?"

"I guess." I stood aside, watching him as he took the tongs and extricated a crucible from the kiln. He set it down gently on the metal surface of the marver and stared into its depths.

Then his expression changed. He peered around, then picked up a pair of metal tweezers and poked at the little pile of stones in the crucible. He picked one out and set it reverently on the marver, then turned to me.

"Look at this. Please."

I moved next to him and looked at the stone he had set apart. It did look darker than it had the day before, but I was no expert. "It's darker, right?"

"Yeah. But look more closely. Wait." He fished in his backpack and pulled out a small, high-powered magnifying glass. "Use this."

I took it from him and held it over the stone, which was suddenly much bigger. "What am I . . . oh." Yes, the stone was a richer green, but deep inside there was a sort of golden glow. "The gold color?"

"Yes. Yes! I knew it. I knew it was possible. Nobody's seen anything like this. Em, please, you've got to let me have more time with the kiln. This is just the start. I'll pay you, I promise. When I show people what I've done, it'll be worth plenty. Just a couple of days. Please?"

Now I was on the spot. He had undeniably changed the stone, but I had no idea what that meant — or what it might be worth. It was intriguing, but I had work to do, and he was annoying me. "Listen, Denis. I agree that it looks like you're onto something, but you still owe me. You come back tomorrow with the balance of what you owe me so far, and we can talk."

Denis looked like he wanted to burst, but after a long pause he said, "Okay. I'll be here in the morning. I promise. Oh, and keep this quiet, please?" He swept up his stones, then scurried out the back door like a man chased by demons.

CHAPTER 10

Peridot is said to help the bearer to find happiness and to overcome anger and jealousy.

Somehow I was not surprised to find Denis waiting yet again when I got downstairs on Thursday morning. Mutely he thrust more bills at me. "This should cover it. Can I work today?"

"This morning, I guess. If you want to leave stuff in overnight, that's okay."

He nodded, more to himself than to me. "Good, good. Longer seems to work better. I can do that." Then he focused on me again. "Thank you, Em. I mean it. I'm close, I know it."

Yeah. Whatever. Still, I'd been paid. I let him into the studio, then went up to say good morning to Nessa. I handed her the wad of bills. "Count this, will you? He says we're square. But I'm not sure I want him around once he's used up his first twenty hours."

The day passed quickly, even without the usual browsers and buyers. I booted Denis out of the studio after lunch, made a few pieces myself, grabbed a bite, took care of the dogs, and worked some more. Finally I straightened up the studio and went around turning things off — the glory holes, the lights. It had been a good day, and things felt almost normal. Maybe I had finally licked the jet lag. I left the kiln on, since I assumed Denis wanted that. I took one last look around, then exited through the front, leaving on only the lowest of security lights in the shop. I made sure the door was locked, then went around the side of the building to the stairs.

I almost jumped out of my skin when a figure materialized out of the dark, and it took me a moment to realize that it was a familiar one. Allison McBride.

"Allison? Why didn't you tell me you were coming?" I tried to see her face in the dim light. Did I want to hug her or punch her?

"Oh, Em — I was afraid you'd . . ." She took the decision away from me when she wrapped her arms around me and held on tight.

I realized that I wasn't really mad, so I

134

hugged back. But I let go before she did. "Why don't we take this inside? How long have you been back? Where's your stuff?"

She took the easy answer first, as I fumbled for my keys. "The plane got in a couple of hours ago, and I dropped my bags at my apartment. And then I came straight here."

I managed to get the door open, only to be swamped by the dogs, who were not in the least interested in me. They swarmed past me to greet Allison, who, to give her credit, knelt down and did right by them. I moved into the room and tossed my keys on the table, and looked up to see Frank standing in the middle of the room. Allison finally disentangled herself from the welcoming committee and followed me, then stopped dead at the sight of Frank.

"Come give your uncle a hug, for all that it's been no more than days since I've seen you."

Allison complied, but I noticed she glanced around the room and looked disappointed when she saw no one else. Aha. So she'd hoped to find Cam here.

I gave the happy reunion another ten seconds, then said briskly, "Okay, Allison, are you hungry? The food on those flights is pathetic."

"I could do with something, if it's no trouble," she replied. "I hoped you'd still be up."

"And starving," I said promptly. "How about you, Frank? You need anything?"

"A beer if you've got it. Other than that, I'm good. Sit down, Allison — you're making me nervous with your fidgeting. He's not here." Clearly Frank had seen what I had.

I rummaged in my refrigerator and came up with salsa, guacamole, and chips. And more beer. That would have to do. Allison sat down at the table, looking rather dazed, and Frank settled himself beside her. I dumped all the food and bottles in the center and sat down myself. I didn't see any point in formality. "So you haven't heard from Cam?"

Allison turned to me eagerly. "I tried to call when I reached the States, but all I got was his voice mail. Have you . . . ?"

I took my anger out on a tortilla chip loaded with salsa before I answered. "Yes, I passed on your message, and he took it just about the way I expected. He said something about a project he was working on and disappeared, last Saturday. I haven't heard from him since."

"Oh my."

When I stopped to count, I realized it had been five days now since I'd heard from Cam. "Did you try to get in touch with him to tell him you were coming back?" *Or that you were sorry, or that you loved him?*

Allison stared at her hands and shook her head. "That I didn't. I hadn't made up my mind, you see, until yesterday, and then I'd just had enough, so I called the airlines and they cobbled together some flights for me."

"So you'd had your fill of the McBrides?" Frank asked, a grin on his face.

"Well, they were all very nice, but . . ." And then she smiled ruefully. "Yes, a little of them goes a long way. Do they never stop talking?"

"Never. Why do you think I fled to Australia?"

Happy families, yadda yadda. I broke in on their warm and fuzzies. "Are you planning to stick around this time, Allison?" I was too tired to beat around the bush.

This time she looked at me squarely. "I am. I'm sorry, Em, for putting you in such a difficult position. It was wrong of me, but I was so overwhelmed by everything, and seeing my mother's grave and all . . ."

I put up a hand. "Apology accepted. I know it must have been difficult, taking it all in, especially after so long, and you're right to have wanted to reconnect with your family. But I'm glad you're back. As I'm sure Cam will be, whenever he shows up."

"Am I still welcome in the shop, then?" she said.

"Of course you are. And things will start getting busier as soon as this blasted Gem Show is over. Speaking of which, Frank, I think Denis is on to something."

"Is he now? Is this what he tells you, or have you seen the results?"

"He showed me a stone that he pulled out of the kiln. It was a darker green, but the really interesting part was that the core seemed to have changed color, to kind of an orangey gold."

That definitely got Frank's attention. "Really, now? That would be worth seeing. If the color holds stable, and if he can repeat it."

"One small glitch, though — he seems to be out of money. His check didn't clear. I wonder if he could use some outside investors?"

"Don't get yourself into that, Em. Might as well pour your money down a rat hole."

I thought briefly of my new nest egg — carefully and safely invested. "I don't plan to, believe me. But if he's onto something good, somebody should be interested.

Anyway, he's paid me most of what he owes me, in cash. I don't know if I want to give him any more time, though — I think he's more trouble than he's worth."

Allison had been watching our discussion as though it was a ping-pong match. "Whatever are you talking about?"

I realized I had probably been indiscreet. Denis had asked me to keep this quiet, and now I'd blabbed about it not only to Frank but also to Allison.

"This doesn't leave this room, okay, Allison? A guy from the university came to me earlier this week and asked if he could rent my studio, or more specifically, my kiln, to experiment with altering some inexpensive stones, to see if he could improve their color. Apparently he's succeeded, and he wants more time, but he's had trouble paying for the time he's used. If you're in the shop tomorrow, you'll probably see him." I wasn't about to say any more, and I thought it wise to change the subject. "So, tell me how you tore yourself away from all your kinfolk."

Allison proceeded to recount the events of the last few days, but it was clear that she was drunk with jet lag, and I took pity on her and interrupted her tale. "You want to crash here tonight? You look wiped out.

Frank's been sleeping in Cam's room, but you can have the couch."

"Uncle Frank's staying here?"

"Sure. I can tell you've never tried to find a hotel room in Tucson during Gem Show."

"If you're sure you don't mind."

"Allison, you know me. I wouldn't have asked if I didn't mean it. I'll even lend you a nightie."

"Thank you, Em. It's good to be home."

I put what was left of the food away and let my two guests duke it out for bathroom privileges. When I headed for my own room, I ran into Allison in the hallway. "Em, I'm glad we're okay, the two of us. But I'm still worried about Cam. It isn't like him to run away like this, is it?"

I felt a prickle of fear. She was right: I had never known Cam to simply disappear. Sure, he had been hurt by Allison's inability to talk to him, but I hadn't considered the possibility that his continuing silence could be due to something else. And I had to admit I had no idea where to even begin looking for him. Was he lying in a ditch somewhere? Or had he gone on a bender and ended up in a Mexican jail? I didn't know where to start.

"Maybe I could ask Matt what we could do, in the morning?"

She gave me a tremulous smile. "Could you? I don't mean to trouble you, but I really do need to see him, to explain."

"I'll call Matt first thing in the morning. You get some sleep."

But I went to bed with a nagging worry in the back of my mind.

CHAPTER 11

The Romans wore peridot to protect themselves from enchantment and also to ward off depression.

The next morning, Allison and Frank were up before me and busy in the kitchen area. More jet lag, no doubt. At least I would get a good breakfast out of it.

"Good morning," I said, reaching for the coffee. "Sleep well?"

"Until I woke up at three. I guess I'm still on Irish time," Allison said.

"It'll pass," I said wisely, based on my vast experience of the last week. "Give it a few days. Hand me the phone, will you?"

She passed the handset to me, and I punched in Matt's home number. When I got no answer there, I tried the station and was put through with only a short delay. "Hi, stranger," I greeted him when he answered.

"Hey there. Everything all right?"

"What, I can't call you just to chat?"

"I'd love to, but I've got to get to work."

I went on quickly. "Listen, there is something I'd like to run by you. Do you have time for a quick lunch?"

He sighed. "Don't count on it. You know we always have security issues around the Gem Show, and I don't know if I can get away."

I thought briefly. "I know, and I wouldn't ask if it weren't important. How about I bring some sandwiches by?"

"Sounds good. Maybe around one? There's an all-hands meeting at eleven, and who knows how long that will run."

"Deal. See you then."

I turned to find Allison watching with a half-smile, and no sign of Frank.

"Did Frank leave?"

"He did. He said he had business to attend to. Things going well with Matt, then?"

"I think so. We had dinner at his place on Monday."

"Ah," she said and then fell silent.

"I'll ask him what to do about Cam. If anything. I mean, we don't have any real reason to worry — it seems silly to get the police involved, if he's just gone off to mope." I hoped. Was I trying to convince

Allison or myself?

"I hope you're right. You know him better than I do, of course. He wouldn't do anything . . . to harm himself, would he?"

"No! Don't even think like that. It's more likely that he just got so involved in whatever project he's working on that he lost track of time, and he'll show up this weekend. I just want to talk to Matt and see what . . ." I dribbled to a stop. I wasn't sure what I was asking, but I just wanted to cover all the bases. In case. A few months ago I would have laughed at my own fantasies, but the last couple of months had been stressful, so I thought it better to be safe than sorry.

I decided to change the subject. "You ready to go downstairs?"

"I thought I'd run home, change clothes and such. I should be back around ten, if that suits?"

"Fine. I'll tell Nessa. You know that she and Frank are . . ." What? Dating? Seeing each other? Flirting?

Allison's mouth twitched. "I guessed as much, not that Uncle Frank has said a word. I think it's . . . sweet."

"As long as he does right by her." When I heard myself, I almost laughed out loud. Nessa definitely did not need protection.

144

"He's a good man, from all I've seen of him. Even the relatives had nothing bad to say, although they were a bit ticked off that he'd stayed away so long. But I gather they're used to that. The memories some of those people have! They'll be telling me about Aunt this and Cousin that, and then they mention it was all in 1938 or some such."

"I get the feeling that things move more slowly in rural Ireland. You sure you don't want to go back?"

"Maybe once or twice a decade. No, Em, my life's here now. Whatever that may be." She stood up quickly and started clearing the dirty plates and cups from the table. "I'll be on my way, and see you in a bit. Right?"

"Good. I'll walk the dogs and head downstairs. Allison — whatever happens, I'm glad you're back."

"Thank you, Em. I didn't want to let you down."

I think we had succeeded in embarrassing ourselves sufficiently for so early in the day, so I headed for the shower while Allison slipped out. Once dressed, I walked the dogs, then returned them, made sure they had food and water, and headed downstairs, where Nessa was already waiting.

She looked up when I came in. "Good morning."

"Good morning, Nessa. Guess what? Allison's back. She'll be here in an hour or so."

Nessa studied my face. "Is that good news?"

"I think so. She says she's back to stay."

Nessa hesitated before asking, "Has she heard from Cam?"

I shook my head. "No, and she hasn't been able to reach him. But at least now they can work out . . . whatever. Oh, if Denis shows up, send him to me, okay?"

"Do you think he will be back?"

"I'm pretty sure he will — I've still got some of his stones. I'll be in the studio."

From the studio I kept an eye on the shop. Shortly after noon, I wrapped up the piece I was working on, stowed it in the annealer, then went out to get food. Still no sign of Denis. I wasn't sure whether to feel relieved or disappointed. I had to admit I had never seen anything quite like the stone he had showed me the night before. But Frank had hinted that it might not be a stable change or that Denis might not be able to replicate it. There were a lot of "ifs" involved, and I had the feeling that Denis would need a lot of kiln time to work them out. If he couldn't pay for the time, what would he do? The kilns weren't all that expensive, but if he couldn't afford my studio time, how was he going to pay for a piece of equipment?

Loaded with an assortment of sandwiches, chips, and cold drinks, I presented myself at the police station and was waved through to Matt's office. He was on the phone when I arrived and held up a finger, telling me to wait. I busied myself laying out our repast while sneaking glances at his face. He looked frazzled.

He hung up the phone at last, then stretched out in his creaking chair, flexing his shoulders. "This looks great," he said, eyeing the food. "Things have been crazy the last few days, and I think there were a couple of meals that didn't happen. How you doing?"

I grabbed half a sandwich and popped the top of a soft drink. "Good, I think. At least the jet lag is gone. And Allison's back."

"When?"

"Last night. Frank's still around."

I watched as Matt inhaled half a sandwich in record time. When he had finished chewing, he asked, "You wanted to talk to me about something?"

"Yes, I needed to run something by you, as a hypothetical."

He picked up another half sandwich. "Go on."

"I don't want to be a nervous Nelly, but I haven't heard from Cam since he stormed out on Saturday, when I told him about Allison. I figured he needed time to lick his wounds, so I didn't think much about it. But now Allison's here, and she hasn't heard from him, and his phone is going straight to voice mail."

"What is it you want me to do, Em?" Matt said neutrally, ripping open a packet of chips and eying the remaining sandwich. I pushed it toward him.

"Right now, nothing. I guess I'm asking . . . when do you decide someone's missing, and what do you do about it?"

He munched his way through a handful of chips before answering. "I know Cam, and I know the circumstances under which he left. I don't think there's any way you — or I — could say he's officially 'missing.' He's an adult, he left under his own power, and he has good reason to avoid you and his girlfriend."

I knew he was right, but that was small comfort. "Okay, how about this? I know that Cam is a responsible person, and he's expected at a new job on Monday. If he hasn't shown up by then, would that be sufficient grounds to take the next step? And what would that step be?"

"You're serious, aren't you?"

"Matt, you know I wouldn't waste your time."

"Fair enough. All right. First we'd check his known locations."

"He has none here, except my place. He gave up his apartment in San Diego, and he hasn't started looking for one here yet. And before you ask, he doesn't know many other people around here. Professional colleagues maybe, but no friends."

"All right. Does his phone have GPS?"

"I have no idea. Probably, because he likes techy things like that, and I know his phone is pretty new."

"Do you know what service he uses?"

I stared at Matt, frustrated. "I barely know what service *I* use. And, before you ask, no, I haven't seen any bills forwarded to him at my place. He only arrived last week. And for all I know he pays everything online."

"If you can get access, we could find out whether he has made or received any calls since you've seen him."

"Doesn't that take a search warrant or something?"

"Maybe," Matt said noncommittally. "And we could see if he's used his credit cards.

What about his car? What's his license plate?"

"Matt, I don't know any of this stuff."

"I understand. But my hands are tied, officially, unless you file a formal missing persons report. Is that what you want to do?"

I thought. "I guess that's why I'm talking to you. Should I?"

"It depends. This is a guy with no history of instability, and there's no evidence of a crime. It's hard to justify using police resources under those conditions."

He was making sense, whether or not I liked it. And what could I give him to work with? Cam was an average-looking guy, and his only distinguishing feature was a scar on one elbow that he'd gotten when he fell off a bike when he was eight. I had no idea if he had any friends or confidants back in San Diego. He had never committed a crime, never had a drug problem or sought psychiatric help for any reason. I couldn't imagine that his fingerprints would be on file anywhere. Cameron Dowell was about as vanilla as a person could be, except maybe smarter than average. So where the hell was he?

Matt had watched me as I worked my own way through this. Finally he said gently,

"Em, I'm sorry. I wish there was something I could do."

"I know. This isn't your fault. And I'm probably worrying for nothing. You must see a lot of that in your job."

"I know you're not the hysterical type, and I am taking this seriously. Give him a couple more days, and if he hasn't shown up, then you can file the report and we'll start the gears turning. All right?"

"Okay. Matt, there's one other thing. . . . Can you check the morgue?"

Matt looked at me with something close to pity. "You really think that's necessary?"

I shook my head. "I just don't know. But it would make me feel a lot better if we could eliminate that as a possibility. I'm sorry, I don't mean to be a bother." I stood up.

"It's okay, Em — that's an easy call."

Matt stood up, came around his desk, and wrapped his arms around me. Maybe there was nothing practical he could do, but he was doing a great job of making me feel better, and that was something.

I was the one to break it off. "You have time for dinner tonight?"

"Let's try for tomorrow, and I'll let you know if something comes up."

I gathered my stuff. "I'd better get back

to the shop and make sure things are okay. I'm glad Allison's back, and I think she's had her fill of Ireland for the moment. I'll see you tomorrow."

"Count on it. And you let me know when Cam comes walking in the door."

"Believe me, you'll hear me yelling from here."

CHAPTER 12

A dream about peridot signifies a need for caution.

When I walked back into the shop after lunch, two pairs of anxious eyes turned to me. "Sorry — nothing new, and Matt says there's not much we can do right now. You?"

Two sets of shoulders drooped. "No, no word," Allison said. "I'm sorry, Em. This is all my fault."

"No, it's not. Anyway, Matt and I agreed that if Cam hasn't surfaced by the time he's supposed to start his new job, then we can start the official process and look for him. Right now let's just assume the best and go on about our business. Assuming we have any. Nessa?"

"The same."

"Which is zero. I'm going to go to my office and pay a few bills and then inventory my supplies. You know where to find me."

"Office" was probably a misnomer. The ground floor of my middle-aged brick building was divided between a large open studio and a smaller display area; storage and my business-work area was squeezed in behind the shop, along with a bare-bones bathroom. The actual work area in the office consisted of a scarred countertop with a rickety rolling chair in front of it, and it was laden with a computer, a phone, and a lot of stacks of paper — supply catalogs, invoices, bills, and other records. At least it had a door, not that I ever closed it.

I managed to lose myself in necessary paperwork for an hour or two. I definitely needed more supplies, and I also needed a new trucker to deliver those supplies on a regular basis. I'd had bad luck with my last two. Would the third time be the charm?

I stood up, stretched, and ambled toward my work area in time to hear pounding at the back door. Why was I not surprised to find it was Denis? Funny — every time I saw him he looked a little bit worse, and I'd only known him a week. But he didn't seem dangerous, just deeply distressed. Like he hadn't slept, eaten, or even bathed for a couple of days. Didn't the man have a day job? How could he be spending so much time at my place in the middle of a semester? I opened the door for him.

"Hi, Denis. How're you doing?" It was a rhetorical question, and I wasn't sure if I wanted an answer.

He pushed past me, already rummaging through his pockets. He fished out another wad of bills and thrust it at me. "Here. That brings us even for now. You said we could talk about going forward?"

"All right," I said cautiously.

"Look, Em, I need those stones I left here, and I need more time. I think I'm really onto something with this technique."

I was beginning to wonder if I needed to call somebody about him. And I was certainly ambivalent about having him around the studio. The man needed some serious R & R. "Denis, are you all right?" I said gently. "Can I get you some food, something to drink?"

He ran his hands over his face and slumped against the marver. "No, no. I'm sorry. Things have been difficult lately, and I've had a lot on my mind. I know I must sound like a lunatic." He straightened up and looked at me squarely. "Look, I really need just another few hours with the kiln, and I need to leave another batch of stones in overnight, see if I can replicate the last couple of runs, build up some volume. I can't pay you right now, but I swear I'll be able to in a week or two. Can you trust me that far?"

Anytime someone used the word "trust," it suggested the opposite to me. I wavered. But I really did feel sorry for him, and I didn't have much to lose. "Okay, Denis. I'll give you tonight, and some time tomorrow. But the weekend is really busy here, so that'll have to be the end of it."

He straightened up. "Oh, thank you, thank you, Em. I'm so close! That should be plenty of time. You won't be sorry. Look, I'll get out of your hair now, but I'll come back around six, okay, and I'll put another batch in, and then I'll be back in the morning, okay?"

"Breathe, Denis, breathe. That's fine. I'll be here."

The man was all but quivering with excitement as I escorted him out the back door. I hoped I hadn't made a big mistake.

After I had locked the door behind him, I restacked the piles of paper on my desk area and went back to the shop. Nessa was nowhere in sight, and Allison was straightening pieces on the shelves.

"Was that the man you spoke of last night?"

"Yeah, that's Denis. He's pretty high-strung. I told him he could come back and leave some stuff in the kiln overnight, and then he'll be back tomorrow to look at it. He thinks he's got some wonderful new technique."

"And you didn't have the heart to turn him down." Allison completed my statement but with a smile. "You're a good person, Em."

"I try," I said. "But he really is making me nervous. He's stretched pretty tight, and I don't want to pick up the pieces if he snaps."

"What more do you know about him?"

"Not much. He said he teaches at the university — English, I think. And he has a wife named Elizabeth — he brought her with him once. That's about all I know. But, heck, I don't ask my students for a full profile when I let them in. Anyway, he paid me what he owes, so I guess the next day is on credit. Or maybe my gift to him." I extricated the wad of small bills from my pocket and handed it to her. "Looks like he's been pawning the family jewels. Poor guy. Frank says the type of gem he's using isn't expensive. Of course, for all I know he's bought tons of the stuff." I tried to imagine a ton of rough stones and gave up. Luckily a couple of lookers came in, and I approached them with the intent of turning them into buyers. "Hi, I'm Em Dowell, and I'm the glassmaker. Would you like me to explain this technique to you?"

As promised, Denis was waiting once more at the back door just before six. This time he looked almost cheerful. "Hi, Em," he greeted me as I unlocked the door for him. "Thanks for letting me keep working. I'm sorry if I was a little crazy earlier, but I've been juggling so much stuff. But I'm close now, and I'm really excited."

I closed the door behind him. "Well, if what you showed me is any indication, I can see real possibilities. Do you know much about the gem business?"

"Not a whole lot, but I know people who do, and once I get the technique worked out, they'll help." He set down his backpack and started fishing packets of stones out.

I perched on a stool to watch. "So, once you've got the process nailed down, are you going to go into business?"

"What? Oh, no. 'Don't give up the day job,' you know? But it would bring in a little extra, and it's kind of fun, seeing what's possible. Maybe you get that kind of feeling, working with glass?"

This was the first time he'd actually asked a personal question, and I was happy to answer. "I think so. I'm always experimenting, and there's always more to learn. That thing you're doing, with changing colors — there's a glass technique called amberina that's like that. The glass starts out yellow — or amber — but if you heat it differentially it turns red. You can get some interesting effects that way. I gather it's due to the gold content in the glass."

"That sounds cool. Oh, bad choice of word — glass is hot, right?"

"That it is." Denis seemed . . . silly, I thought. I wondered if he was on some kind of mood-altering drug. Still, it wasn't any of my business, and I'd been paid. "Well, I'm starving, so I'm going to go up and find some food. I'll be back in an hour or so. Will that be enough time?"

Denis looked up from the small piles of stones he was sorting. "What? Oh, sure, fine. I just want to get these into the kiln and make a few notes. I really appreciate your letting me come back. And I'm sorry if I freaked you out earlier. Things should go better now. You go ahead."

"See you in a bit, then." I left him in the studio, exiting through the shop to make sure that things were shut down, and then went up the stairs to my place. When I entered, there was no sign of Frank. I fed the dogs, then walked them, taking a round-about route to see what my colleagues and competitors were up to, and noting that Madelyn Sheffield's stained-glass shop had a for-rent sign posted in the window. Wonder what would go in, in her place? It was a nice site, but I was happy where I was.

After the dogs had exhausted all the good smells of the evening streets, I took them back home, refilled their water dishes, then looked at my watch. An hour had passed, and if all Denis had planned was to put some more stones into the kiln, he should be done by now. Back I went, down the stairs, and around to the back. The lights were on, but when I unlocked the door and went in, Denis was nowhere to be found. But the kiln was shut neatly, and his back-pack and notebook were gone. As I straightened a few tools, I spied a pebble lurking under one of my glass nippers. No, not a pebble — one of Denis's treated tones. As I held it up to the light, I could see the golden glow in the center, though the stone was less than a quarter inch in size. I slipped it in my pocket to show Frank, whenever he showed up.

Which was sooner rather than later, because he was waiting when I let myself back into my home. I wondered, not for the first

time, just what he did with his days, although I guessed that Nessa might have
played a part this afternoon. But I wasn't
going to snoop. "Hi, Frank. Have you
eaten?"

"I have."

"That's good. Oh . . ." I hesitated a moment before pulling out Denis's stone from
my pocket, but then said, "Can you take a
look at this?"

He took it from me, rolled it in his palm,
then held it up to the light. Then he pulled
a loupe from his pocket and walked over to
the lamp by my couch and peered through
the stone. "Interesting," he finally said.
"This is your pal's work?"

I nodded. "He left it behind by mistake.
What does it look like to you?"

"Definitely peridot — you can tell by the
double refraction in the crystal, if you know
what to look for. And it's got that yellow-
green cast. But I'd guess it's darker than it
started, and the internal color is unusual.
He might have a shot at selling it."

"If he doesn't have a nervous breakdown
first. Let's assume Denis is on to something
entirely new, never seen before. What does
he do next?"

Frank handed the stone back to me, sat
down on the couch, and leaned back, link-

ing his hands behind his head. "He's an egghead, right? So he doesn't have connections in the gem business. If he's smart, he'll find a partner who knows the trade and let him sell the stones. Hope he knows some good cutters. The stones will sell better if he can flash the finished product."

"How does he find somebody?"

"Plenty of small dealers in town for the Gem Show. He'd be in good shape to go that route."

"So why is he in such a hurry? Unless he's already cut a deal and he's afraid he'll lose it."

"That I can't tell you."

"Okay. Like I said, maybe he's just nervous. I'll see that the stone gets back to Denis when he stops by to pick up his next batch. It may be his last, although he said he wanted more kiln time. What kind of dollars are we talking here, if he can put together a batch of rough stones?"

"If you're lucky, he'll net enough cash to buy a kiln of his own and get out of your hair."

"Amen to that." I stood up. "I'm heading for bed. Oh — I talked to Allison this morning, and we agreed that if we haven't heard from Cam before Monday I'd think about filing a missing persons report. That's what

Matt suggested."

"You're that worried?"

Reluctantly, I nodded. "It's not like him, not to contact me at all. I don't want to think that there's anything wrong, but I'd rather do what I can, you know?"

"I'm sure he's fine, but I agree with you. No harm to it. Well, good night to you — see you in the morning."

CHAPTER 13

One of the key characteristics of peridot is its double refraction: Objects seen through it appear double.

Somehow my dreams were colored by sparkling stones, which flashed and twinkled and then dissolved as I tried to grab them. When I finally dragged myself out of bed, I decided I couldn't wait until Monday to officially start the search for Cam. We had been raised by parents who could most kindly be called indifferent, and my brother and I had banded together early, despite the eight years' difference in our ages. As adults we didn't call each other every night and chat, and I didn't hover over him: we both had satisfying and busy lives. But these circumstances were different, and I expected him to let me know that he was all right and planned to return in time to start work on Monday. That's all I wanted.

So where was he?

Allison was in the shop when I arrived. We didn't even need to speak: we just looked at each other and shook our heads. Okay. No news was not good news, but didn't have to mean bad news. No news was just . . . no news. I picked up the phone and called Matt.

I was surprised that he wasn't at home, since this was Saturday. When he answered at his office after the usual delay, I said abruptly, "Matt, we've got to start looking for Cam."

"No word from him?" Matt sounded distracted, distant. "You want to come down and file a report today?"

"Wait — it's Saturday. What are you doing there?"

He sighed. "The Gem Show always brings extra trouble, so we've got a full crew here. You can come in today."

"All right." We said terse good-byes and I hung up, unsatisfied — a feeling that was compounded when I realized I had forgotten to ask him about his morgue search. Or maybe I hadn't forgotten; maybe I really didn't want an answer to that. Still, somehow filling out a piece of paper with Cam's particulars did not feel like taking action.

Allison was watching me anxiously. "Will

he help?'

"As much as he can. It's not exactly high on his priority list, and I can't complain about that. I know, I know — I want to do more, but I have no idea what. You?"

"No. Cam's made no effort to call me. I thought perhaps he might have written me, but there's nothing from him. Oh, Em — he's got to be all right! I'll never forgive myself if . . ."

"Stop. Don't go there. He's probably camping out under the stars howling at the moon and cursing all women, me included. This is just a precaution." I almost smiled at Allison looking for a letter, since Cam was such a computer guy, but then I remembered that Allison didn't even own a computer and probably had no e-mail address anyway.

I collected my car keys and made my way to the police station. Inside I was greeted by Mariana, the desk sergeant, who knew me fairly well. "Oh, hi, Em — the chief left this for you. He's in a meeting at the mayor's office, about security for the Gem Show, and he wasn't sure how long he'd be." She passed me a large manila envelope with my name on it. "Trouble?"

"Thanks. I hope not. I'll just fill this out and give it back to you, then."

I sat down in one of the unyielding plastic chairs in the waiting area and pulled out the form. It felt wrong, reducing Cam to a list of words on a page. White male, six foot one inch, 180 pounds (maybe?), gray eyes, blondish-brownish hair (varied depending on how much time he had spent in the sun recently), scar on left elbow. No jewelry. Clothes? Would guessing that he was wearing faded jeans, a button-down shirt with its sleeves rolled up, and ratty running shoes help or hurt? Car: I could give make and model, but damned if I had memorized the license plate. I barely knew my own. Last seen? A week ago, at my place. Permanent residence? He didn't have one at the moment. Place of employment? Nowhere, until next week. Relatives? Me, and only me. I didn't know whether to get mad or depressed by the stupid form, so I did both.

I finished filling in the blanks as best I could and handed the form back to Mariana. She glanced at it, then at me. "Your brother?"

I nodded. "He's supposed to be moving to Tucson to start a new job, but I haven't heard from him in a week. And that's not like him."

"I can see that you'd be worried. I'll see

that the chief gets this as soon as he returns."

"Thanks, Mariana. I'll see you." I turned and left more abruptly than I might have, not wanting to face the concern in her eyes. I just wanted to get on with finding Cam — and I hated that there was nothing else I could do. So I went back to the shop.

Allison was out, presumably at lunch; Nessa was in. I didn't feel like eating, so I said, "I'll be in the studio, if anyone needs me." If I couldn't do something about Cam, I would do something with glass.

"That's fine, dear," Nessa said. "We've got the shop covered."

The air was heavy with things we weren't saying, so I fled to the studio and started working.

A few hours later I managed not to drop the piece I was transferring to the annealer when there was a sharp rap at my back door. Denis, no doubt. I carefully stowed the hot glass piece and shut the annealer door before answering. It was indeed Denis, and the fact that he looked terrible, like warmed-over cheese, penetrated even my preoccupation. "You okay?" I asked.

He shoved past me without answering. "My stuff's still in the kiln?"

"Yes. I haven't touched it. Let me . . ."

168

Before I could do anything more, he had grabbed a pair of long tongs and opened the top of the kiln, reaching in to extricate one of the small crucibles. He dumped the contents on the metal marver and started poking through them with a pair of long tweezers, sorting them into two piles, one larger than the other. I caught the glint of gold from the smaller pile — ones he had successfully transformed? Nevertheless, apparently he wasn't happy. He returned to the kiln for first one, then a second crucible, until he had gone through the same steps for each, all in grim silence. I watched without saying a word, afraid he might snap like a bowstring if I interrupted him.

When he had sorted through all the stones he stood frozen, staring at the two piles. "It's not enough, damn it," he muttered, although loud enough for me to hear him.

I was getting stiff, trying to hold still. Besides, this was *my* studio, so why was I walking on eggshells? "Problems?" I said.

Denis turned to look at me, his expression bleak. "The process works, but not often enough. I need more. I can't make any money on this unless I have money to make more stones. And I don't have the money. Isn't that stupid? And I still need to get the stones cut and polished. What am I supposed to do? Em, I need more kiln time. And I need it now. Look, I'll pay you as soon as I sell some stones. Or I'll pay you in stones now. Whatever you want. But I've got to create more, and fast."

I studied him. Nice, respectable professional, my age. Good, steady job. Was I supposed to feel sorry for him? He'd gotten himself into this mess. Maybe under different circumstances I would have said yes, but I was worried about Cam, and Denis's check had bounced, and I wanted to get some of my own work done — and I was tired of being a pushover. "Look, Denis, I think you're going to have to find another kiln to use, or even think about getting one of your own if you're serious about this gem thing. I just don't think this is working."

Denis didn't say anything, and he had a peculiar expression on his face. Anger? Frustration? Calculation? Was he trying to figure out what he could offer me to change my mind?

Finally he spoke with a curious calm. "Em, I understand your position, and I know I must sound like a madman. I'm not really like this. It's just . . . money pressures, I guess, and I'm so close to making this technique work. If I could find another way, I would, really. I know it's not your problem, is it?"

I felt relieved — and as though I had backed away from a cliff. Poor Denis really was wound up about this gem thing. Was this kind of mania part of the whole precious-stones thing? I'd have to ask Frank.

Apparently my mind was wandering, because Denis had gone on talking and I wasn't following. "Excuse me?" I said.

"I was saying that I'd be interested in meeting your brother."

My antennae went up. "My brother?" I said.

"Yes. Cameron Dowell's your brother, isn't he?"

"Yes, he is. Do you know him?"

"We have some mutual colleagues who've talked about his work. Sounds like interesting stuff. He's moving to Tucson?" Denis's face gave nothing away.

"Yes, he is." I liked this less and less. How many people knew that Cam was moving here? Not many, I would guess. "Someone at the university knows him?"

"I guess that's where I heard about him. He's done some work with people there, hasn't he?"

"I think so." Heck, I didn't know. "Denis, why are you so interested in Cam?"

He held my eyes and smiled slightly. "Just

curious. He sounds like a guy with a lot of interests."

"Maybe I can introduce you, when he gets here," I said, my voice tight.

"Sure. You expect him soon?"

"Any day now." Okay, maybe he was just being polite, trying to soften me up so I'd give him more kiln time. Maybe he really did know people who did know Cam — it wasn't unreasonable. So why was I so uneasy?

"Good. I'm sure you'll enjoy having him around. Listen, Em, about the kiln time. I know I'm asking a lot, for you to trust me, but I believe that it will all work out, and soon. All I need is maybe another couple of days, a few more runs, to fill out the first batch. I'll be out of your hair soon, I promise. Can you give me that much?"

I wavered. I liked Denis less and less. But if he really did know who Cam's local friends were, I would have something to give the police — if it came to that. Which it wouldn't — would it? "Okay. Fine. You do what you need to do. You have until Monday and then we're done. Understood?"

He still had the same mirthless smile. "Thank you, Em. I'll be back later to start another batch. And I sure hope your brother's all right."

I stood frozen in place as Denis gathered up his stones, slipped them into bags, slid the bags into his backpack, then let himself out the back door, at an unhurried pace. By now all my interior alarms were sounding. Why had he had brought up Cam's name now? And why would he use those words: "I sure hope your brother's all right"? Was he trying to send me a message? Did he know something about Cam's whereabouts? Or was I just being paranoid and overreacting to an innocent comment? How was I supposed to know?

Too many questions, not enough answers. Time to talk to Matt again.

CHAPTER 14

The Aztecs, Toltecs, Incas, and ancient Egyptians believed that peridot could balance the energy of the physical body.

Once Denis had disappeared into the night, I headed back upstairs in a daze. No Cam, no message. No Frank either. I was feeding the dogs when I was interrupted by a knock on the door. The dogs raced to the door, looking eager, so it probably wasn't an enemy. I didn't have any enemies, anyway. Did I? I didn't dare hope it was Cam.

I opened the door to Matt. Wordlessly I, well, not exactly threw, but propelled myself into his arms, startling both of us. He patted me awkwardly but held his ground.

Reluctantly I let go, embarrassed, and peeled myself off him. We backed into the room and I shut the door behind us.

"Bad day?" he asked, watching my face.

"I've had better. Any news?"

"No, I don't know anything more. Though I did follow up with the ME's office to see if they'd found any unknowns lately."

"And have they?"

"Only one in the right time frame, and before you ask, it wasn't your brother. He was Hispanic, maybe ten years older than Cam."

"Well, that's something, I guess. Is he the one I read about in the paper the other day — the one with the pebbles?"

"That's him."

"Poor guy." *But at least it isn't Cam, thank God.*

"Hey, you hungry?"

"Definitely. How about Elena's?" Not only was the food good, but most tourists hadn't discovered Elena's small and informal restaurant, so we might have a chance at some privacy. And I could use the ten minutes it would take to walk to Elena's to make up my mind about what to say to Matt about Denis, who was definitely creeping me out.

We filled the brief walk with meaningless and rather disjointed small talk, both of us distracted by our own thoughts. As I had hoped, Elena's was only middling busy, and she directed us to a booth at the back. Once we had ordered and the waitress had re-

175

treated, we both sat back and stared at each other. Matt looked tired; I had no idea what I looked like.

"You want to go first?" I ventured, stalling.

"What?"

"You look like warm spit. Problems?"

He shrugged. "Nothing out of the ordinary. The Gem Show always stretches us thin — with all those stones, and a lot of cash floating around, we get more than the usual share of petty crimes, and there's also extra traffic to worry about. And don't forget the usual: politics, complaints. Penny-ante stuff that keeps us from working on the big stuff. It's been a long week. You?"

Okay, decision time. I understood that Matt had a lot on his plate at the moment. But I was worried about my brother. "Matt, what do I do about Cam now? I have to do *something*."

"You've filed the report — that's the first step. What do you know about Cam's new job?"

"We haven't had a chance to talk about it a lot." I searched my brain for the name of the company and came up blank. "Some sort of 'Save the Desert' organization. He connected with them pretty fast, once he decided to move to Tucson. I think the people there figured Cam would be a good complement to their existing staff — he has some standing in the ecology community, and he's a whiz with modeling natural systems, or so I understand."

"It's not affiliated with any of the local colleges or the university?"

"I don't think so. Cam thought he could have more impact with a small independent organization. Besides, he's not into that whole structured academic thing. Too much other baggage attached — he likes more independence." Like me. "I'm sorry I can't tell you more, but he hasn't even started working there yet."

"No hard feelings with the company he left?" Matt said. "He did give notice pretty quickly."

"I don't know. He might've said something to Allison. Maybe you should be talking with her."

"I will, if I need to. But let's not worry her at the moment."

"She's already worried, and she feels guilty on top of that. She thinks his disappearance is all her fault."

We sat in glum silence for a minute or so. Finally I said, "Matt, you know Cam — he's Mr. Squeaky Clean. I don't think he's done anything illegal in his life. I suppose it's barely possible that somebody knows about my windfall and is planning on shaking me down for money, but if so they're taking their sweet time about it."

I was still vaguely troubled by Denis's obscure comments, and though there was nothing Matt could do about them, I trusted him to tell me if I was completely off track. "Matt, can I run something by you? At least on a personal level, if not a professional one?"

"Of course."

He heard me out as I explained my first contact with Denis and described his rapid disintegration, ending with his cryptic comments about Cam. When I finished, I waited for Matt's response, which was slow in coming.

He poked at his cooling food, and I poked at mine. Finally he said, "Em, if I heard this from anybody else, I'd say that person had an overactive imagination with a dash of paranoia thrown in. But I know you, and I know Cam, and I'll agree that you have cause to be concerned. But we don't know for a fact that anything has happened to Cam. Maybe this Denis guy *is* acting a little strange, but that doesn't mean much. I'm not saying you're wrong, but what can I do?"

"How about checking out Denis?"

Matt nodded. "I can do that, within limits. I have no excuse to look at any of his records, much less subpoena them, but I can sniff around, see if he has any kind of history with the police."

It was a crumb, but I still sighed. "Somehow I doubt it. He's probably exactly what he says he is: an ordinary college professor playing around with an idea."

"Run through what he's doing again?"

"Heat-treating peridot, to make the stones more valuable. I asked Frank about it, and he says it's legal and it's done all the time. Maybe there's a kind of gray area if you don't state up front that the stones have been altered, but that's one of those 'buyer beware' situations. The buyer should ask that question."

"Where are the stones coming from?"

"I don't know. Denis hasn't said, and I never asked. I figured it was none of my business. He did say they were easy to buy."

"You know where most peridot comes from?"

"I didn't, but I do now, thanks to Frank — the San Carlos Reservation."

"You think maybe Denis is stealing from the reservation?"

I laughed. "You haven't seen Denis. He doesn't look like the type to go creeping around the reservation harvesting stones. And he has a day job at the university, presumably. Besides, he's got to be smart enough to know that someone is going to ask about his source."

"Maybe he's buying them from some middleman, who asked him to pretty them up. Even someone from the reservation. They sell to middlemen all the time. What was it Denis wanted you to do? Give him free access for the next couple of days?"

"Yes. He said he'd be done by next week. I told him I was cutting him off after this weekend. He kept muttering that he didn't have enough of the enhanced stones. So I guess he thinks he can produce the right number fast. Maybe he's got some kind of deal with someone who's in town for the Gem Show and who's leaving soon?"

Matt was staring at some spot over my head, until he said slowly, "I'll bet the Apaches keep a pretty close eye on peridot sales — after all, they make good money from them. So if something new pops up, they'll be right there asking questions."

"Great," I said glumly. "Now we've got a local Indian tribe in this mess. Is there anyone else you'd like to throw into the mix? The CIA maybe, or international jewel thieves?"

"Em . . ." Matt said simply.

I knew he was trying, and that made me feel a little better. "I'm sorry — this is not your fault. You know, if Cam were here, I'd ask him to do some computer snooping, about Denis, and stones, and the San Carlos group. I don't have the skills or the time or the patience to do that, and you can't ask your people to do it. I suppose I'm just hoping there's a loose thread somewhere that will untangle this."

Finally Matt said, "Em, I agree that there's something here that doesn't feel right. I don't like coincidences, because they usually aren't. And Denis mentioning Cam right now is definitely a coincidence."

I didn't know whether to cheer or cry. The good news was, Matt believed me and he was going to help, officially or not; the bad news was, that meant he believed that Cam could be in trouble, and we didn't have a whole lot to go on. But it warmed me that he was on my side. He'd even said "we." I slid my hand over his, across the table. "Thank you."

"For what?"

"For believing me. For not telling me I'm overreacting. For taking this seriously. I'm sorry I'm dumping it on you at such a busy time."

"Em, I know you're not a hysterical female, and I know you care about your brother. We'll work this out."

The warm and fuzzy interval lasted about thirty seconds, and then I withdrew my hand and sat back in my chair. "Now what?" I asked.

Matt rubbed his hands over his face. He still looked tired. "Is Frank still around?"

"Yes. He hasn't said when he's leaving. Why?"

"Because Frank's the best resource we have about the gem community. I may help deal with security for the Gem Show on occasion, but I wouldn't know a ruby from a gumdrop."

"Want to go see if he's home?"

"I guess. And if he isn't, maybe we can find something else to do?" He made a brave attempt at a leer, but it fell a bit short of the mark.

I appreciated the sentiment anyway. "Let's go."

After Matt had settled the bill (hey, he'd asked me to dinner), the walk back took little time. When I let us in, Frank was settled on the couch, engrossed in a journal of some sort, with reading glasses perched on his nose. I was a little bit disappointed to see him — I could have used some quality time with Matt.

Frank looked up and greeted us enthusiastically. "Em, Matt! I wondered when anyone would show up. What's the word?"

"Not much." There was no point in beating around the bush, and I knew Frank liked to be direct. "Frank, when I saw Denis today, he mentioned Cam, and it bothered me — he made some sort of explanation about how they know the same people, but I didn't buy it. Denis was pretty coy, but I had to wonder if he was trying to pressure me somehow. Anyway, I thought it was time to call for reinforcements, at least unofficially. I've brought Matt up to speed on Denis and what little I know about him and what he's doing, but Matt thought we could both use your expertise with stones, if you're willing to help."

"Of course. What d'ya need?"

Without asking, I went to my refrigerator and located three bottles of beer. Looked like Frank had done a little restocking, bless him. I distributed them and sat down.

"Frank," Matt began, "I'm the first to admit I don't know much about gems, but this is what Em has given me so far: Denis has a supply of peridot, and apparently the ones he has can be altered artificially, to his advantage. He's in a hurry to turn out a certain number of treated ones, which may be related to the end of the Gem Show. Maybe he's got a buyer who's leaving? Who'd be interested, and why the rush?"

Frank thought for a moment before answering. "Might be another thing — maybe his source doesn't know he's got the stones, and your man wants to get them off his hands as fast as he can."

"If he's got them illegally, you mean? Hmm . . . most of the local stones come from the San Carlos Reservation, but they're pretty tightly controlled. You think Denis's come from there? It's not illegal to buy them."

"He could buy them up front, no worries. But then he wouldn't be so anxious, would he? Maybe he's sneaking them off the reservation and doesn't want to be caught. That's more your territory than mine, Matt."

"Not really," Matt replied. "That's outside my jurisdiction, in more ways than one. It's tribal land, and they have their own courts."

"Didn't know that. Interesting. But maybe I can help. Stones from different locations may have different properties, and you can identify the source. So if I had a stone from

Denis's stash, I could compare it with a stone from the reservation, maybe tell you if they're the same. That'd be one more piece of information for you." He cocked an eyebrow at me. "Em, you still have that stone?"

Sweet man, he was trying to protect me. Well, I hadn't actually *taken* the stone from Denis — I'd found it in my studio and I hadn't gotten around to returning it. "Yes, I do. And before you ask, Matt, Denis left it behind, and I picked it up. For safekeeping, you know."

"Of course." Matt managed to keep a straight face. "So if we had a reservation stone, you could look at them both, right, Frank? Shouldn't be too hard to come by."

"Way ahead of you, Matt." Frank fished in his pocket and pulled out a few now-familiar plastic envelopes of rough stones. "Been collecting them all along, sort of a souvenir of my trip. Got samples of all the sources."

"Frank, you are a marvel," I said. I retrieved Denis's stone from where I'd hidden it. "Here's the other one." I handed him what now seemed to be our first — and only? — clue. Then Matt and I sat side by side and waited while Frank located his loupe, found a light source that suited him,

185

and compared the stones. And compared. And compared. Maybe this careful approach made him a good gem dealer, but he was driving me crazy.

Finally he returned his stone to its bag and handed the other back to me. "They could be the same. They're not different, anyway. Definitely not Afghan, Pakistani, or Burmese."

I wondered if I could hit him with something. "So what does that tell us, Frank?"

"I'd guess the stones are local. They came from the reservation or someplace nearby — it would have to be the same geological formation, although that could cover quite a lot of ground."

"Frank, how much more do you think the altered stones would be worth, compared to the unaltered ones?"

"Hard to say, Em. And it also depends on who he tries to sell them to, and how."

"Give me a guess, will you? Twenty-five percent? Fifty percent?"

"The treated one you showed me looks pretty unique to me. Make it a hundred percent, easy, to the right buyer. Maybe more, if the marketing was right."

"So he's doubled his investment, with a couple of hours in my studio. Is that what you're saying?"

"It's possible. Still all completely legal, you know."

I looked at Matt, who looked distracted. "Matt? What're you thinking?"

He shook his head. "I thought I had something, but I lost it. Sorry, Em, but I'm beat. I'll be more useful with a decent night's sleep." He stood up, slowly for him. "I'll talk to you tomorrow. Em, see me out?"

I followed him to the door. "Matt, is there anything I can do?"

"You told Denis he could come back, right? I'm thinking maybe it's time I take a look at the guy. When are you expecting him?"

"Probably early — he wants to produce as much as he can over the weekend. The treatment that seems to work best takes a while, so I'd bet he'll show up early, pick up the ones that are done, and put in some more."

"So I'll be here early. Em, Cam'll be all right. You'll see."

He wrapped his arms around me, and we sort of held onto each other for a while. It was nice. And it occurred to me that he didn't care if Frank noticed either. Definitely nice.

Finally he untangled us and took his leave. I made my way back to where Frank was sitting; he was wearing a restrained grin. "Good man to have on your side, eh?"

"Definitely."

CHAPTER 15

Ancient legends hold that peridot can protect its wearer from evil spirits.

Before I opened my eyes the next morning, I listened, hoping against hope that I'd hear Cam's voice, bantering with Frank or Matt or even the dogs. Nothing. With a sigh I heaved myself out of bed and took a shower.

Spruced up and ready to face the day, I went to my main room. No humans, just Fred and Gloria, and since they weren't nipping at my ankles, I assumed Frank had fed them. When I looked, I found he had left me a note on the kitchen table:

Breakfast with friends. Back later. F.

Short and to the point — typical Frank.

I had made my coffee and eaten breakfast when Matt arrived. "You want some coffee?"

"Please," he replied, then bent down to

greet the dogs. While I made more coffee, I puzzled over his choice in wardrobe: faded jeans, faded running shoes, faded shirt with the sleeves rolled up. I was used to seeing him in his "public" garb — not exactly a standard suit-and-tie but respectable enough to interview a public figure or even appear on the evening news. This was decidedly casual for him.

He sat at the table, and I put a filled mug in front of him. I sat down with another mug. "Okay, why are you here, and why are you in disguise?"

He looked puzzled for a moment, then looked down at his shirt and smiled. "I kind of wanted to blend in. I thought I'd come down and hang around the shop until Denis shows up, catch him off guard. Maybe that'll help me figure out what tack to take."

"You've got something?"

"Kind of." He avoided my eyes, looking into the depths of his coffee while he swirled the mug in his hands. "I remembered what escaped me last night. When we were talking about stones?"

"Okay. What?" I prompted.

"The body at the ME's."

"The one with the pebbles?"

"That's the one."

I nodded encouragement, not sure why it

mattered. As long as it wasn't Cam, I really didn't care much.

Matt went on. "The ME gets pretty backed up, with all the illegals coming over the border and not making it. He usually doesn't have time to process the bodies for a while, especially if there's no ID on them, but he and his staff record the basics. Sad — a lot of the time there's no one to notify that they're dead."

"It's a tragedy, I agree. But what's it got to do with Cam?"

"The ME mentioned the pebbles, and I didn't think much about it. But then when Frank was showing us those rough stones, it hit me. . . ."

"You think the pebbles might actually be peridot?" I finished his sentence. That didn't sound good.

"Right. Long shot, I know. But I stopped by the morgue on the way here — I called in a favor and talked the ME into authorizing me to take a couple of the pebbles. This is what he gave me." Matt pulled a small plastic ziplock bag out of his shirt pocket and tossed it across the table to me.

Even before I picked it up, I was pretty sure what I was going to see. I held the small packet up to the light, watching the green glints within the dusty stone. "Rough peridot. The guy at the ME's office had no idea what they were?"

"Nope, not when the body came in. Not that it mattered to him. It didn't tell him anything useful about the dead guy."

"Did you ask where that body was found?"

"Of course. A dry canyon east of Summerhaven, in Pima County. The reservation is a good ways north of there. The body wasn't on reservation land, which would be a whole different can of worms."

"And how long had he been out there, before they found him?"

"Maybe a day. The body was in good shape."

"Still no ID for him?"

Matt shook his head. "As I said, there are a lot of bodies that come in, and there was nothing remarkable about this one. When you asked me to nose around, and I came across the report on this body, I did ask the ME to take a closer look, see if he could determine cause of death. Most of these are just written off to exposure and/or dehydration, so they don't look too hard, but this guy didn't look like he'd been out there long enough for that."

"Who found him?"

"A regular patrol. They look for the vultures."

192

I pushed that ugly thought out of my head. I was reluctant to frame my next question, but I had to. "Do you think this dead man is somehow connected to . . ." What? So far I had a creepy college professor with some peridot, and a missing brother. Not much to go on.

"I'm not even going to guess at the moment, Em, but peridot keeps popping up here, and you know I hate coincidences."

"I know. Matt, thank you for pulling strings, or whatever you want to call it, on this. I appreciate it. What do we do now? For all I know, Denis is standing outside the back door of the studio as we speak. Do you have a plan?"

"I thought I'd play innocent tourist and just hang out in the shop or the studio — kind of scope him out."

"Be gentle, will you? I don't want Denis to fall apart, because then we'll never learn anything."

"You cut me to the quick, Em. Have I ever been anything but courteous to my suspects?"

"I don't really know. Have you?"

He dropped the bantering tone. "I know my job, Em. Don't worry."

He kept saying that to me. Heck, *I* kept saying it to me. It didn't do any good, and I just kept worrying. "I'm going to walk the dogs, and then we can go downstairs for our little charade."

"I'll wash the dishes," Matt said blandly. I was less than impressed: the dishes consisted of two mugs and one plate. But it was a nice thought.

I made a quick dash around the block, leaving the dogs relieved but less than satisfied, but didn't see Denis anywhere. I returned them to my place, and Matt followed me downstairs as I opened up. Both Allison and Nessa arrived hard on our heels. I needed the extra coverage — not to mention the moral support. They were surprised to see Matt.

He smiled in an attempt to set them at ease. "Pretend I'm just an ordinary customer, all right?" he said.

Allison looked bewildered, but Nessa caught on. "Were you looking for something in particular or just browsing, sir?" she said, her face innocent.

"Browsing, I guess. I've met the artist, and I found her work . . . interesting." They drifted away toward a display, talking about glass, and I headed for the studio. I thought I could get a few pieces done before lunch, assuming I wasn't interrupted, but waiting for Denis made me jumpy and I couldn't focus. I settled for tidying up my frit cans and glass canes, the colors I added to clear glass through a variety of techniques, keeping a watchful eye on the color kiln — as though I expected it to empty itself or vanish — and the back door. It was nearly eleven when Denis finally arrived, looking worse than the day before. The man was running on fumes.

"Em," he said, and made a beeline for the kiln.

"Denis," I replied, then looked over toward the shop window and nodded at Nessa. The door opened and Matt drifted in, looking confused.

"Oh, sorry — the woman in the front said it was okay to come in and look around."

Denis looked up briefly then dismissed him. He had spread out the latest stones on the marver, and he was poking at the piles with the long tweezers.

"No, that's fine," I said to Matt, trying to hold up my end of the ruse. "This is where I create all of our pieces. Let me know if you have any questions, or if you see anything you like."

Matt wandered around the room, picking up a glass piece now and then and admiring it, but getting ever closer to where Denis was working. Finally he drifted toward the marver and peered over Denis's shoulder. "Those glass?" he said.

"No," Denis replied, and clammed up again.

"Gemstones maybe?" Matt prodded.

"Yes. Can't you see I'm working? You're crowding me."

I could see Denis's hand shaking as he sorted the hot stones with the metal tool.

Matt stepped back but stopped at the end of the marver. "They're peridot, aren't they, Denis?"

It took a moment for the full import of Matt's words to sink in, and then Denis turned toward me with an expression that combined equal parts of anger and fear. "I told you to keep your mouth shut."

"Denis, I happen to care about my brother, and I thought it was a little odd that you'd mention him when you did. Oh, maybe I should introduce my friend here, since you don't seem to recognize him. This is Matt Lundgren, Tucson chief of police."

Denis turned an interesting shade of gray, and for a moment I wondered if he was going to pass out. He backed away from the stones and fumbled blindly until he found a stool, collapsing on it. He shut his eyes for a long moment, then opened them again. "I should have known better. I should never . . . I don't know what to do."

Matt stepped closer. "Mr. Ryerson, do you have any knowledge of the whereabouts of Ms. Dowell's brother Cameron?"

"No. Well, not exactly. It's complicated."

"Then maybe you can explain it to us."

"No! I can't. I have to finish . . . Are you arresting me? I haven't done anything!"

"Mr. Ryerson," Matt said patiently, "you are not under arrest. As of this moment, I'm not aware of any crime you have committed. I am simply asking if you know where Cameron Dowell is."

"I'm sorry, I'm sorry. Maybe I should talk to a lawyer. But I don't have time to talk to a lawyer. I don't know what to do . . ." Just as I had feared: Denis looked headed for a complete meltdown, which wouldn't help any of us.

I stepped closer to him and laid a hand on his arm. "Denis," I said gently, "this has to do with the stones, doesn't it? And why you're in such a hurry to produce the altered ones?" When he nodded, I pressed on. "Are they stolen, Denis?"

"No, no, no," he shook his head violently. "They're mine, legally, or ours, I guess. They come from a property we hold title to, at least for the moment."

Matt and I exchanged a glance, and he

nodded slightly at me. Apparently the feminine touch was working. "You said 'we.' Are you working with your wife, Denis? Or someone else?"

"Not my wife — a friend of mine, from the university. Alejandro Gutierrez — Alex. He's in the geology department. You see, we . . ."

Matt interrupted. "Mr. Ryerson, have you seen or spoken with your friend recently?"

"What? No, I guess not. That's part of the problem. You see, we were worried . . . I mean, we had a buyer lined up, but he's here only for the Gem Show, so he's leaving soon. He said if we didn't have them ready by then, the deal was off. But we had trouble working out the kinks in the process, so we fell behind, and I've been trying to catch up. Alex was the one who set up the deal, but I don't know if he's talked to the guy lately. I'm not sure how to get hold of him."

I wasn't prepared when Matt pulled a folded sheet of paper out of his pocket. "Can you give me a physical description of your friend?"

Denis looked at Matt bleakly. "Alex? Uh, maybe six feet, dark hair, dark eyes. My age or so. Pretty fit — he spends a lot of time rock climbing. Why?"

Matt unfolded the paper with deliberation, then slid it, face up, across the marver to Denis. "Is this your friend?"

Denis took one look at it, and then his eyes rolled up in his head and he started to slide off the stool. Matt caught him before he hit the floor, thank goodness.

"I'll take that as a yes," Matt said.

CHAPTER 16

It has been claimed that peridot brings power and influence to its owner.

Two steps forward, one step back. Denis Ryerson had a partner, Alex Gutierrez; Alex was dead. Denis was working with local stones, and he and Alex had a buyer who was leaving town shortly, which was why Denis was in such a hurry. But what did Cam have to do with any of this?

Matt was holding woozy Denis upright on the stool. "Em, can you get him a glass of water or something?"

I mobilized myself and went to fill a plastic cup from the water cooler I kept in the studio — it was important that both I and my students stayed hydrated when we were working with hot glass, especially in Arizona's dry climate, so I always had water on hand. Wordlessly I handed it to Denis, who grabbed the flimsy cup with both shaking hands. At least he managed to raise it to his mouth and swallow, while both Matt and I watched like hawks. I looked at Matt. "We don't need medical help?"

"I don't think so. You okay now, Denis?"

Denis nodded. His eyes stayed open, and he was sitting up all by himself. "I don't know what just happened, but I've been so stressed out lately, and then that picture . . . I wasn't expecting it. He's dead? What happened to him?" He raised his eyes to Matt.

"We aren't sure yet. His body was found out in the desert north of here, last weekend."

"Oh God, oh God . . ." Denis shut his eyes and rocked back and forth on his stool. "When did he die?"

"Maybe a day or two before that." Matt watched Denis critically. "When did you last see him?"

"I don't know . . . let me think. A week? Ten days? We have lunch on campus now and then — we've been friends for years, and business partners more recently."

"Didn't you find it odd that you didn't hear from him for a week, at this particular time?"

Denis shrugged. "No. I told you, he's a geologist. He's always going out rock climbing, looking at stuff. He'd handed off the treatment of the stones to me, and he was going to pick them up when I was done. I can't believe he's dead. What happens now?"

"Obviously there'll be an investigation into your partner's death, now that we know who he is, but that's for the county sheriff to deal with, since the body was found outside city limits. I'll get in touch with him, and with the ME. But right now, I'd appreciate it if you'd tell me what's been going on. Why don't we go upstairs?" Matt looked at me and I nodded.

Matt got Denis onto his feet, keeping a hand on his arm to steady him, but then Denis turned back. "The stones, they . . ."

Oh, right — the ones he'd left on the marver. "I'll collect them for you." I rummaged for an empty frit can and swept the stones off the marver into it before following Matt and Denis out the back, thinking hard. I wasn't an officer of the law or a trained psychiatrist, but Denis's reaction to the picture had certainly looked sincere to me. Did he have any idea *why* Alex was dead? And did it involve the stones? And where the hell did Cam fit in this equation?

I opened the door for Matt — and found Frank waiting for us. Frank stood up when we arrived, and I ushered everyone ahead of me. Was I supposed to offer refreshments, or was this an interrogation? I decided against it, mostly because I didn't want to miss anything.

Matt made perfunctory introductions. "Denis Ryerson, Frank Kavanagh." I noticed he didn't explain who Frank was or why he was here, but Denis seemed beyond caring.

I took inventory of the group: Denis looked miserable, Frank looked cheerful but his eyes were wary, and Matt looked . . . official. He and Frank exchanged some sort of unspoken conversation, which I interpreted as "stay here because I might need you, but keep your mouth shut."

We sat. Matt prodded Denis. "Mr. Ryerson, let's take this from the beginning."

"Wait, wait. You're not arresting me?"

"No, I'm not. I just want some information."

"Okay, okay." Denis closed his eyes for a moment before starting. "I told you I was a faculty member at the university? I've been there about fifteen years now, since I got my PhD. I met Alex years ago at some university function — I don't even remember now. He's — he was with the geology department, but that didn't mean much to me in the beginning. He's not married, and I think he was lonely, and we got to be friends, after a while. Things went on that way for a few years."

Denis stopped and ran his fingers through his already-messy hair. "We were both making decent money at the university, so we came up with this idea to start investing some of it, making it work for us. This was maybe five, seven years ago? And it looked like this whole area was really booming. I'm sure you've noticed — all these housing developments going up around the city, even further and further out. So we started buying up undeveloped land. We weren't in any hurry — we're a long way from retirement, and we don't have any kids to put through college. We could afford to sit on the land and wait for it to appreciate, and it worked pretty well for a while. We turned over a few properties for a nice profit, and put a lot of the money into more."

I could figure out where this was going. Tucson — and the rest of Arizona — had been booming for a long time, with lots of population moving in, and lots of new construction. But over the past year or so, the national economy had slumped, and so had the local economy, if not quite as quickly. Most likely Denis and his pal had been caught with their pants down, so to speak. "And then the market changed, right?"

Denis shot me a glance. "Exactly. We'd gotten kind of careless, I guess, and we overextended ourselves. Now we've got some big balloon loans coming due and no way to pay them off, and nobody's buying land."

While I didn't want to interrupt the flow of Denis's story, it still seemed a long jump from bad real estate investments to tinkering with stones in my studio to a dead body in the desert.

Denis plowed ahead. "So, like I said, Alex was a geologist, and he gets this bright idea, see? Some of the properties we owned were north of here — open ranch land. We got it cheap, but it's probably going to be a while before anybody's going to want to build on it. Anyway, he starts looking at it, poking around, and he finds some peridot here and there."

"That's up toward the San Carlos Reservation?"

Denis nodded. "Yes, but it's definitely not reservation land. We made sure of that."

"You know which piece of land the stones came from, Denis?" Matt said.

"No. I know, this makes me sound stupid. But Alex was the geologist, and he found the stones. I didn't plan to go out there and grub around in the sand. We had clear title, I know that much. Look, you can go over all the documents — we set up a legal partnership, and I've got the articles of incorporation, copies of the deeds. We weren't doing anything funny. Anyway, the stones he was finding were nothing special."

Frank spoke. "Midgrade stones, average color, not big. Nothing to get excited about."

"You've seen them, uh, Frank, was it?" When Frank nodded without elaborating, Denis went on. "He's right — pretty ordinary. But Alex thought maybe there was a way to make them better, and he started experimenting. I guess he liked what he saw, because that's when he told me about it, got me involved."

"You didn't know about the gems before that?"

"No, not specifically. Not my area of expertise. I'm an English lit professor, after all. And it didn't look like they'd be worth much, at least until Alex started fooling around with them."

"Hang on," I interrupted. "I thought you said you couldn't use the university equipment?"

Denis shrugged. "That's what Alex said at

first. Mostly I think he was paranoid that somebody would figure out what he was doing and horn in on it, so he handed the processing over to me. Said any idiot could do it, once he'd worked out the basics. But I didn't mind doing it. I thought the whole idea was cool, and we weren't going to lose anything by exploring the idea, right? So I read up on it, and we started working together on the process."

I had to give myself a gold star for self-restraint. This was all very interesting, but it wasn't getting us any closer to why Cam had anything to do with this, or why Alex had ended up dead.

Denis must have sensed my frustration, because then he said, "And that's when Cameron Dowell got involved."

CHAPTER 17

Some Hawaiian beaches are made of tiny grains of peridot, which to the Hawaiians symbolized the tears of the goddess Pele.

That certainly got my attention. "Cam was working with you?"

"Kind of. Alex had been looking into computer modeling of geological formations."

"What does that mean? I thought mostly people did aerial surveys and drilling samples and stuff like that." Matt glared, but that didn't stop me. This was *my* brother we were talking about.

"Sure they do — not that Alex and I could afford anything like that. But recently there's been interest in nonphysical mapping, taking what's known about an area and extrapolating based on data from other comparable geological formations."

That sounded like something that would

interest Cam, although as far as I knew he specialized in natural systems — plants, animals, weather patterns, and that kind of thing. "But that's not Cam's specialty. How did he get involved?"

"Alex talked to people he knew at the university, asked about a computer modeler. I told you, he was getting nervous about people finding anything out, so he talked in very general terms. What he was asking about fit into his usual research interests, so nobody asked why. What we really wanted to know was whether the formations we had on our land were extensive enough to work seriously, or if we'd just picked up a couple of pretty pebbles that could have come from anywhere. Somebody mentioned Cameron Dowell, and Alex got in touch with him."

"But you didn't ask Em about using her equipment until after Cam had started working on your project," Matt said. "When exactly did you make the connection?"

"I didn't, not really. I needed something that produced certain temperatures, and I couldn't use the university equipment. I thought a glassblower would have what I needed, and Em's the only glassblower in town who rents studio time, so I ended up here. It still took me a couple of days before I put her and Cam together, and even then

I wasn't sure. I asked her about it yesterday. Right, Em?" He turned to me.

He was right — up to a point. "You didn't ask about Cam until yesterday," I agreed. I had no way of knowing when he had connected us.

"Anyway," Denis continued, "when it turned out that he was moving to Tucson anyway, it seemed like a stroke of luck. Alex outlined the project, and Cam spent some time reviewing the procedures, what kind of data he would need. He got back to us and said he'd be willing, and he'd need some time on site to collect hard data from that specific site. He sounded pretty sure he could wrap it up pretty fast."

That certainly sounded like Cam. I turned to Matt. "Right before he left, Cam said he had a short-term project he was working on. This must have been it. He never gave me any of the details." I shifted back to Denis. "Did you ever actually meet Cam?"

"No. Alex set it all up. I couldn't have contributed much anyway — I'm not into that side of things. Alex didn't even tell me exactly when Cam would be working."

"Cam was supposed to give his results to Alex?"

"That was the plan. Like I said, Alex handled it. I think Alex was getting kind of

210

bent out of shape about all of this — he couldn't stand the idea of losing money on this whole real estate deal, and that's why he went off on a tangent with this whole gem thing. Hell, he didn't even have a family to consider. I don't know how to tell my wife about any of this."

Things still weren't adding up. "Let me get this straight. You two owned the land. You had a legitimate right to whatever minerals were on it. You were investigating a perfectly legal way to improve the value of the stones you found. So why is one man dead and one missing? And why are you in such a hurry to crank out the stones?"

"I told you," Denis protested. "There are loans coming due, and if we default, then the bank takes the land back and we lose the whole bundle. We thought we had it all figured out, with these dealers in town for the Gem Show, but not that many people were interested, and our buyer said he'd walk if we didn't get the stones to him. We were running out of time."

My questions were multiplying like rabbits, but Matt interrupted. "Do you hold title jointly or through the partnership? Was there any provision made in the event one of you died?"

I caught a flash of the whites of Denis's

eyes as he rushed to answer. "Of course. We set up everything by the book. And, yes, the whole thing reverts to me now — including all the obligations. But before you even wonder if I might have had something to do with Alex's death, tell me just how I benefit, huh? I'm worse off now than before."

He had a point. "Is there anything that Cam might have found that would make a difference?" I asked.

"I don't know. He told Alex that he couldn't give us much time, because he was starting a new job, right? But his main contact was Alex. I don't even know if he knows how to reach me, although I suppose he could ask around at the university — if he even knows my name."

Knowing my methodical brother, I was sure that he would have checked out the bona fides of Alex, Denis, and their little corporation before committing to anything — and probably demanded to be paid up front. I wondered if there was any way to look at his recent bank deposits. Even so, it sounded as though this was a project that he would have enjoyed, and one he'd clearly thought he could finish quickly. I looked at Matt. "But Alex has been dead for at least a week now, right? Denis, you weren't concerned?"

"I didn't even know Alex was missing, and it's not like we talked every day. In fact, recently we haven't talked much at all, since usually all we had to share was bad news. The last time we talked was when he told me he'd hired Cam and told me how much he was paying him, since that came out of the corporate account — which was getting pretty close to rock bottom."

Denis turned back to Matt. "Alex and I had talked about what we were doing with the stones we did have. He's the one who collected them, and he gave them to me. I've been working out the details of procedures, timing, temperatures — you've seen that, Em. Maybe I'm just slow, but I really didn't get any significant results until a couple of days ago. When things started working with the stones, I called and left Alex a voice message, and he didn't get back to me, but I had no reason to believe there was anything wrong."

Frank broke in. "You know who the buyer is?"

Denis shook his head. "Alex didn't tell me much — I think he had a phone number somewhere. But I know that this guy wants the stones next week, or the deal's off. He really wanted them a week ago. He's willing to take the chance that the stones are what we told him they are. It's all a gamble, isn't it?"

I tried to suppress my budding panic. "Denis, do you know where Cam was staying? Is there a place to stay on this property of yours?"

"Maybe." Denis shrugged. "I've driven through that area, mostly on the way to the casino, but I don't really remember. Truth is, I've never even seen most of those sites myself. I told you, Alex took care of all that."

"Matt?" I appealed to him.

"Em, that missing persons report gives the police the authority to check Cam's phone records and credit card charges and maybe even his computer access, but it's not instantaneous. If he's holed up in a motel out there, the charges might not even have showed up on his account yet. Or he might have paid cash."

"I would have said he'd go into withdrawal if he couldn't get online for more than a day, but maybe he really did want to get away from everything." *Including me.* "What do we do now?"

Denis stood up abruptly. "Are you charging me with anything, or am I free to go?"

Matt couldn't ask the obvious question, but I could. "Where are you in such a hurry to go?"

"I've still got to finish up with the supply of stones on hand, and if Alex isn't going to be bringing me any more now, I better hope like hell that I can figure out who the buyer is. And I need the stones downstairs back. If you won't let me use your studio, I'll have to find some other way."

I looked at Matt, who shrugged imperceptibly before answering Denis. "You're free to go. But I'd suggest staying around town for the foreseeable future. And I'll give the ME's office Alex's name — and your contact information. If Alex has no family around here, you might need to identify the body."

"Great," Denis muttered under his breath. Then he straightened. "Sorry, you're right. I owe Alex that much. I'll give the ME's office a call."

"Thank you for answering our questions. I'll get back to you if we need anything else."

Denis summoned up a weak smile. "Thank you for treating me politely. I was expecting maybe rubber hoses." When nobody laughed, he held up both his hands. "Joke, joke. Em, can you let me in downstairs so I can collect the other stones? Please?"

I had no reason other than petulance to deny him, and I wasn't about to stoop that low. "Sure. Follow me."

I led him back down the stairs and around to the back door. Inside, I retrieved the stones from where I'd put them, decanted them into a glass jar with a screw top, and handed them to Denis.

After safely stowing the jar in his pack, he looked at me. "I'm sorry about your brother, Em. I really didn't know he was missing. I wish I could help, but I left all the geology stuff to Alex, and he was the one who dealt with your brother. I'm sure Cam's all right, wherever he is."

"I hope so. Good-bye, Denis." I ushered him out the back door and shut it firmly behind him. Now at least I knew how Denis was linked with Cam, but the story seemed kind of thin. If he was a smart college professor, why did he let his friend and partner handle all the business details? I had to wonder just how much money was involved here. Something didn't smell right.

I turned and realized that Nessa and Allison were standing in the doorway that led to the shop, staring at me expectantly.

"Em, I think we deserve some explanation," Nessa said. "What was Matt doing here this morning, and whatever did he say to Denis?"

Nessa was right — I owed her at least the

bare outline, which was just about all I knew. I took a deep breath. "This might take a while. Can we sit in the studio here?" There wasn't a customer in sight. Blast the Gem Show.

"Of course, dear," Nessa said. She locked the register, and they settled themselves on stools in the studio, while I leaned against the marver facing them. "Okay, here's the deal. You know that Denis has been heat-treating stones, and he seems to have some kind of deadline? When he asked me last night about giving him more time in the studio, I told him I wanted to cut him off — he's been making me nervous. And then he said something odd." I swallowed and glanced at Allison. "He asked me about Cam."

Allison gasped. "Does he know him?"

I shook my head. "I don't think so. But it bothered me that he knew Cam existed, and that he chose that particular moment to bring him up. So last night I decided to tell Matt about what had been going on, and he agreed to look into it. The problem is, there wasn't any crime — that we knew of." *Yet.* I thought of the grainy picture of dead Alex. "Which means that Matt had no reason to launch an investigation, officially. He was just doing me a favor." I stopped, unsure of how to go on.

Nessa knew me well. "But that's not all, is it?" she prompted quietly.

"No." I swallowed again. "Matt had asked the medical examiner to see if there were any unidentified bodies that had come in recently. Only one had, last Sunday, and he wasn't Cam. But . . . well, he had some pebbles in his pocket, and nothing else, and the ME mentioned it in passing when he talked to Matt. Then Matt put two and two together, and got hold of a few of the pebbles, which turned out to be rough peridot. So Matt got a picture of the dead guy and when he showed it to Denis, Denis fell apart. Seems that the dead guy was a colleague of his at the university, and apparently they had some shared real estate investments and were working on this gem deal together."

We all fell silent for a moment. Nessa looked thoughtful, and I thought I saw a glint of tears in Allison's eyes. "Did he know anything about Cam?" she said in little more than a whisper.

"Sort of. He said Cam was doing some kind of computer consulting work for them, but that he, Denis, had never met Cam — his partner Alex handled all that, and now Alex is dead." That didn't sound good even to me.

"Isn't there someone else involved — a buyer or a dealer?" Nessa asked.

"Yes, but Denis claims that Alex handled all of that too." Denis sounded like a real idiot, didn't he? He'd put up money, and then let his partner handle everything else. And now he was stuck with the whole mess, and a dead partner.

I needed to get back upstairs and see what Matt and Frank had made of the interview. "Look, let me find out what happens next, and I'll call down, okay? Right now I want to see what Matt thinks he can do."

When I entered my place, Matt was talking on his cell phone. He looked up when I came in, his eyes dark. More bad news? I was staring out the window over the sink at the darkness beyond when Frank joined me.

"Something's rotten there," Frank said in a low voice.

"You think so too? Denis is either lying or covering up something, but I have no idea what. Are these stones worth it, Frank?"

"Who's to say? They're worth what somebody'll pay for them."

Not worth a life. Had Alex really died for a bunch of pretty green gravel?

Matt finally snapped his phone shut and announced, "We've got a problem."

"What?"

"That was the ME's office. You remember I asked the ME to take a closer look? He sent one of his assistants in, as a favor to me, and he just gave me the results. Alex didn't die of exposure. His skull was fractured — a blow to the back of the head, but it didn't show up until somebody took some X-rays."

Well, well. Frank was right: something here was rotten. "Was it an accident? Maybe he fell off something out there and hit his head?"

"Not where he was found, out in the open, on flat ground."

"So it's murder?"

"I'm afraid so. Damn! The guys who collected the body sure as hell weren't looking for evidence, and I doubt there's anything there now."

I sat down heavily on the couch. "What happens now?"

Matt crossed the room and sat next to me, watching my face. "I need to have another talk with Denis. I'm not sure he's told us everything."

"I thought he looked pretty surprised when he found out about his colleague, but does he have any idea why Alex is dead?"

"Maybe Alex didn't tell him everything. It

sounds like Denis still hopes to pull off this gem deal; maybe he doesn't want us to spook the buyer. Right now we don't have a lot of facts. But we've got more latitude to look into things, now that we've got a suspicious death. You let me do my job, not that it's going to be easy — this mess involves more than one jurisdiction. The Pima County sheriff takes the lead, but they're keeping me in on it. At least we know there's a crime now, but we're a long way from connecting it with Cam or the stones."

"What — you don't think all this is connected? That the guy who hired Cam is found dead in the desert with peridot in his pocket, and Cam just happens to disappear at the same time?"

"Em, I'm not downplaying your concerns. I'm doing what I can."

I leaned against him. "I know. I just feel so helpless, and I hate that."

"I know you do." He put his arm around me and kissed my forehead.

"Hey, lovebirds, I'm still in the room, you know."

"I'm sorry, Frank." I almost *had* forgotten he was here. "So what's your take on all this?"

"I think Alex had the right idea — scope out how big the deposit might be before getting too excited. By hiring Cam, an outsider, he was keeping it quiet. I can see why he started tinkering with the stones. Of course, maybe he didn't know what could be done with them, when he hired your brother."

It took me a second to make the next logical conclusion. "So Alex might have had a reason to shut Cam up, if he realized the stones could be more valuable than he thought?"

"I didn't say that. Besides, they might have signed some sort of confidentiality agreement — not uncommon where gems are concerned. And Cam would have stood by that."

"But how would Alex know that about Cam? Still, it's Alex who's dead, not Cam." I hoped. And no way could I see my brother killing anyone — besides, if he had, he would have turned himself in to the closest authorities immediately, not tried to cover things up. Cam's like that.

"Em," Matt interrupted, "you're getting ahead of your facts. Let's take this one step at a time. The ME will report the homicide to the sheriff, and I'll tell him that we know who it is, and why. The sheriff will investigate. I will contribute what I know to the investigation, and hope that the sheriff will share what he finds. And that's as far as I'm willing to speculate at this time. Let's find out who killed Alex, and then maybe we'll have more to go on."

"Easy for you to say — Cam's not your brother," I muttered.

"I'm sorry, Em. I know this is hard. Right now I'm going to head for Denis's place and let him know that Alex's death is officially being considered a murder."

I felt a sense of relief, reluctantly. I needed a little time to mull over what we had just learned.

"Em, I'll keep you informed, I promise. And, Frank, can you do something for me? Sniff around the Gem Show and see if there's any buyer who's said anything about fancy new stones?"

"Already on it, Matt." Frank looked pleased to have been included. "I talked to a couple of mates this morning, and they'll get back to me. Could be the buyer made promises to others that he can't keep thanks to Denis and Alex, and now he's pissed."

"Thanks. Em, walk me out, will you?"

Matt stood up. It took a major effort to get myself off the couch, but Matt lent a hand. I followed him toward the door; the dogs followed both of us, hopeful. At the door he turned and said, "It may not feel like it, but we have made some progress."

"I suppose I should be glad that my instincts about Denis were right, but that doesn't get us any closer to finding Cam."

"Actually it does. We know more than we did. I'll contact you if I hear anything new." Frank's presence did not deter Matt from bidding me a proper farewell.

CHAPTER 18

Peridot set in gold may protect its owner from night terrors.

I called Nessa and Allison, giving them permission to shut down the still-empty shop for lunch, and they arrived in less than three minutes. Poor dogs: Fred and Gloria had seldom seen so much company in the space of a few hours, and they were beside themselves with excitement. They were particularly fond of the latest arrivals, so the exchange of greetings took another few minutes. Finally we all found seats for ourselves (dogs included).

"All right, let me give you the condensed version." I outlined what Matt had heard from the ME's office as well as our mutual speculation about Denis, with a few small corrections from Frank. The women didn't interrupt until I had run out of steam.

Nessa was the first to respond. "So, in a

nutshell: Denis Ryerson and Alex Gutierrez were business partners. Alex is dead, murdered by an unknown person. Alex hired Cam to do some work for them; Denis did not know Cam but knew *of* Cam. Everything we know that Denis has done has been legal, but he's acting very nervous. Matt agrees that there's something going on, and he shares your concern about Denis. Do I have it right so far?"

"You've got it, Nessa. And don't forget that there's someone else involved — this mystery buyer. That does explain why Denis is so eager to produce the stones he's been working on: he needs the buyer's money to pay off his debts, or at least part of them, or the bank may seize the property. And that buyer may not want to wait around after the Gem Show is over. What do you think, Frank?"

Nessa nudged Frank gently, and Frank awoke with a start from what looked suspiciously like a nap. "What? Oh, right, love. Makes sense. Denis needs him — he can't wing it because he doesn't know the market or the players. On his own he'd get bottom dollar, and I doubt he's got enough stones yet to cover whatever he owes. Since it sounds like Alex had the head for business, he probably checked out the buyer. I'd like to know who this guy is."

"So would I. You think you can find him, Frank?"

"If he's here, I'll smoke him out. If he thinks he has something hot coming, he'd be spreading the word, with or without the product to show. He could stir up a bit of excitement in advance, like. Besides, the good stuff doesn't necessarily show up on the convention floor — there are deals going on all the time."

"Maybe Mr. Whoever took out his frustrations on Alex, or was trying to send a message, because they didn't deliver when promised," I suggested.

"Maybe but not likely." Frank didn't sound convinced. "Like you said, why kill the source? Not worth it."

I knew I was grasping at straws, but I really didn't like what I was hearing. Apparently I'd had the right idea all along: stay as far away as possible from the whole gem trade. "Frank, is this really what your business is like? I mean, would somebody kill for something new and different?"

"Ah, Em, that's a hard one. On the one hand, it's a big business, big dollars — look at the international diamond trade. At the other end of the scale, there are a lot of people out there on their own, following leads, sinking their own money into exploration, hoping to make that one big find. Even if they do, things don't always work out — they can be pressured by the big guys to sell out or else risk being shut out of the market. It happens, and I wouldn't rule it out in this case."

Not what I wanted to hear. "If Denis doesn't make his deadline, what's going to happen?"

"The buyer will most likely go on about his business and leave town. It means more to Denis than to him."

"I know that makes sense, but Alex is dead. Why? Are the stones that important, or is there something else going on that we don't know about?" Another thought slammed me from the side where I wasn't looking. "Damn!"

"What?" Nessa and Allison said in unison.

"Maybe it's farfetched, but what if this buyer *is* the one who went after Alex, and he still wants something from Denis? How would he pressure him?" Before anyone else could speak, I answered my own question. "Denis has a wife — Elizabeth. If the partner's dead, she's the closest person to him, so if this unknown of ours wants to lean on Denis, he could go after her next." How were we to know how desperate this silent partner was? "If I was Denis, I would have gone straight home, collected her, and headed to parts unknown. He's in way over his head, and he was pretty rattled even before he found out that Alex was dead, let alone murdered."

I found my cell phone and punched in Matt's number. He answered on the fifth ring. "Em, I don't —"

"I know. Where are you?"

He sighed. "In front of Denis Ryerson's house."

I was almost afraid to ask. "And?"

"He's gone. His wife is gone. His car is gone. They've flown the coop."

"Any signs of violence?"

"Nope. Neighbor said he and his wife came out of the house with suitcases and drove away."

"Are you going to go looking for him?"

"I can't — it's the sheriff's case, and technically Denis isn't even a suspect. I'll tell him what I know, and it certainly looks suspicious. But that's all I can do."

I could think of several things that would be satisfying but unquestionably illegal to do to Denis — if only we could find him. "Well, thanks for trying."

"Right. And Em? Keep your eyes open, will you? Maybe your feeling is contagious, because this just keeps getting weirder to me."

"Will do. And I've got Frank to protect me." I looked over at him, and Frank winked. "I'll talk with you tomorrow."

I shut the phone and tried to figure out what I felt. The good news was Denis and his wife were alive and traveling under their own power at the moment, according to a witness. The bad news was Denis was our only real source of information, and now he was in the wind.

"They're gone?" Nessa asked.

"They are. They must have moved fast, since Matt wasn't far behind them."

"Well, it looks as though Denis is either guilty of something or afraid of someone."

"I don't know which I prefer."

"But what about Cam?" Allison chimed in. "We still don't know where he is."

When Frank spoke, we all turned to him. "We may yet have a lead, Em. The stones are local, and Denis said Alex found them on a piece of land they'd bought together. We locate their properties, we can make a good guess. And I can probably eliminate a lot of places where that kind of stone just couldn't be, based on rock formations or lack of 'em."

I could have kissed him. "Frank, you're a

genius. I knew we were keeping you around for a reason. If we find where the stones come from, maybe we find Cam's trail. How do we find out where the properties are?"

"Depends."

"On?"

"On how fast your local government records property transfers — purchases and sales. Know any local real estate agents?"

"I do." Nessa smiled a Cheshire Cat smile. "My son-in-law."

Maybe we'd finally caught a break. "Can we call him now and tell him what we need?" I asked.

"Of course," Nessa said. "I'll call right now. Alex Gutierrez and Denis Ryerson, right?" When I nodded, she pulled out her cell phone and retreated to the other end of the room for privacy. She returned a few moments later. "He'll get right on it, but he may not have anything for us until tomorrow."

"Thank you, Nessa — it helps. And thank you all for being so patient. I'll talk to Matt tomorrow and I can run by him what we've figured out, and maybe he'll have some new ideas. I guess you two should get back to the shop."

I ushered the women out the door, then turned to face Frank. "Am I crazy, Frank? I mean, to be so worried? It was bad enough when Cam was just missing, but now that we know someone might be willing to kill . . ." I couldn't finish the thought.

"Em, don't borrow trouble. I can tell you there's funny business that goes on in the gem trade, but this could be something completely unrelated. And Cam might have done his work, left, and be sitting on a beach in Mexico right now drowning his sorrows with a bucket of margaritas. We'll do what we can tomorrow, but right now there's little to be done."

"So we wait," I said glumly. "I guess I'll try to get some work done. What about you?"

"This and that," he said. I didn't press him.

"I'll take the dogs out." I sighed, then rounded up the pups and headed out. Normally I enjoyed our walks — the streets were usually bustling, and I felt safe, especially with two dogs, even if they weren't exactly Rottweilers. But this week all the foot traffic had taken itself off to the Gem Show, and there were few pedestrians in my neighborhood. And after the last couple of days I was left wondering: How many other unseen plots and schemes had I missed? I liked Tucson, and I had built a life for myself here, but had I ignored the darker parts that I just didn't want to see?

Cam, where the hell are you?

CHAPTER 19

Peridot is the only gemstone to have been found in meteorites.

I spent the afternoon making a lot of simple glass pieces, which was about all I could handle. Finally I gave up and went back upstairs. No Frank. I threw together a haphazard supper, walked the dogs, and went to bed. Unfortunately sleep did not seem to be on the schedule. I heard Frank come in an hour or so later. I had finally fallen into restless dreams when I was dragged back to reality by a loud pounding on the door. I found the light switch, wrapped a robe around myself, and stumbled out into the big room. Frank had roused himself as well and hung back in the doorway to the bedroom, at the ready. He looked surprisingly alert, all things considered.

"I'm coming, I'm coming. Stop making

all that noise!" I yelled as I neared the door. I looked through the peephole: Denis. I pulled the door open, fast.

"Can I come in?" he blurted, and then shoved past me without waiting for an answer. He was alone. I shut the door behind him and turned to find that Fred and Gloria had blocked his path. Fred was growling low in his throat. He may not be large, but his teeth are sharp, and Denis didn't seem inclined to challenge him.

"Denis, what the hell are you doing here? And where's Elizabeth?"

"Elizabeth? What?" Light dawned slowly in his eyes. "Your police chief friend was looking for me?"

"Yes, he was, and he knows you left your house, with your wife *and* suitcases. He was coming to tell you that the medical examiner took another look and decided that Alex was murdered."

Denis went pale again, and I wondered for a moment how I was supposed to catch him if he fell. "How?" he whispered.

"Somebody hit him over the head before they dumped him in the desert. Denis, what's going on?"

"I need to sit down."

I guided him to the couch, and he dropped heavily onto the seat. Frank remained where he was, silent and wary.

"You thought I was running? No, no — I put my wife on a plane. Elizabeth's going to stay with her parents back east. I didn't want her to get caught up in all this. Now I'm really glad I did — this is worse than I thought."

"Does she have a clue what's going on with you? What you've been doing? How could she not?" I was working up a good head of steam. I don't like being dragged out of bed in the middle of the night. But then I remembered that odd scene when Denis and Elizabeth had stopped by the studio, and he'd told his wife a clumsy lie about what we were doing.

"She trusts me."

The woman was either an idiot or willfully oblivious — maybe she just didn't want to know what Denis was up to.

"I told her it was important but that I didn't have time to explain it all, and I took her to the airport. But she got on the plane, I made sure of that, even though she had to charge her ticket on her own credit card, because mine's maxed out."

That's right — Denis had no money, especially after he'd scrounged up the last bit of what he owed me. That would make it hard for him to pull a disappearing act.

"So why are you here?"

Denis's gaze darted around the room, stopping briefly on Frank, who was still leaning against the doorjamb, looking wiry and tough in a sleeveless T-shirt and crumpled chinos. "I need a place to stay. I didn't want to go back to my house. Em, there's a killer out there somewhere! He might come after me next."

So now he wanted to put *me* at risk too? "Denis, why on earth should I want to help you? You disrupt my life, you make vague threatening hints about my brother, your partner turns up dead in the desert — why should I do anything other than shove you out the door and kick your sorry ass down the stairs?"

"I didn't know where else to go." Denis looked like a schoolboy about to burst into tears. Didn't this man have any other friends? But I realized that I really would rather have him under my watchful eye than out wandering the countryside where this unknown killer lurked. Maybe if I kept him here I could actually find out something.

In the morning. Nobody was functioning very well at the moment. In fact, Denis was swaying slightly and looked like a slight push would topple him. "Okay, here's what we're going to do. First: sleep, or at least rest. Denis, you get the couch. In case you're wondering, I have no cash or weapons or anything any self-respecting pawnshop would want, so you can't rip me off and disappear into the sunset — or maybe I mean sunrise — again. And if you do try to sneak out again, I wash my hands of you forever. If your mystery man tries to kill you, that's your problem."

"Huh?" Denis looked confused, and I realized he probably didn't know that we knew . . . No, it was too much to sort out now.

I tried again, sticking to one-syllable words. "Denis, lie down on the couch and try to get some sleep. In the morning I will call the chief and we can try to make sense out of all of this. Bathroom's that direction." I pointed, then without looking back I stormed back to my room and shut the door — leaving Frank and the pooches to keep an eye on Denis. After getting into bed and turning off the light, I lay in the dark listening for a while, but I heard nothing and drifted off surprisingly quickly.

Monday morning. Since my second-floor apartment is higher than most of the surrounding buildings in this commercial district, I'd never bothered with curtains on this side. Usually I enjoyed watching the light grow in the morning; this morning I could have done without it. I peered at my clock and was surprised to see it was almost eight, late for me. I heard low voices in the other room, so I decided it was time to get the show on the road.

After a detour to the bathroom I emerged and found Frank and Denis sitting across from each other at the kitchen table, apparently talking about gemstones. There was coffee, and Frank had laid out eggs, onions, peppers, and a few other odds and ends I had forgotten I even had. He, as usual, looked ready to wrestle crocodiles, blast him.

He jumped up when he saw me coming. "I'll handle breakfast, Em. Denis here was just telling me about how he and his mate worked out the stone treatment."

"Goody, goody. Is this something I need to know?" I filled a mug with coffee and sat down next to Denis. "You get any sleep?"

"Some. Look, Em, I'm really sorry about all of this. I had no idea . . . I mean, I'm not like this, not really. I'm just an average guy, with a job and a mortgage and all that. And I thought I was being smart, getting into this land investment thing — I mean, do I look like a land baron? I never thought it could end up like this."

"Who does?" I muttered to my cup. Then I took pity on him. After all, who was I to throw stones? I'd had my life derailed more than once recently, and I had never seen it coming. "Denis, I appreciate your apology. Besides which, it's too late to go back and change anything, so we'd better figure out where we go from here. You're willing to talk to Matt? Full disclosure? Because I get the feeling you haven't exactly told us everything."

"I promise. You're right. Besides, keeping my mouth shut is what got me backed into this corner in the first place. How is it you're so tight with the police chief?"

"Long story, but suffice it to say we have a relationship. Which is damn lucky for you." I stood up and retrieved my phone from where I had left it, turned my back on Denis (and Frank, now whistling cheerfully as he scrambled more eggs), and called Matt.

"Wha'?" he said coherently.

"Good morning to you too. Would you like to come over for breakfast?"

"What time is it?" he barked.

"After eight. You must have had, oh, maybe three hours of real good sleep, right? But I've got a surprise for you."

"Do I want to know?"

"Yes. Denis Ryerson is here."

"Denis Ryerson?" The change in his tone was immediate.

"The same. He said he wasn't doing a bunk but merely taking his wife to the airport to send her out of harm's way. And he promises to tell all, if you get your butt over here."

"Be there in fifteen." He hung up. A man of few words is Matt.

He was on time. When he came in, he made civil noises to us all, but I could tell he was itching to get down to it with Denis. Frank had apparently made enough food for an army, or at least for four sleep-deprived people, so we first dispensed with eating, and I distributed refills on the coffee so we would all be appropriately fueled.

Once the plates were cleared, Matt pulled out a small notebook and put on his serious face. "Denis, are you ready to explain what's been going on for the past week or two?"

Denis nodded. "As much as I can. I'm beginning to realize how much Alex didn't tell me, but I'll give you what I know. Where do you want me to start?"

"We know you two were partners and that you jointly owned undeveloped property north of Tucson. Do you have copies of your

241

property records?"

"Uh . . ."

"You didn't keep your own copies?" I burst in, incredulous. How could anybody manage a business without records?

Denis looked embarrassed. "Alex took care of a lot of that. He had a good accountant, and the accountant did our taxes. I just signed things, because I trusted Alex. Okay, it was dumb of me, right? I'll admit it. But can't you just get hold of the records? Or go to the city recorder's office?"

"Yes, but that takes some time," Matt said with admirable patience. "We could use a line on locations sooner than that. Okay, let's move on to the gemstones. You said Alex found them on one of your properties. Tell me again why you started experimenting with them."

"Alex knew that the stones, left untreated, were kind of average and not worth much, but he thought if we could play around with them a bit, we could make them more valuable. I agreed that it was worth a try. And it was kind of fun, almost magic, you know? You take this ordinary stone, cook it a bit, and presto, it turns into something else."

"Got it. But why the deadline?"

Denis looked down at his hands, and I wondered if this was a sticking point.

"The buyer was calling the shots. I've got big bills coming due, and the buyer isn't going to hang around if I'm any later. I've got to sell the stones, fast — I need the money. Alex found someone who would buy them, but the buyer said he was leaving soon. And I don't have the time or the contacts to shop them around now. We were supposed to have things worked out in time for the Gem Show, but it took longer than we thought."

I flashed Matt a quick look, before turning my attention back to Denis. "Who's your buyer?"

"I told you yesterday I don't know. Alex dealt with him, not me."

I wanted to strangle the jerk. I managed to control myself and I asked, "When and where were you going to turn over the stones?"

"Are you angling for my job, Em?" Matt said. I glared at him but shut up. Matt focused on Denis again. "Can you answer her question?"

Denis slumped back in his chair. "Here's the deal. A few months ago, when the real estate market started going south, we got a little panicky. We started hitting the casinos. I know, stupid move. And if there is such a thing as luck, we should have known that ours was in the tank anyway. I stopped before I got in too deep, but I can't swear that Alex did, although I hope to hell it was his money and not the partnership's. So after a month or two he comes to me and says, listen, there's this guy and he's offered us a deal — he'll pay off what's coming due in exchange for all the gemstones we find."

"And what did you do?" Matt asked.

"Well, I can tell you I didn't look a gift horse in the mouth. We owned the stones, and we had every right to sell them."

"Did you ever meet this man?"

"No."

"Did it ever occur to you to ask why he was willing to help you?"

"I figured he thought he could sell the stones and make money off 'em. I wasn't going to complain. Heck, he could have 'em all, as long as Alex and I didn't go bankrupt."

"Did you ever see any of his money?"

"Some. He gave us enough to pay off the first round of loans — called it a good faith deposit."

"Did you give him any stones, in exchange?"

"What we had. Look, in the beginning we didn't have many of the treated ones. We were kind of stumbling around in the dark, trying different techniques, until we finally found a combination that worked. And then once we figured that out, we were supposed to produce a whole lot more, but Alex wanted to work someplace where people weren't looking over his shoulder all the time. That's when I came to you, Em."

I looked at Matt, who asked, "If what you were doing was legal, then why is Alex dead?"

"I don't know!" he replied vehemently. "You think I haven't been going crazy trying to figure this out? We haven't missed our deadline. Maybe the guy was pissed that he couldn't make a big announcement at the Gem Show. But killing Alex? That makes no sense. But . . ."

"What?" Matt said.

"Alex and I, well — I guess he didn't trust me completely. He didn't tell me everything. Maybe he thought we were safer that way, or maybe he had some idea of cutting me out. I just don't know. With Alex dead, I have no way of finding this guy, and he's never going to get his stones, even what he's paid for. I mean, I can't pay him back, not until I get enough stones. And if he killed Alex, what do you think he's going to do to me?"

Roast you slowly over an open fire? I managed not to say that out loud. Matt and I exchanged a glance; we were still missing a piece of this puzzle.

"Denis, I still don't see any motive for killing Alex," Matt said slowly. "Unless he had lied to you about where he got the stones?"

The whites of Denis's eyes were showing. "I've told you all I know! I know we own properties, but how can I prove where the stones came from? I thought Alex was my friend, but maybe he was pulling a fast one."

"I think our first priority is to track down this mystery man that Alex was working with," Matt said. "And since Alex is the victim, we — or should I say, the sheriff — will have access to Alex's records. You're saying that all this started after you began hitting the casinos?"

"Does that make a difference?"

"Maybe Alex lied to you — he could have been borrowing money from someone, off the record, and he put the stones up as collateral. Maybe he got in deeper than he admitted to you. Or, as you suggest, he could have been using the partnership's funds to gamble with. Or he could have put up the land, without your consent. Plenty of possibilities. I hope you haven't signed anything lately?"

"No, nothing like that. You mean that he

might have forged my name or something?"

"Could be. Or he could have just entered into a business agreement with someone he met at the casino or elsewhere. That's more or less what he told you, right?"

"Well, if it was business, like I said, I never signed anything, and Alex told me not to tell anyone. He didn't say it was illegal, but he didn't want word to get out."

"So now what, Matt?" I figured I should keep my foot in this conversation.

"I've got to fill in the sheriff. He'll want to talk to you, Denis. We can arrange for protection for you, if you want, until this is cleared up. We can get into Alex's files — you happen to know whether he kept them at home or at the university?"

Denis shrugged. "I'd guess at home. His office at the university is a mess, full of rocks and stuff. And people are in and out of there all the time."

"What about whoever it was who does your taxes?"

Denis brightened. "Yeah, I've got copies of those papers. I can give you the guy's name, and he should have more information."

"Matt, what about Cam?" I felt like a little girl tugging at his sleeve, but my brother was my first priority, and I wasn't about to lose sight of that.

Matt thought for a couple of seconds. "Look, the way I see it, we've got two main avenues: find the guy Alex was working with, or find out where the stones are coming from. Either one could lead us to Cam."

Now I was faced with a dilemma. I knew that Matt meant well, and he could muster all the combined forces of local law enforcement. But that was a mixed blessing, because law enforcement had to follow the law, which meant there were procedures that had to be observed. Which, as a good citizen, I supported, but official procedure took time, and I wasn't sure what kind of time we — or Cam — had.

"When do you think you'll have anything?" I asked.

He gave me a look that mingled frustration and sympathy. "My people will talk to the recorder's office today. We can call the accountant at home, I guess. But I still have to bring the sheriff up to speed."

"Denis, what about your deadline?"

Denis shrugged, looking miserable. "I don't know. I was going to give what I had to Alex and he was going to deliver the stones this week, before the show ended. I don't know what happens now."

"Matt, somebody's going to search Alex's

house, right? Maybe he left some information about the buyer?"

"Of course. As soon as we figured out who's handling what. We're headed to the sheriff's office next. Denis, you ready to go?"

Denis stood up shakily. "I guess. I'm sorry I've made such a mess of things. I should have paid closer attention to what Alex was doing."

I tried to feel sorry for him but gave up. "You just tell the sheriff everything you know and let him and Matt sort things out. Matt, you'll call me?"

"When I can. Come on, Denis."

He and Denis took their leave, and Frank and I were left behind. "Well," I said.

"Well, indeed," he replied. "I take it we're still hunting for the properties?"

"Of course."

"You didn't mention that to Matt."

"No, I didn't. He has to go through channels, and I don't want to wait. We're not doing anything wrong. When Nessa comes in to work, I hope she'll have something for us from her son-in-law. And maybe you can replicate what Cam was working on? Map out where the stones might have been found?"

"I'll give it a try. You don't happen to have

a geological map handy?"

"No, but the Internet is a wondrous thing, and I'm sure you can find something on-line."

He looked as disgusted as I felt about computers, but at least we could get started. If Cam was anywhere near the right kind of geological formations, we'd track him down.

CHAPTER 20

In the Middle Ages, peridot was said to give people divine inspiration and to protect them from evil.

Frank was pecking away at my computer in the corner when Nessa arrived at eleven the next morning.

"Hi, Nessa. Thanks for coming over on your day off," I said, grateful the shop was closed on Mondays — we wouldn't be rushed. I got right to the point. "Was your son-in-law able to find us any information?"

"Yes, dear. Arthur was able to access those property transfers online." She handed me a large envelope, then went over and laid a hand on Frank's shoulder, peering at the computer screen. They exchanged words, she nodded, then turned back to me.

"Good news?" I asked her, hefting the envelope.

"Some, I think. But there are a number of

properties involved, scattered around over a wide area, and most are completely undeveloped, which means there is poor access."

"Dirt roads?"

"More or less. Arthur thought that Denis and his partner paid a fair price for most of the parcels, but they weren't good for much, which is why they were affordable. And as we already knew, the market has since dried up, so they would be having trouble selling them again."

"Any idea how much Denis and Alex owed on them?"

Nessa mentioned a dollar figure that made me gulp. "But of course, they put only a small portion of that down, expecting, no doubt, to sell the properties quickly before the balloon payments were due. Arthur says they weren't the only people to make that assumption."

"Of course not. No shortage of get-rich-quick schemes, or of suckers to sink their money into them."

"Too true. Anything new on your end?"

"Yes. Denis showed up here in the wee small hours."

Nessa's face lit up. "Really? So he wasn't running?"

"No. He said he was worried about his wife, so he took her to the airport and shipped her off to her parents to keep her safe, and then he came to me, saying he was scared to go home. I called Matt this morning, and he came by and picked Denis up. They went off to tell the Pima County sheriff all about it."

"Thank goodness! Did Denis have anything useful to say?"

"Not much. Apparently he left almost everything related to their investments and the peridot to Alex. Alex met this unknown man, Alex cut some sort of deal, Alex kept all the documents, Alex hired Cam, and so on. I don't know whether he's covering up something or he's just an idiot. Either way, he didn't tell us much."

"Oh dear. That leaves us no further along, does it?"

"Yes and no. Matt and the sheriff can put their heads together and pool their information. Bless you for finding the land records. Frank's looking into geological formations, and we think that if we match the geology and the properties, we can narrow down where the stones came from and maybe find Cam somewhere in the vicinity. Matt still thinks he may just be sulking."

Nessa was quick to protest. "Oh, Em — I don't believe he would go this long without contacting you. Cam knows you would worry. He would contact you if he could."

"That's what I think. Which means he's either stuck somewhere out there without computer or phone access, or someone is stopping him." I stood up abruptly, not wanting to dwell on the other possibility: that Cam had met with Alex's fate. "I can't just sit here — I've got to do something. Frank, you have anything?"

"Maybe. Some ideas, anyway, but I'd have to see the land to know. Rough land out there?"

"Some, I guess. I haven't exactly done a lot of off-roading, you know."

"Em, can I take a look at the property records?" Frank held out his hand, and I handed him the envelope. He moved to the table and spread out what he had printed out next to the papers Nessa had brought.

"Shouldn't you wait for Matt? Or Denis?" Nessa asked.

I laughed. "Denis knows squat, or if he knows something, he doesn't know he knows it. I'll leave him to Matt, and he and the sheriff can dig up whatever documents Denis might have. Frank, you up for a road trip?"

"Grand," he replied promptly. "I've got some ideas."

"Did you have plans for today, Nessa?"

Her eyes flickered briefly toward Frank before she answered. "Nothing special. Is there something you'd like me to do?"

"Maybe you could hang out here? I don't know how long we'll be, but I'd feel better if I knew you were here."

"I'd be happy to. If Matt should call, is there anything I should tell him? Or not tell him?"

I shrugged. I had faith that Matt would do whatever he could, but he couldn't include civilian me, and I couldn't sit still. "I'll fill him in when I see him — we shouldn't be more than a few hours. We're just kind of scouting things out at the moment. Frank, let me dig out my road maps and get dressed, and we'll head north."

A short while later we said our good-byes to Nessa and sallied forth. I didn't know what I expected to find. Maybe I clung to the illogical hope that I would be able to home in on Cam by some natural instinct. Mostly I just couldn't stand sitting around talking and waiting anymore. Besides, this excursion would allow Frank to see the land, which was always better than studying a map, or at least so I hoped. Since this was a preliminary expedition, so to speak, I was willing to take my battered car. If at some point we needed to head overland, we'd have to reconsider our choice of vehicle.

I had moved to Tucson ten years ago mainly for its thriving crafts community and good climate for glassmaking, but I had not been prepared for the monochrome austerity of Arizona mountain and desert. I had come to love it and had never regretted my choice. Still, I hadn't spent a lot of time driving around the countryside admiring the cacti; Cam was the one who preferred long-distance treks, which was lucky, as it meant he usually came to visit me, rather than the other way around. In any case, I didn't know the land that lay beyond Tucson very well, so I couldn't give Frank a lot of guidance.

"You have any idea what you're looking for here?"

"Peridot's usually found in basaltic formations. The whole of Peridot Mesa, where the reservation is, is a single huge basalt flow, with masses of olivine — that's the peridot."

"The stones are embedded in solid rock?" I tried to sound intelligent.

"Yup. The olivine — that's another name for peridot — has a high melting point, so it crystallizes inside molten rock. Either the basalt weathers away over time and the peridot crystals wash out, or you can get at the crystals by drilling and blasting."

"Okay, so you've got crystals inside the mesa — I get that — and either they fall out or are blasted out and collected. But what are *we* looking for?"

"Basalt is volcanic — and you can have big flows and small flows. I'm guessing that what Alex stumbled on — if he was telling Denis the truth — was a smaller basaltic intrusion away from the main body of the mesa."

"Ah. And you can identify that just by looking?"

"If you know what you're looking for."

I scanned the empty horizon rimmed with low hills. "Alex and Denis must have been crazy to think they'd be able to resell this land for a profit. Who'd want to put a housing development way up here? It looks like the back of beyond."

"Maybe they were thinking they could use it for grazing land," Frank suggested.

I tried to picture Denis managing a herd of cows and almost laughed. Besides, there probably wasn't much return from leasing land for cattle. No, they must have had some optimistic expectation that the Tucson housing boom would eventually spread this way. Certainly, some people had done well — investors with a better sense of timing than Denis and Alex.

We passed quickly through the nearer towns like Oro Valley, then followed Route 77 when it branched off slightly east after Oracle Junction, then through Oracle and Mammoth. Even to my novice eye it was clear that the topography changed, and changed again. I was also very aware that we kept crossing county lines, and was reminded of the problems of jurisdiction. Maybe Matt was buddies with the Pima County sheriff, but what about his counterparts in Pinal and Gila Counties? Where exactly had Alex died, and who covered that? Matt's connections could only extend so far.

The land was fairly flat after Oracle Junction, but as we neared Oracle, the hills rose up to our right, and at Mammoth we found ourselves paralleling a dry riverbed, with the land rising higher yet to our north.

"Anything useful, Frank?" I asked. There was no point in my taking my eyes off the road, because I couldn't distinguish one rock from another. Not that there was much traffic to distract me out here — I'd be more likely to hit a roadrunner than another car.

Frank had spread out maps and printouts on his lap, and his gaze darted back and forth between those and the sere landscape.

"Maybe, maybe. Still working on the big picture. Where's the reservation from here?"

"East-northeast of here. I thought I'd go as far as the casino, since Denis mentioned that."

"There a lot of gambling around here?"

"The various Indian tribes in this state manage a number of small casinos. There are a couple around Tucson that belong to the Tohono O'odham tribe. I don't pay a lot of attention to them, because I don't gamble. At least, not in casinos. I think there are enough risks in running a small business, and I can't see throwing money away. It's not my idea of fun. What about you?"

"Seen a couple in my day, but I guess I'm like you — plenty of excitement in the gem business, without all the bells and flashing lights."

Past Winkelman the road branched again, and we passed quickly through Christmas, hitting a long empty patch before Route 77 dead-ended at Route 70. To our east lay the aptly named town of Peridot and the San Carlos Reservation, including the Apache Gold Casino. Even I could tell that the land in that direction rose higher: the mesa, I assumed.

A few miles later we came to the casino complex. Signs advertised the golf course, which I found slightly bizarre, since I knew how much water it would take to maintain anything like grass out here. The casino building itself was a low blocky building incongruously surrounded by palm trees; the parking lot surrounding it was well filled, although the majority of the spaces were occupied by not-new sedans and a scattering of pickup trucks.

I had visited one or two casinos around Tucson, out of curiosity, and this looked no different. I knew that stepping inside would be like entering a different universe, one filled with artificial light and noise; one that deliberately cut hapless visitors off from the real world and tried to keep them trapped in the crazy world of slots and tables, where they were supposed to become so mesmerized that they emptied their pockets. It was interesting to me as a phenomenon, but I had no desire to participate.

"Frank, you want to go in?"

"Why not?"

I eyed him dubiously. "You know, we aren't authorized to ask questions. We don't have pictures of any of the people involved. What can we accomplish?"

"Ah, Em — I just want to get the lay of the land. Get a sense of how busy it is, and how much someone like Alex would have stuck out. Can you handle that?"

"I guess." Not my favorite idea, but Frank seemed to have pretty good instincts, and he'd probably have better luck worming information out of people than I would.

We entered the casino and were greeted by the noise and lights that I'd expected. Frank headed toward the bar while I drifted among the infernal machines. Next time I looked toward Frank, he was deep in conversation with a guy who looked to be Native American. I took a look at my cash supply, then headed for a nickel slot. If I hit a jackpot, would that use up all my luck for the day?

I didn't. I kept feeding nickels into the silly machine and pushing buttons without even thinking, and had managed not to lose all of the five dollars I had set as my limit when Frank popped up next to me. I was happy to quit. "Anything?" I asked.

"Said Alex was a regular, and wasn't a big loser. Came in with a woman now and then. He didn't remember Denis."

"Well, at least some small part of Denis's story is true. Did he say if it was one woman or a whole raft of them?"

"We didn't get into details, but I gather it was only the one."

"Huh." That didn't add much to our

treasure trove of knowledge, except that now we had an unknown woman in the mix.

We were on our way to the door — if we could find it through the maze of machines — when I noticed another man behind the bar. I nudged Frank. "Is he the one you talked to?" I asked, pointing.

"No. Looks like he just came on."

"He's the guy we saw at the Gem Show, talking with the owners of the San Carlos peridot booth, isn't he?"

Frank squinted. "You're right. Interesting."

We started to head in the man's direction, but just as we did, he slipped through a door marked "Employees Only." After ten minutes, he still hadn't reemerged.

I wasn't sure what we hoped to accomplish even if we did talk to him. What were we supposed to ask? Who are you, and why do we keep running into you? "Well, this seems like a bust. Shall we go now?" I asked Frank. "I want to get back to looking for Cam."

"Fine by me. Me, I know rocks, so let's keep looking at rocks. You know anyone who'd give us a guided tour of the reservation?"

"No such luck. But let's find a place to sit down and make a plan." Anyplace but here

— I couldn't think in the casino, with all the lights and noise.

"Sounds good to me."

I drove back toward Globe. The main street was lined with one- and two-story buildings that in a perverse way reminded me of the small New Jersey town I had grown up in, though the street itself was at least twice as wide, and New Jersey didn't have mountains like these in the background. We settled on a nondescript diner, and Frank and I snagged a corner booth where he could spread out his maps. We ordered sandwiches and coffee, and then we huddled over the maps.

Frank lined up the printouts he had made of the geological maps alongside the roughly outlined property maps. I'm glad he was handling this, because I would have been lost on paper, not to mention the sites themselves. "What do you see?" I asked.

"Okay, here" — Frank stabbed at the map with a pencil — "here, and maybe here, you've got what might be basaltic intrusions, places you're most likely to find peridot. If you look at the topographic maps, you can see which way the gullies run, so we might also look at the downstream bits, where stones might have washed out."

I studied the maps. "That's still a lot of

territory."

"It is. Nobody said this'd be easy."

Our sandwiches arrived and we took a moment to refuel. When we'd taken the edge off our hunger, I asked, "So what do we do now? Call in helicopters? Guys on horseback? What?"

"Impatient, aren't you?" Frank grinned at me.

"Shouldn't I be? Cam may be out there, in trouble."

His grin vanished. "Sorry, Em — you're right. But we've hardly given your Matt time enough to rally his troops for a full search. Which means we're on our own. There are a couple of sites that look likely, and there are roads, if only bad ones, leading to them. If your brother doesn't have an ATV, I'd wager he didn't go far from a road. It's a start, isn't it?"

Frank looked so enthusiastic that I didn't have the heart to discourage him. One discouraged person at the table was plenty. The two of us hunting through how much desert? Yet we were it. My watch told me it was just noon, and if we were going to do any searching it would have to be before dark, which gave us maybe five hours.

"Where to first?"

CHAPTER 21

Holding a peridot under the tongue was said to reduce the thirst of a person suffering from fever.

After our lunch, equipped with a couple of bottles of water and a full tank of a gas, Frank and I set off to retrace our steps along the mostly empty highway. Frank was intent and focused, and every few miles he would point to a small road running off perpendicular to the highway. I would turn and follow the road for as long as I could. Some petered out to sand after a mile or two, and I figured if I couldn't make it any further, neither could most people without an ATV. Cam's middle-aged car certainly couldn't have handled them.

After the fifth or sixth try, the sun was low in the sky. I stopped at the end of yet another nowhere road, turned off the engine, and got out of the car. I guess I'd been clutching the steering wheel hard, because my neck was stiff. It felt good to be standing in the open air — but that just drove home how futile our task was. We were very small, and the desert was very big. I wrestled with a wave of despair.

"Frank, are we crazy to think we can find anything at all out here?"

Frank was scanning the horizon, and judging from the deep wrinkles that settled around his eyes, he'd done this plenty of times before. Without looking at me he said, "Em, if you know what you're looking for, you can read this like a book."

"You mean all those old television shows I watched when I was growing up were right? You can look at a bent twig and tell me a six-foot-two man who walked with a limp and was blind in his right eye passed this way a week ago Tuesday?"

Frank glanced at me and smiled slightly. "Not quite. But I can tell you that nobody's passed along these roads in the last week or two. Or at least, nothing human. So I think we can pretty much write off these parcels."

"Well, I guess that's something. How many more did you flag?"

"Three. Might get them in before dark, or we can pick up again in the morning."

I wanted to keep going until all options

were exhausted; I couldn't take another night of uncertainty. But neither did I want to miss finding a trail because it was too dark. "Maybe when we get back, Matt will have something." I hoped. Oh, how I hoped.

We made the rest of the drive back to my shop in silence. Upstairs we found Nessa settled in an easy chair, the dogs at her feet; she had been joined by Allison, which didn't surprise me. They all looked up as we came in. "We covered about half the sites, and we thought we'd try again tomorrow. Have you heard from Matt?"

"He called to say he'd be by after six," Nessa said.

"Maybe we should all hunker down and plan?" I suggested.

"Why don't I go get some takeout?" Allison volunteered. "I'm sure you don't want to cook."

Smart woman. "You've got that right. Okay, I'll take care of the dogs and you'll get food and Matt'll come, and we'll solve all the problems of the universe." I caught myself: I was sounding a little ragged. "Sorry — it's been a long day on top of too little sleep. I'm sure if we pool our resources we can come up with something. I'll see you in a bit, okay?"

I grabbed the dogs' leashes, hooked them

up, and fled before I could say anything else stupid. I really was tired: the steps seemed to go on forever. Once down the stairs, I took the dogs around the block, but even they seemed subdued, or maybe they were worried about me. As we were coming home, I met up with Nessa and Allison returning with the promised takeout, which smelled wonderful. And no sooner had we distributed plates and food on the table than Matt arrived.

He looked tired too. But then, he'd looked tired when all this started, and things had gone downhill from there. At least I had the sense not to bombard him with questions immediately, much as I wanted to. "Sit down. You want a beer? Or are you on duty?"

"Yes, and no. Beer would be great."

Nessa beat me to the refrigerator and retrieved a six-pack, which she set on the table. We all settled ourselves around the table, and I had a strange wish to say grace. *Please bless those gathered here with wisdom, insight — and a big shot of luck. Amen.* We dug into the ample food and paid it the attention it deserved, for the first few minutes anyway. I thought I saw Matt loosen his belt buckle, but I wouldn't swear to it. Funny how much better everything looks with a full stomach.

Finally I thought I had been tactful long enough. "Okay, gang, time to share. Matt, how did your meeting with the sheriff go?"

"He's busy, I'm busy, two heads are better than one, et cetera. I don't think he's been giving Cam's continued absence much attention, but he's going full bore on Alex's murder. Alex was a respected member of the Pima County community, and this will not be tolerated, and so on. He's good at that."

"What did you two do? And what about Denis?"

Matt helped himself to another bottle of beer. "Denis went over his whole story again, but he didn't have much to contribute. Alex did this, Alex did that. The sheriff kindly delegated to my department the privilege of going through Alex's office at the university and his home, since both are within city limits. That is going on as we speak. We did get a few crumbs."

"Yes?" Nessa, Allison, and I said in unison. Matt certainly had an eager audience.

"We checked with the DMV. Alex had a car registered, but he also had an RV. Denis told us Alex liked to use the RV on his geology field work — saved on hotel bills, and I gather some of the places he went didn't

269

exactly have convenient hotels. The RV wasn't parked at his home, so we've put out an APB for it. But, Em, there's something else. . . ." Matt hesitated.

I didn't like the look in his eyes. "What?"

"We found Cam's car parked in Alex's garage. That made the sheriff pay attention."

That was something I had not expected to hear. It took me a moment to process the simple fact, but Allison's reaction was quicker — and more heartfelt. "Oh, Matt, what does that mean, that his car was there?"

"Allison, I wish I knew. The car looked fine, and some of Cam's stuff was in it, but I'd guess not all."

"His computer?" I asked sharply.

"No computer."

I relaxed a little. If Cam had taken his computer with him, there was a better chance that he was all right. Cam might not worry about clean underwear, but he would never let his electronic friend out of his sight.

"So what's your guess?"

"The most innocent explanation is that Alex volunteered to take Cam out to the site he was supposed to study, either because he thought it would be easier than explaining how to get there, or he thought the trip would be too hard on Cam's car. And I'm betting he parked the RV wherever the stones are."

Frank and I exchanged a quick glance.

"Let's say Alex offered to let Cam stay in his RV," I said. "Wouldn't that have to be somewhere reasonably accessible? I've never driven one, but I'd guess they aren't easy to maneuver, especially not on rough ground."

"That'd be my guess," Matt agreed. "Not that it narrows down the choices much."

"Hey, I'll take anything I can get. Can we run through the time line? Cam shows up here last Saturday, I tell him about Allison" — I sneaked a glance at her, and she looked away — "so he hightails it off to meet Alex, whom he'd already contracted with to do this computer-modeling project. Matt, how long did the ME think that Alex had been dead when he was found?"

"A day or two. Hard to be precise, when a body's left out like that."

"So it's possible that Alex took Cam out to wherever the RV is parked, the same day he left here, and promised to come back and collect him in a few days. Except he died shortly after that, so he couldn't. Which means Cam might be sitting out there somewhere in the desert, wondering where the heck Alex is. But why wouldn't he just

271

walk out? It's not high summer, and Cam's in good shape. Surely he had food and water." I was more or less talking this out for myself, but everyone else was following me closely.

"Maybe someone wouldn't let him." Matt's voice was quiet, and I could tell he knew that I didn't want to hear that.

"Our mystery buyer? Why would he detain Cam?"

"Em, we don't know. We still don't know anything about him. There's no paper trail that we know of, and we have only Denis's story about what Alex told him. Maybe — if he exists — he thought Cam had discovered too much or was trying to horn in on the find."

I sat there, stewing, my dinner turning to lead in my stomach. There was a chance that Cam might have innocently blundered into something he knew nothing about, and he might have paid heavily for it. No. I was not going to think like that. We still had paths to follow. "I . . ." I began and then stopped, horrified when my voice cracked. I swallowed and looked at Frank. "Tell him what we did today."

Frank turned to Matt. "Em and I took a drive north, toward the San Carlos Reservation. We were looking for sites where the rock formations might be right for peridot, where they overlap with properties that Alex and Denis own. We got through a few before we lost the light, but those looked pretty much undisturbed, so I think we can rule them out. There are three or four likely ones we might try tomorrow. If that's all right by you."

"You got hold of the land records?" Matt's voice was ominously quiet.

"Yes." Frank nodded. "With a little help."

"That would be from me, or more precisely, my daughter's husband, who's in real estate," Nessa volunteered.

Matt looked like he was swallowing a lot of words. He was silent for a long time, his expression carefully blank. I had a pretty good idea what he was thinking: that we should not be interfering in an official investigation; that if we, or rather the sheriff's crew, didn't act quickly, it might be too late; that the missing RV might be the murder scene where Alex was killed, and our finding it might compromise evidence. I felt for him, really I did — but Cam was my brother. Once again I think he read my mind.

He sighed. "Em, if I say no, you'll probably go anyway. No, don't say anything yet. This isn't my investigation, it's the sheriff's, and it's not a good idea to tick him off. But having said that, I can't stop Frank from taking a drive to see the desert, can I?"

I thought I heard a qualified "okay" in there somewhere, so I picked up where Matt had left off. "And of course he needs a helpful local citizen to direct him. It would be a shame if Frank got lost, wouldn't it? And if he and his helpful guide were to happen to stumble over anything that might be of interest to the sheriff, we would know enough not to touch anything or move anything, and we would contact the sheriff immediately."

"That about covers it. I guess it's not worth saying that I'd rather you didn't put yourself in the middle of this? One man is dead, you know." Matt looked at me, his gaze steady but unreadable.

"I'll be careful, Matt, and Frank will be with me. All we want to do is check out a few more sites, and now that we know there might be an RV, we can look for that too, and sites that would accommodate one. There's no guarantee that we'll find anything."

"Take my vehicle," Matt said.

"What? The police cruiser?"

"No, my own — my truck. It's got four-wheel drive, and it's a lot sturdier than

274

yours. I'll take yours tonight." Matt yawned, then looked contrite. "Sorry — not much sleep. I should go. Em, can you give me your car keys?"

"Sure, and I'll walk you out."

Outside in the cool darkness, I asked Matt, "Was there anything you didn't want to say to the group up there?"

"No, not really. I think Denis has told us what he can. The sheriff is disinclined to think that Cam's been the victim of foul play until it's shoved in his face, and I can't say that I blame him. He's pulling out all the stops on Alex's death, anyway. I'll get a report on what my guys find at Denis's and Alex's homes, and maybe there'll be something there."

"You're searching Denis's house too?" I said sharply.

"Of course, and his office. He worked with Alex. He didn't object. Em, it'll be all right — we'll find Cam."

I wasn't really sure that Matt believed his own words, but even if he was only being kind, I'd take it.

He pulled me close, under cover of darkness. "Be careful, will you? You know people get in trouble all the time in the desert around here. There are a lot of dangerous things out there. Tarantulas, snakes, that kind of thing."

Reptiles or human snakes? I relaxed against him. It was kind of nice, having someone to lean on, both literally and figuratively. "I know. I'll try. But Cam's more important to me than he is to the sheriff, so I'm going to do all I can."

"That's about what I figured."

A few minutes later I watched him drive off in my car, fumbling only slightly with the gears. *I think I got the better of that trade,* I thought as I glanced over at Matt's dusty midsize pickup truck, which looked as though it could climb walls. If Cam was anywhere out there on Denis and Alex's land, Frank and I would find him.

I hoped.

CHAPTER 22

The reflection of light from the surface of a gem has been described as adamantine, metallic, greasy, waxy, and pearly.

After another restless night I was beginning to wonder if I'd ever get any sleep. I thought of my studio with a brief moment of longing, but I knew that I wouldn't accomplish much worthwhile there as long as Cam was still missing. I sometimes used making glass as therapy, losing myself in the fascination of shaping molten glass, but right now I was too distracted. Would the mystery buyer try to get in touch with Denis? The deadline was approaching fast — the Gem Show ended in a few days. I had to assume the police had that possibility covered.

Frank and I ran into each other in the kitchen early. We communicated economically.

"Coffee?"

"Please."

"Food?"

"I'll do it."

Finally I managed to string together an entire sentence. "We should refill the water bottles if we're going to be out for a while."

"Good idea."

That, apparently, was our quota of words for the first hour. Luckily I didn't need words to communicate with Fred and Gloria. The rattle of kibble meant food; the jingle of leashes meant walk. Finally, fed, watered, and equipped with detailed maps, Frank and I were ready to set out.

"You want me to drive?" I asked, not sure of what answer I wanted. I don't like unfamiliar vehicles, and I don't know much about driving on bad roads or sand. Put those all together, and I had my doubts about setting out in Matt's truck.

"Nah. I think I've got the general idea. Not too many roads anyway, are there?"

"No, and not too many people either." I handed him Matt's key ring and we set off.

Since we'd started from the northernmost end of the highway yesterday, it seemed simplest to start at the southernmost today. That took us some five miles outside of city limits. Catalina was the first town past Oro Valley. To the east of the highway it's a thriving town; to the west, there's nothing but open land. Unfortunately Frank and I found . . . nothing. And when the few roads leading in that direction petered out, Frank and I headed north on the highway again. This time I held the maps, but Frank didn't seem to need them, relying on some internal sense of direction. Or maybe the rock just called to him. It didn't say a damn thing to me.

Again we took the fork at Oracle Junction and headed toward Oracle. I knew Oracle was a fair-size town, although it was set back off the highway. We had gone less than a mile beyond Oracle when I swear Frank's nose twitched.

"That road off to the left — where's it go?" he asked.

I traced my finger over the map in my lap. "Looks like . . . Old Tiger Road."

Frank slapped the steering wheel with one hand, making me jump. "Of course! The old Mammoth-Saint Anthony Mine. How could I have forgotten that?"

"Huh?" I said intelligently. "Frank, do you know everything about every mine in existence?"

"Not quite, but this one was famous in its day. Opened up in 1879, mostly for gold. But they found something like ninety kinds of minerals there, back in the day. Not open now."

I looked back at my map. "It looks like there's a pit mine a bit further ahead."

"Nope, we want this road. Pit mine's not what we need — different geology."

I lay down my maps and concentrated on the landscape. The road veered to the left, skirting the flank of a hill, then right to follow the gully along the fold between two hills. It wasn't in good repair, and I couldn't imagine that it went anywhere, except maybe to a ranch. We followed the road a mile, then two, bouncing around in our seats like popcorn. I was ready to suggest we turn around before we trashed Matt's suspension, when Frank stopped the car and pointed. "There."

I followed his finger and at first saw nothing. Then a patch of brown resolved itself into the man-made lines of a small RV, covered with dust. "I see it! Can we get closer?"

"If it got there, we can get there. Hang on." Frank started up again and crept forward until we were within twenty feet. It was a small Winnebago, not new. I didn't see anything like an electric line, although that would have been a lot to expect out here. Frank turned off the engine and quiet fell on us. I climbed gingerly out of the car and studied the RV as Frank came up beside me.

I realized my heart was pounding. Odds were good that the RV was Alex's, but I was scared to take the next step. It looked pretty deserted, and nothing moved.

Frank relieved me of the decision. "Halloo in there! Anybody home?" His voice sounded shockingly loud in the empty landscape. Still, it didn't produce any response.

We looked at each other. "Matt didn't want us to interfere with it, if we found it," I said dubiously.

"Gotta make sure there's no one in there, don't we? Somebody might be in trouble and need our help."

"Oh, definitely. We should be sure. We don't have to touch anything else, right?"

"Right." Frank strode toward the metal door, with me following closely.

We stopped again when we reached the door. It was closed and didn't look damaged.

"A five-year-old could open this lock, you know."

Was I really so transparent? "Then open the door."

When Frank carefully covered his hand

and tried the door, it wasn't locked. It opened out, and Frank took a cautious step into the interior. He stood still for a moment, and then he stepped forward and beckoned me to follow. I climbed in and stopped beside him.

Silence. There was nobody there. At least, not anyone living. I had never been in a vehicle like this, and under other circumstances I might have admired the compact and efficient use of space. I spied a microwave, a stove top, and a small television with a DVD player set into the wall. But I had other things on my mind. I nudged Frank. "Bathroom?" The presumably tiny bathroom was the only enclosed space and the only part of the vehicle that we couldn't see from where we stood. I was holding my breath when Frank pulled open the door, and I let it go when I saw that it was empty. There was no one here.

But there had been, and not long ago.

Frank returned to my side and we looked at the small open space. "What're you thinking?"

"For a start, someone has been here recently. And not just in and out — the surfaces aren't covered with dust. Out here, it doesn't take long for dust to accumulate, and this place is anything but airtight."

"Couple of days, max?" he asked.

"I'd say so. And it looks pretty tidy in here. I'll have to ask Matt what Alex's house looked like, but Denis said his office was a mess. So somebody cleaned up?" I realized as I said it that that could be taken in more than one way. Either the place had been occupied for some time by a neatnik, or someone had done a thorough job of removing evidence of . . . something.

As I shoved that unpleasant thought out of my head, I looked around again. "No electric wires. What keeps this place going?"

"Built-in generator, runs off the gas tank. Looks like this has been here for a bit, so whoever was using it wanted to have all the comforts of home. And he probably kept his power use low." Frank gestured toward a propane lamp on a shelf. "There'll be a water tank too. Pretty sweet little setup, actually."

I wandered over to the tiny refrigerator, which wasn't running, and opened it with one finger. Inside I found several jugs of water and not much else. Opening a cupboard with the same one-finger technique, I saw cans and packages of pasta and quick meals-in-a-bag, and a couple of rolls of toilet paper. This was definitely a bachelor hangout, and if someone spent time here, he probably went into one or another of the nearest towns for real food. Assuming, of course, that he had a car. Nobody would walk this far, not in Arizona, unless they were desperate.

Nothing I saw screamed "clue" at me. No bodies, no blood, no weapons. Maybe I should be looking at what *wasn't* there — starting with people, Cam in particular. I didn't see anything that looked like my brother's computer, and that spurred another question. "Frank, if there's a generator, would that be enough to power a computer? A laptop, anyway?"

"Sure. Nobody travels without a computer these days, right?"

"But there isn't one here, in any case." I scanned chair backs, hooks — anyplace that might be used by a guy to drape something and forget it: nothing. "Frank, what does this look like to you? The place is clean and tidy. There's no fresh food and no clothes."

"Looks to me like somebody came along and took any and all of the personal stuff."

"I was afraid you'd say that. I agree. It all looks perfectly innocent — but it looks too good. What the heck are we dealing with here?" I tried to picture myself explaining to one or more law enforcement types that I was suspicious because the RV was too tidy.

That would go over really well.

I was running out of ideas. *Cam, if you were here, can you send me a message or something?*

I opened a few more cabinets, and then I got lucky: there was a plastic wastebasket tucked in one of them, under the sink. I pulled it out slowly and peered in: fresh plastic bag, empty, but stuck to the side of the container there were a couple of pieces of torn paper. "You have a handkerchief, Frank?"

Like a good Boy Scout he fished out a clean handkerchief and handed it to me. I covered my hand, reached into the trash container, and pulled out a piece of paper with writing on it.

I recognized the writing: Cam's.

The flood of mingled relief and fear that swept through me then was almost nauseating. My brilliant deductive reasoning had been right: this had been Alex's desert camp, and he had brought Cam here. Cam had been here. But now Cam was *not* here, and it looked as though somebody had gone to some length to conceal that he ever had been. That scared me.

"What've you got?" Frank's voice startled me.

"It's Cam's handwriting. He must have

been working here at some point — this looks like some kind of calculation — so that pretty much fits what we figured out. But then he left . . . with or without help."

I looked around me at the too-tidy space and wrapped my arms around myself. "Frank, before we get ahead of ourselves, can you take a look around the place, outside, see if anybody was kind enough to leave us footprints?"

"Right." Frank stepped carefully out of the RV, studying the ground, then moved off in a clockwise direction. I looked around inside again and considered my options. Which were pretty close to none. There were no clues of any value that I could see. I assumed the proper authorities would be able to "see" better and could look for fingerprints and other things. Cam had not left a neatly signed note saying "Help! I have been abducted by thugs! Please send assistance to . . ." It was time to call in the big guns and let them do their stuff.

I stepped down from the RV and pulled out my cell phone. It was fully charged, but it got no signal at all, which did not surprise me. It also confirmed my suspicion that Cam couldn't have called me even if he'd wanted to. And obviously, he hadn't had his car, so he couldn't have driven to a phone

— or someplace with a Wi-Fi connection. He could conceivably have walked the few miles back to the highway and sought help. But how long would it have taken him to decide that he needed help?

I could picture him here, nursing his wounded heart, distracting himself by digging into whatever modeling problem Alex had handed him. I could imagine him losing all sense of time. After all, he had food, water, and enough power to run his beloved computer, right? What more did he need? Maybe after a few days, when he had finished whatever he had to do, or Alex had missed a scheduled rendezvous — because he was dead — Cam would have begun to worry, a little. How long would he have waited before setting off to find civilization? And how quickly had he been interrupted by . . . who? Alex was dead, and Denis didn't know where the RV was. Had Alex given someone information about where to find it? And had that information included the fact that Cam was there? Or was it purely coincidental that someone had stumbled on the RV? Or had Cam cleaned up before heading out and then gotten waylaid? Or worse, lost?

Frank came back. "Nothing like usable footprints, but it looks like one guy came, two guys left."

"It didn't look like one of them was resisting, or possibly being dragged?" When Frank shook his head, I went on. "I guess it's time to call Matt. He'll know who should cover this. I'm not even sure what county we're in. My cell phone doesn't get a signal out here, so we've got to go back to Oracle." The town could be counted on to have working telephones and cell phone service.

We drove back in silence as I mulled over what I wanted to say to Matt. Oracle turned out to be a nice sleepy town. I knew it had become something of a bedroom community for Tucson, since it was just under forty miles away (although I much preferred my commute, which could be measured in feet), and I seemed to remember something about an Oracle Pumpkin Festival.

When I finally found a signal, I punched in Matt's cell, and he answered quickly. "What've you got?"

I matched terse with terse. "We found the RV, outside of Oracle. Nobody home, but it looks like somebody worked hard to tidy it up. No dust, no mess. If this was Alex's home away from home, there should have been junk lying around. There's nothing personal there at all." I swallowed. "Matt —

288

I found something with Cam's handwriting on it. I'm pretty sure he was there."

Matt's sigh echoed over the ether. "Pinal County. Figures. Okay, I'll get the ball rolling. Can you find someplace in town to sit tight until I get there?"

"Will do. See you soon. And, Matt? Can you hurry?"

CHAPTER 23

Cleopatra's famous emeralds may actually
have been peridot.

Matt called my cell phone when he arrived
in Oracle and met us at the pizzeria where
Frank and I had taken refuge. He dropped
into a chair and ordered a cold drink before
asking, without preamble, "Where is it?"

"A couple of miles outside of town, to the
west. It's back in an arroyo, so you can't see
it until you're pretty much on top of it. Who
are we waiting for?"

"The rest of the troops are coming. They
had to do some song and dance about who's
in charge. I just gave them the general
outline and told them to meet me here. You
okay?"

"Good enough. FYI, I found the papers
with Cam's writing on them in the wastebasket under the sink. Before you ask, I
didn't touch them directly, and I left them

where I found them. We didn't mess with anything else except to make sure no one was hiding in the bathroom. Frank looked around outside and found some footprints. Matt, I know it doesn't seem like much, but like I said, the RV is just too clean. If this was Alex's place, I would have expected junk lying around. How does that match up with Alex's home?"

"Night and day," he said absently. "Frank, you get anything that Em missed?"

"I would have missed the 'clean' part." He grinned. "Outside? People have been around, not too long ago. Still plenty of gas for the generator, and water in the tank. Nothing out of place."

Matt's eyes were on a Pima County sheriff's vehicle that had pulled up outside behind his cruiser, followed shortly by a Pinal County one. "Show's about to start. Frank, you can guide us out to the site. But, Em, I think you ought to stay out of this — go back to Tucson."

"Go back and tend to my knitting while the big boys do all the work?" I said, angry even though I knew it was unreasonable.

"You know I don't mean it like that. But this is going to get crowded, fast, and the fewer civilians, the better. I will pass on that you identified the writing as your brother's and that there is good reason to believe that he was there. But it's going to be bad enough just explaining what you were doing there."

I was pissed, but I knew that he was right: I'd only get in the way. "All right," I said, trying not to grit my teeth. I stood up. "See you later, if you aren't too busy." I stalked away before Matt could say anything else, or before I said something I would regret.

On the drive back toward Tucson, all by my lonesome, I wondered just what I could do now. I'd been doing my part, giving everything I found to the right authorities. What did that leave me with? Not much.

What advantage did I have? I knew Cam, although a lovelorn Cam might not act exactly normally. And . . . I had Denis's confidence. He had come to me when he was scared. I had counseled him to come clean to the cops, and he had. Could I use that trust?

The police had searched Denis's and Alex's homes and offices. But had they really "looked" at them the way I had looked at the RV? I had noticed how clean the RV was — and that was not typical of a bachelor like Alex. So maybe, just maybe, I could find something that they'd missed at Denis's. It was the best — or more like the only — idea I had at the moment.

I knew Denis's address from the form he had filled out at the shop, and I turned and headed in that direction, hoping that he'd actually be home. I assumed that in the midst of an investigation, he might have decided not to show his face at his department on campus and would be lying low at home. It was worth a try.

Denis's house turned out to be a cookie-cutter adobe in a development maybe ten years old. Not awful, but nothing special. There was a car in the driveway, which was a good sign. I parked behind it, marched to the front door, and rang the doorbell.

"Oh, Em!" Denis said as he opened the door, clearly surprised to see me standing on the other side. "What are you doing here?"

I pushed past him without waiting for his permission. "I wanted to talk to you." *And scope out your house.* "How are you holding up?" It wouldn't hurt to be civil to him.

He closed the door behind me. "Okay, I guess. You know the police were here?"

"Yes, Matt told me. Do you know what they were looking for?"

"Mostly anything that had to do with Alex and the investments. But they went through just about everything. They were very

293

thorough. I had to spend most of the night putting things back the way they were."

"Yeah, they can leave a mess behind. And with your wife out of town . . ." I tried to look sympathetic.

"Exactly. She's very particular about how she wants things. She would have gone ballistic if she had seen it the way they left it."

Ah. She probably had him well trained. "It's a lovely place" — which I couldn't have described three minutes after I walked out — "and she's done a nice job with it" — if your idea of interior design was beige on beige. "How much have you told her about what's going on?"

"Very little. Mostly that Alex and I had run into a little trouble, and that Alex had been killed."

"How did she take the news that Alex was dead?" I remembered that Denis had spirited his wife out of town before Matt had learned that it was murder.

"She was upset, of course. We go back a long way. We were all friends." Denis shrugged. "I wasn't sure how much was safe to tell her, with Alex's killer roaming around. Elizabeth hadn't seen her folks for a while anyway, and she had vacation time coming. I haven't told her about the search here yet."

"Denis, did the police find anything, take anything with them?"

He shook his head. "I told you, and I told them, Alex kept all the records. I had copies, and they took those. But it's not like Alex was being secretive or anything — I mean, I trusted him. I just wasn't that interested in the business side of things. I signed the tax forms each year, and I kind of eyeballed them, reviewed the bottom line, but I don't have a mind for financial stuff. I never really looked at the copies, just filed them. I think the police took those. Hey, you want something to drink? Water, soda?"

"Water would be fine," I said. Denis seemed relieved at the opportunity to play host rather than interrogee, but I wasn't going to let him off that easy. "Did they find Alex's records at his house?" I asked as I followed him into the kitchen. There, Denis opened a cabinet. I noticed that all the glasses were lined up according to size.

Denis took out a tall glass, filled it with ice cubes from the freezer, added tap water, and handed it to me. "No, but they didn't say much anyway. Mostly they asked where things were, like my own records. I let them look at everything. I don't have anything to hide."

"And they looked in your office, and

Alex's, at the university?"

"That's what they said. What are you looking for?"

"Denis, to be honest, I'm not sure. I just hope I recognize it when I see it. You told the police about Alex's RV, right? Was it Alex's or the partnership's?"

Denis shrugged. "Alex's, I think. Though I'm pretty sure he claimed it as a business expense. Does it matter? I never saw it."

"We found it. The police are searching it now."

"Hey, that's good, isn't it? Was there anything there?" he asked eagerly. If I'd hoped for some sort of incriminating reaction from Denis, I was disappointed.

"Did Alex have any other place for storage? A rental unit somewhere?"

"Not that I know about. Maybe you can find out from payment records or something?"

If there was, I was pretty sure the police would track it down. I was rapidly running out of ideas.

"What about your car? Do you keep anything in that?"

"The police looked there. I try to keep that neat, because Elizabeth doesn't like to ride around in a messy car."

Another dead end. I remembered the

information Frank had gotten at the casino, about the woman — or women — Alex came in with occasionally. "Do you know if Alex was seeing anybody? Is there a girl-friend we should know about?"

"Not right now. He dated women — I mean, he wasn't gay or anything — but nobody ever lasted long. I think he really liked to be alone, when you come right down to it. All that time by himself out in the desert or wherever. He thought he was a lone wolf. And most women weren't too excited about that."

I certainly hadn't seen any feminine touches at the RV — other than the unusual cleanliness, it had screamed "bachelor." "So there's nobody else you can think of who Alex might have shared information with?"

"I'm sorry, Em, but no. I've been thinking about this ever since I found out he was dead. I thought I was his best friend. I can't imagine why anyone would want to kill him. I always considered Alex a pretty honest guy. I don't want to find out that he was screwing me over, or he got me into some-thing illegal."

It was nice that Denis felt some loyalty to his late friend and business partner. But my goal was not to find out how nice a guy Alex had been, but to find some thread to follow that might lead to my brother. I was getting desperate. I sipped my water and cast my eyes around the kitchen, looking for an idea, any idea. Had the police sifted through the flour canister? Melted all the ice cubes, in case there was something hidden there? Could you hide peridot in lime Jell-O?

My eye lit on an untidy stack of mail on the kitchen counter. That would definitely displease Elizabeth, if she saw it marring the pristine purity of her kitchen. "That new?" I nodded toward the pile.

Denis looked and then all but blushed. "Oh, that's the stuff from my university mailbox. I stopped by and grabbed it this morning, in case there was anything important, but I didn't stick around. I know the police have talked to people in my department, and I didn't want everyone staring at me, whispering, you know?"

I deposited my empty glass next to the sink and then leafed casually through the stack of mail — apparently the only thing in the house the police hadn't searched, since it hadn't been there earlier.

In the midst of the pile there was a midsize cardboard envelope. No return address, no postmark, so I assumed it came from within the university — or had been hand delivered. I picked it up and felt the contents:

thin but hard, square shaped — a CD case? Without turning, I said, "Denis? When was the last time you picked up your mail, before this batch?"

"Uh, a week and a half ago, maybe more? I don't check all that often. Most of us use e-mail these days, so the stuff in the box is mainly advertising or university notices, that kind of thing."

I turned to face him, then handed him the envelope. "Open this."

Clearly bewildered, he looked at the envelope in his hand, then at my face. "What is it?"

"I don't know, Denis," I said, struggling for patience. "It was in your mail. Why don't you open it?"

Thankfully, he did before I lost whatever self-restraint I had. He reached in and pulled out a CD in a case. There was a sticky note on the outside of the case, and I leaned over to read it: "Thought you should have a copy of this stuff — Alex."

Bingo!

CHAPTER 24

In ancient Egypt, only pharaohs, high priests, and nobles were permitted to own glass, and used it to decorate their thrones, funeral masks, and mummy cases.

"What do I do now?" Denis said plaintively. "Do I read the disk?"

I was sorely tempted. I really wanted to know what was on that disk and whether it would help me find Cam, but I could almost hear Matt's voice in my head: *Do not tamper with evidence.* Besides which, I knew the limitations of my computer skills, and I'd probably manage to destroy the precious item before I even accessed a file.

I took a deep breath. "Denis, this is potential evidence in a murder investigation. You will get in your car, and you will take it to police headquarters immediately. Do not pass Go, do not collect $200. Tell the person at the desk that it's important that Chief Lundgren see it as soon as possible. I'll try to call him now, to let him know you're coming. Got that?"

Denis nodded, obviously relieved that he didn't have to make any decisions for himself.

I turned away and fished out my cell phone, intending to leave Matt a message, and miraculously got through.

"Em? What do you want?" Matt all but barked.

"Nice to talk to you too. I'll cut to the chase: Denis found a CD from Alex in his campus mail today. I told him to take it directly to your office. Where are you?"

"Not far — I'm on my way back. I'll meet him there. Thanks, Em. Uh, you haven't looked to see what's on it or anything, have you?"

"No, sir, I have not. I have not even touched it, just the envelope it came in. We'll leave it to you and your forensic wizards."

"Thanks. Talk to you later." He hung up.

I turned back to Denis. "Go. He'll meet you there. Take the disk and the case and the envelope in came in. Put the whole thing in a bag. And take good care of it." When he had bagged the precious disk, envelope and all, I shepherded him out the front door to his car. I watched his car depart, then went back to mine. I had done the right thing, right? I had followed appropriate procedure.

I got in my car, and even though half my brain was somewhere else, I made the trip through the gathering dark without mishap. Back at the studio, I pulled into my usual parking space behind the building. I sat for a moment, collecting my energy, then got out and locked the car and made my way around the side to my staircase.

And stopped in my tracks. There was someone sitting on my steps.

As a responsible home and business owner, and a woman living alone, I had of course installed floodlights for safety. Unfortunately they didn't do me much good from where I stood behind the stairs: all I could see was the dark outline of a male figure sitting at the bottom of the metal staircase.

An outline that looked familiar, even from the back. I moved fast, to the front of the stairs, hoping against hope . . .

"Cam?"

"Hi, Emmeline, sister of mine. Hey, that rhymes. How ya doin'?" He grinned, a singularly sweet and silly grin.

Unquestionably my brother — in one

piece, grubby, and (I noticed as I came closer) a little ripe, but at the moment I didn't care. I just hauled him to his feet and flung my arms around him and hugged as hard as I could, just to make sure he was real.

And then I pushed back. "Where the hell have you been?" I demanded.

He swayed slightly but didn't seem to notice. "I was out in the desert. Do you know, you have some beautiful desert around here? I mean, it's so big and quiet. Except for the lizards. They were kind of loud."

My first surge of euphoria over, I took a harder look at him. Something was not right. Even allowing for the dimness of the surroundings, his pupils looked awfully large. Holding him, I could feel heat radiating off him, and his heart seemed to be racing. Heatstroke? Was he on something? What, I had no idea. But he was still Cam and he was still here, and I was ecstatic.

First things first. "Let's go upstairs, okay?"

"Sure, sounds great. Wow, look at those stairs! They just go on and on. . . ."

As I guided him up the outside stairs, I wondered if he needed medical help. If he'd been wandering in the desert, could he be dehydrated? Should I do something about it? I decided to call the EMTs and then Matt. Better to be safe than sorry.

I dug out my keys and opened the door. Predictably the dogs went berserk at the sight of their much-loved Uncle Cam, who sat down on the floor and (I swear) exchanged sniffs with them. They rolled around in an orgy of excitement, with staid sober me watching the show. I made a beeline to my phone and called 911, and someone promised to have an ambulance at my door in minutes.

They were right — they must have been in the neighborhood, because they arrived before I could even reach Matt. I opened my door to a pair of paramedics.

"What's the problem?" one of them asked.

"It's my brother. He's been missing for a few days, and then he just showed up and he's not acting normal. I was worried that it might by hyperthermia or something — he may have been out in the desert for a while."

"We'll take a look."

I stood back as they introduced themselves to Cam, who greeted them like long-lost friends, and then did assorted medical stuff — took his temperature, checked his pulse and heart and lungs, flashed lights in his eyes. After a few minutes they came back to me.

"He's okay?" I asked.

I could have sworn they were struggling to hide smiles. "He's high. Mescaline, most likely."

"But Cam doesn't do drugs!" Had the events of the last week driven him over the edge?

The older paramedic shrugged. "We see a lot of it around here. But no question, he's toasted." When I looked blank, he volunteered, "Baked? Cooked? Wasted? Not much we can do — just keep an eye on him until he comes down. May be a while."

"Thank you!" I called out as they went down the stairs. Then I turned to my very stoned brother. "You hungry, Cam? Thirsty?"

He looked up at me with a beatific expression. "Hungry?"

"Yes, hungry. When was the last time you ate?"

"I don't know. What day is this?"

"Tuesday."

"Oh, wow. I thought it was Friday. I ate on Friday, I think."

Fred and Gloria were still circling around Cam, enjoying the strange and wonderful scents he must have brought with him. Too bad they couldn't tell me where he'd been, based on those scents. I decided he could stand to lose a few of them.

"Cam?" It took him a few seconds to tear his attention from his renewed lovefest with the dogs and look at me. "I think you need a shower. Why don't you take a shower while I fix us something to eat?"

"Shower. Oh, great idea. I love the sound a shower makes, don't you? All swooshy and wet."

I held out my hand and hauled him to his feet, then turned him and pushed him toward the bathroom at the back. "Shower, that way." He ambled in the right direction, with a few small detours, and finally found it, closing the door behind him.

I seized the moment to call Matt on my cell again.

"What?" he said, sounding snappish. "Denis is here. We've got the disk."

"Matt, shut up. Cam's home."

"What?" At least I'd gotten his attention. "You found him? Is he okay?"

"He was sitting on my steps when I got home. He's high on something — the paramedics thought it might be mescaline — but otherwise seems to be all right."

"Sit tight. I'll be there in, oh, half an hour."

When he hung up, I turned to the refrigerator. It looked like scrambled eggs and sausage were the best I was going to manage, and at least I had plenty of bread. I fed the dogs, then started mixing eggs and frying sausage. After about ten minutes, I realized the water had been running continuously in the bathroom. Maybe Cam had managed to drown himself like an idiot turkey?

I moved the sausage pan off the heat and went down the hallway to knock on the bathroom door. "Cam?" I didn't hear anything other than the water. I opened the door a crack. "Cam, are you all right?" We might be brother and sister, but I clung to a few shreds of modesty.

"Em? I'm fine. I'm wonderful. Your soap smells so good I can hear it."

Whatever he was on, he was having a grand time. "Time to get out of the shower, Cam. Dinner's almost ready. I'll bring you some fresh clothes." I quickly went into what had been Frank's room for the last week and riffled through the clothes Cam had left stashed in the dresser. I grabbed some underwear, a pair of sweatpants, and a T-shirt, and discreetly tossed them into the bathroom on my way back to the kitchen.

Cam was sitting, clean in body and clothing, at the kitchen table with a heaped plate in front of him when Matt arrived. Cam gave Matt another sweet grin. "Hey, Matt. Good to see you. How've you been?"

Matt and I exchanged glances. "Are you hungry, Matt? I made plenty."

"Why don't I help you?" he replied, taking me by the arm and steering me toward the stove. When we were more or less out of Cam's hearing — not that he was paying the slightest attention to us, being more interested in feeding bits of sausage to the dogs at his feet — Matt said, "You had him checked out?"

"Of course. We don't know where he's been. The paramedics told me he was high and there wasn't much they could do for him."

"What's he been like?"

"Very happy. He said he could hear the soap."

"Dilated pupils? Fast pulse?"

"Yes to both."

"Sounds like mescaline all right. Does he do drugs?"

"Cam? His limit's about two beers."

"He's been under a lot of stress lately — maybe it pushed him in the wrong direction."

"Why don't you ask him?"

"I'll try, but he may not be making much

sense. Or he may not remember much —
peyote messes up your short-term memory."

"Great," I muttered. "This just gets better
and better, doesn't it?"

Matt took a seat next to Cam at the table.
"Cam, where've you been hanging out the
past few days?"

Cam turned to look at him and gradually
focused. "Matt. Where? Um, out in the
desert. There was this really cool camper.
Maybe I'll get one of those. It was so
compact and efficient, you know?"

"Yes, Cam, I've seen it. It's very nice. Were
you alone there?"

"Well, sure. That was the deal. I was working. Oops!" His eyes darted around the
room. "I'm not supposed to tell anyone
about that. It's a secret."

"Does it have to do with the gemstones?
The peridot?"

Cam's face fell. "You know? I didn't tell
you, did I?"

"No, Cam, I found out myself. Did you
see anybody else out there?"

Cam shook his head vigorously. "No. And
I waited for days. And nobody came. I was
about to go looking when this guy showed
up."

If Matt had been a dog, I swear his ears
would have swiveled toward Cam. "What

guy? Was it someone you knew?"

"Nope, never saw him before. But he was real nice, offered me a ride into town. Even gave me a cup of coffee too."

Matt leaned forward in his chair. "Then what, Cam?"

"I, um . . ." Cam's brow wrinkled in concentration. "I'm not sure. We went somewhere for a while. And then there was this woman. She was nice. And then I was here. What day is this?"

"Tuesday, Cam," I said quietly. I looked at Matt. "He asked that before. Is any of this helping you?"

Matt looked defeated. "I don't think I'm going to get anything coherent out of him now. If it's peyote, he should be more rational by morning. I might as well wait until then to talk to him. At least we know he met a guy out there at the RV and there was a woman involved somehow. And since he didn't identify the guy, it's probably no one he knows." Matt rubbed his hands over his face. "I should go. Keep an eye on him, okay? He'll probably just go to sleep."

"Have you gotten anything from the disk yet?"

"Not yet. We're working on it."

"You'll come back in the morning?"

"Count on it."

We said good night with more weariness than passion, and I shut the door behind him and turned back to Cam. He'd cleaned his plate, and mine, and the plate of toast I'd made. "Em, I'm hungry. Can I have some more?"

"I've got toast. Is that okay?"

"Sure. You have any of that pink jelly?"

"The prickly pear stuff? Sure." I fed more slices of bread into the toaster and retrieved the cactus jelly and put in on the table in front of Cam. When the toaster popped up, I buttered the toast and set in on the plate in front of him.

He picked up a piece and starting spreading jelly on it. And kept on spreading jelly on it, swirling it around with the knife, his expression rapt. "Isn't it pretty?"

"Yes, very pretty, Cam." This was beginning to feel like entertaining a cheerful five-year-old. "Are you going to eat it?"

"What? Oh, sure." He bit into the jammy toast, and a look of bliss spread across his face. "Oh, that's good!"

How long was this going to last? I wanted answers as much as Matt, but clearly I wasn't going to get any soon.

Cam had finished a fourth piece of pretty pink toast when I heard the sound of a key in the lock, and Frank walked in — followed

311

by Allison.

I hadn't managed to think ahead far enough to plan how to tell Allison that the lost was found, but now that decision had been made for me. When she saw Cam, Allison stilled, and I watched expressions chase across her face in quick succession. Cam took a moment longer to look up at her, but when he did, he stood up abruptly and lost the silly grin he'd worn since he'd walked in the door.

Then like magnets they began to move toward each other, slowly at first, then faster until they collided in the middle and wrapped themselves around each other. I had to look away from the sheer intensity of their reunion. I caught Frank's eye and we smiled at each other. He gave me a thumbs-up gesture. So far nobody had said a word. Even the dogs were fascinated by this weird human behavior.

I wondered if there was a protocol dictating how long we should wait. If there was, I chose to ignore it, but after about fifteen seconds, I said, "Cam? I think maybe you and Allison should talk privately, don't you? Go on." I nudged them, still entangled, toward Cam's bedroom. Allison pulled back a minimal distance, laid a hand on his arm, and drew him toward the door. It closed behind them.

I took a deep breath. "Well."

Frank echoed, "Too right. You wouldn't have a drink handy, would you now? I think we've got some catching up to do."

"I do, and I'll join you. And I'd guess you'll be sleeping on the couch tonight."

CHAPTER 25

In the past, ground peridot has been used as a treatment for asthma.

I finally managed a decent night's sleep and awoke to the sound of voices: I could hear Allison's fluting accent, Frank's rumble, and an intermittent word or two in Cam's baritone. I knew that there were still a lot of unanswered questions, starting with who killed Alex, but having Cam back, safe and sound, made a huge difference in my outlook on life. I wondered when Matt would appear — and that thought prompted me to get out of bed and face the day.

I scurried to the blessedly free bathroom, showered, and emerged clothed, ready to take on bears. In the big room Cam and Frank were seated at the table, while Allison hovered, bringing food and refilling coffee cups. Everyone looked at me as I approached.

"What? Is my hair on fire or something?" I helped myself to coffee. "How are you feeling, Cam?"

"Foolish. Kind of weird. Was I talking strangely yesterday?"

I smiled into my coffee. "You might say so. You said you could hear the soap."

"What the hell happened to me?"

"I was kind of hoping you could answer that. The best guess was that you'd taken some mescaline. You were really out of it, baby brother."

He looked stricken. "But I don't do stuff like that — you know that, Em. How . . . ?"

"Cam, I don't know. Do you remember anything?"

"No — it's all really fuzzy."

"Matt said that was normal, but you should be okay today." I wondered if Cam would ever reclaim the memories of the last few days, but I wasn't going to stop him from trying. I concentrated on eating. "So, you two make up?" I sneaked a glance at Allison, who had scooched her chair as close to Cam's as possible without actually climbing into his lap.

Allison blushed. Cam blushed. It was very sweet.

"Do you want me to fill you in on what you missed? I mean, after you disappeared?"

"I guess. Why do you say 'disappeared'?"

"Because you stalked out of here without telling me where you were going, you dummy. We had no idea where you were."

He glanced briefly at Allison. "Sorry about that. I was mad — at Allison, at you, at the world in general. But I did have this short-term consulting deal set up, and Alex said he had a camper or RV or whatever that I could use, out in the desert, and it seemed like a good idea to just get away from everyone and think." Suddenly he looked stricken. "Where's my laptop?"

"I don't know. Didn't you have it with you?"

"At the RV, sure. Was I carrying anything last night?"

"Not a thing. And it wasn't at the RV either."

"How do you know?"

I sat back in my chair and stared at my clueless brother. "Cam, you disappeared. I figured at first you just wanted some time to work things out, so I didn't think too much about it. But after a week, when I knew you had planned to start work, uh, two days ago, and you hadn't phoned or e-mailed or anything, I got worried. I reported you missing to the police on Saturday, but it was Frank and I who found the RV."

"Alex knew where I was. Oh, that's the guy it belonged to, the guy I was working for. He took me out there, the day I left here. Alex Gutierrez. I guess you didn't know that."

A heavy silence fell, and Frank and I exchanged a look. Finally I said, "Cam, Alex is dead."

"What?"

"He was found in the desert, and not anywhere near the RV. If we hadn't been looking for you, probably no one would have gotten around to identifying his body for quite a while. But when I reported you missing, Matt asked about recent bodies, and we found Alex at the morgue. Cam, he was murdered."

Cam paled noticeably and shut his eyes. Allison laid a hand on his arm, watching his face. It was a few moments before he spoke.

"How much do you know about what I was working on? Because I signed a confidentiality agreement with Alex, and I think he had a partner."

"He did. His name's Denis Ryerson. We've been talking to him. I think we're pretty much up to speed on the whole gem thing. Frank's been amazing."

"You flatter me, Em," Frank said. "But

gems are my business. Plus Denis filled us in on the property deal. Said Alex handled most of it, though."

Cam studied the tabletop, thinking out loud. "Alex knew what he was talking about, when it came to the geology. I wasn't sure I could help much, but I think I did a respectable job, given what I had to work with, and the time limitations. And I think he would have been pleased with the results — which are on my laptop. Damn!"

"I have to admit that I wondered how you would manage without an Internet connection." I helped myself to more of Allison's homemade bread.

"The RV had plenty of power, and I really didn't need anything from the Web. Alex was kind of secretive, didn't want me doing too much searching on my own. I wasn't getting any connection out there anyway. But he handed me a lot of data that he'd collected, and he was very thorough, so I had more than enough to work with. I was kind of happy to be alone for a while. He did have a really sweet little unit, even if it was kind of a pigsty."

Frank and I exchanged glances again: what we had seen in no way resembled a pigsty.

A knock on the door, followed by the

pups' enthusiastic response, heralded Matt's arrival. I went to let him in.

"How's he doing?" he asked in a low voice.

"Fine, I think. He seems to remember what happened early on, when Alex took him out to the RV. We haven't talked about what happened after that."

"Good. Sorry if I've been snappish, but there's a lot going on here, and coordinating with the sheriffs' offices hasn't been a picnic. I don't know if having Cam back is good or bad in terms of the investigation — but I claimed first right to interview him."

"You want us to stick around or to vanish?"

"You can stay as long as you promise to keep your mouth shut."

"What, me interfere?" I grinned. "And I don't think we can pry Allison off him with a crowbar."

"Things back on track there?"

"Looks like it."

"Then let's get to it." He headed toward the table. "Cam, you look a lot better than you did last night."

Cam stood up. "If you say so. I don't remember a lot. And I'm sorry to hear about Alex. I'll do whatever I can to help."

Silently I put a mug of coffee in front of Matt and sat down. Matt pulled out a pad and cleared his throat.

"Let's start with a time line, since we still aren't exactly sure when Alex died. You left here on Saturday, the sixth?"

"Yes. When Em told me that Allison was still in Ireland, I decided to go over to Alex's house. We went out to the RV that afternoon, before dark. He said it was kind of a rough road and suggested that he do the driving, to spare my car — I'd told him how it had been acting up on the road, going back and forth from San Diego. The original plan was that I would work on mapping his site, based on the data he provided and what I could review myself on the ground, and then come back here the next weekend and review things with him before I started work. When was Alex found?"

"Last Sunday, in the desert," Matt said. "Because there was no ID on him, the ME originally assumed that Alex was another illegal who had crossed the border. But it turns out he had some rough peridot in his pocket, so I asked the ME to take a closer look, and when I showed his partner Denis a picture, he identified the body. The ME found that Alex's skull had been cracked."

"Wow." Cam shook his head. "The way we left it, Alex was going to come back and pick me up on Friday — our contract was for a week. I wasn't too worried when he didn't show, but by Saturday morning I was getting nervous, so I thought I'd walk to the nearest town and find a phone, since my cell didn't get a signal. We'd driven through one on the way in, so I knew it wasn't more than a few miles. Except . . ."

"What?" Matt prompted.

"I'm sorry. That's when things get kind of fuzzy. I can remember getting ready to hike into town and then a knock on the door."

I think we all leaned forward to hear what Cam would say next.

"I figured either it was Alex, or he'd sent someone to pick me up," he went on. "I mean, if you've seen the place, you know people just don't happen to wander by. I opened the door and there was a man I didn't recognize standing there who said Alex had sent him to give me a ride back. So I collected my stuff, shut the door, and followed him to his car."

"Make? Model? License plate?" Matt snapped.

"Hey, I wasn't paying attention, all right? I think it was a four-door, not dark, definitely not new. It had lousy shocks. I really didn't think it was necessary to get his license number."

"Sorry, Cam. It's been a rough few days.

So you got in his car and he started driving, right?"

"Right. He offered me a cup of coffee — he had a thermos. I hadn't had any decent coffee for days, so I accepted. Oh, shit — is that where the stuff was? The mescaline?"

"Probably. The coffee would mask the bitterness. Then what?"

"I think we went back to the nearest town, and he volunteered to buy me lunch — said Alex would want him to. And that's really about all I remember."

"Nothing between lunch on Saturday and when you showed up on Em's stoop last night?"

"Fragments, flashes. Nothing I'd trust, really."

"Don't beat yourself up, Cam. Mescaline messes with your memory. Em told me that you mentioned a woman."

Cam closed his eyes for a minute, I assumed to try to recreate his memories. "There was a woman somewhere in there. And she and the man argued, but it was kind of like I was hearing it under water. None of it seemed real. Will something come back, Matt?"

"Maybe. The stuff affects people differently. You have any recollection of how you got here?"

"I think the woman drove me here and dropped me off, but I really can't be sure."

Matt sighed. "About what I expected. It's not your fault, Cam. I'd guess that they picked that particular stuff to achieve exactly that result. Either you wouldn't remember anything useful, or if you did, it would be so garbled it would be worthless. If they'd wanted you dead, we probably never would have found you. Maybe they didn't want another body on their hands."

After that sobering statement, we all fell silent. I noticed that Allison's hand tightened on Cam's arm.

Finally Cam broke the silence. "What now?"

"Cam, I've got to take you to talk with the sheriffs, or at least the Pima County sheriff — his department's the lead on this. I'll vouch for you."

"Thanks, I guess. Will I need that?"

"I hope not. You ready to go?"

"I guess."

Before Matt could drag him away, I grabbed Cam for another hug. So did Allison.

CHAPTER 26

Roman glassmakers used glass to imitate crystal and other stones, especially for cameos, which were carved to reveal contrasting colors.

Nessa had only to look at Allison and me as we walked in to know that we finally had good news. Her face lit up. "Cam?"

"He's back." I couldn't stop smiling. It felt so good to be in the shop without the awful black cloud of uncertainty hanging over me. Sure, there was still that pesky matter of dead Alex, but selfishly I was just happy that my brother was home safe.

I set about filling in the blanks for Nessa. "He just showed up last night, high as a kite on what the EMTs said was probably mescaline," I began, "and unfortunately he can't remember much about the last couple of days. Matt says that's to be expected, but there shouldn't be any lingering aftereffects."

"Well, that's good to hear. Allison, have you seen him?"

I swear Allison blushed again. I stifled the bad joke that popped into my head: I was sure she had seen all there was to see of Cam last night.

"I have."

Nessa probed gently, "And is everything all right?"

Allison nodded, unable to suppress her own smile. Then she grabbed a duster. "I'd better get the dust off these shelves." She busied herself at the far end of the shop.

I finished the rest of the story for Nessa, ending with "and the next thing Cam knows he's sitting on my stairs contemplating his navel or the galaxy or something. He did mention there was a woman involved somewhere in there. And that is about the sum total of what he could tell us: a man who knew about Alex and the RV, and who drove an ordinary car, and possibly a woman somewhere in the mix. And two days of real pretty pictures in his head."

"Oh my. Well, I'll keep my fingers crossed for him. Oh dear — look at the time. I'd better open up."

"And I'm going to try to make some glass, if you don't need me up here. You're both in all day, right?"

"We are," said Nessa, counting the small bills in the register. "Although it seems a bit silly to have both of us here when there are so few customers."

"Nessa, I don't think Allison would leave right now even if I paid her to, and I'm not going to make her go. If you'd like to take a little time off to spend with Frank, that's fine."

"We'll see. You go get some good work done."

"I'll do my best." I headed for the studio; it felt as though I hadn't been there in weeks, rather than only two days. Blessed peace, at last. I turned on one of the glory holes and went over to the cabinet to contemplate my frit and wait for inspiration. What color was today? A lot brighter than yesterday, no question. What would Cam have seen, under the influence? Maybe he could help me recreate his visions in glass — plenty of swirls and pretty colors. That could work. I picked up a warmed blowpipe and opened the furnace for my first gather. I had been experimenting with a new technique that involved fusing individual rods of different colors into a single long one, then using segments of the rod to blow out into individual pieces. The end result — when it worked — was a wonderful swirl of rainbow colors. Perfect for Cam's recent psychedelic experience.

Three hours later I closed the annealer door on a nice clutch of glassworks. I realized that I'd missed lunch, and I was starving. I could see Nessa in the shop and assumed that Allison was at lunch.

"Have you eaten?" I asked as I closed the studio door behind me.

"I have, and Allison's getting her own lunch now. I'd have brought you a sandwich, but I didn't want to interrupt you."

"That's fine. I was finally back in my rhythm, and I got a lot done. I'll run out now and get something."

Fifteen minutes later I returned to the shop with a bulging plastic bag filled with tasty stuff. Allison hadn't returned yet, and Nessa had busied herself by the register while a lone customer browsed the shelves. "I'm back," I said, stating the obvious. "I think I'll go into the office and eat."

"Oh, Em, before you go," Nessa said, beckoning to me from behind the counter.

Curious, I walked around the counter and put my head close to hers. "What's up?" I said in a low voice.

"I'm not really sure," she replied in the same tone. She indicated the customer with the tiniest of nods. "The lady came in a few minutes ago, and she's been kind of drifting around since, looking, but I don't think she's really interested in the glass, if you know what I mean."

I tried to check out the woman without being obvious. Middle height, close to my age, long dark hair, casually but nicely dressed in pants and a pressed shirt. Something about her said "not a tourist," but that was about all I could tell. Except that she seemed nervous: she kept looking around the room, now and then casting a sidelong glance toward us. I had to admit we looked a bit suspicious ourselves, huddled behind the counter, whispering.

I agreed with Nessa's feeling she hadn't come here to buy art. Was she casing the joint? But that was absurd, because it wasn't easy to walk out with a batch of glass items — they're both heavy and fragile. We never had much money in the register, and most of our buyers paid by credit card anyway. There were plenty of other stores around here that had better pickings for a burglary. So what was she doing here?

I crossed the room toward her. "Hi, I'm Em Dowell, the glassmaker. Did you have questions about any piece in particular?"

"Oh, no, no. I'm just looking. You have

some lovely work here."

"Thank you. Do you own any glass pieces?"

"Not art pieces, no. But I've walked by your shop before, and I was in the neighborhood and had a few moments to spare, so I thought I'd stop in and take a look."

She seemed sincere enough, and I'd learned over time that some people don't like to be crowded when they look at art. "Then I'll let you enjoy the pieces at your own speed. Let me know if you have any questions."

"Thank you," she replied politely, moving away as quickly as courtesy permitted. Definitely a nervous lady.

She must have sensed my eyes on her, because after a few more minutes she grabbed a piece off the shelf, almost at random, then approached the register. "I'll take this," she said curtly.

It was a medium-size bowl in one of my favorite techniques — a swirl of multiple colors, with a line of aventurine glass that added a subtle sparkle. "Oh, I'm glad you like that — it's an interesting pattern, don't you think?"

"Yes. Nice." She handed me a credit card, and I processed the sale while Nessa carefully swathed the piece in bubbled plastic.

She put the wrapped object in a box, and the box in a bag, just as I handed the woman her credit card and charge slip. Out of habit, I looked at the name on the credit card: Beverly Harrison. That didn't ring any bells. When her hands were free, I handed her the bag.

"I hope you enjoy it. And please come back again."

The woman left without a further word, and I turned to Nessa. "What was going on with her?"

"She seemed so fidgety. I was surprised when she actually bought something."

Before I could snag my lunch and disappear to my hidey-hole to eat it, Matt and Cam came around the corner and let themselves in.

"Hi, guys," I greeted them. "Everything go all right?"

"As well as could be expected, all things considered," Matt said. "Unfortunately Cam couldn't contribute very much, which didn't make anyone happy."

"I'm sorry, Matt," Cam protested. "How many times do I have to tell you that? I just can't remember."

"And how many times do I have to tell you that I understand? It's just frustrating that you're the best lead we've got at the moment, but there still isn't much to work with. It's not your fault, Cam, and thanks for your help. Em, I'll talk to you later. Oh, hang on — we need to switch cars again."

We exchanged keys, and Matt left. I gave Cam a nudge. "Cam, you have any plans?"

He looked at his watch. "I suppose I should go talk to the people at SDE and explain what's been going on — at least, as much as I know. Then I've got to start looking for a place to live."

"Where's SDE based?"

"They've got a building on the south side of town. Maybe I'll just drive around that end of town and see what the neighborhoods look like."

"Small problem — your car's still at the police lot, isn't it? But you can take mine." I crossed the room and gave him yet another hug. "Be careful, will you? The last time you went anywhere, you disappeared for a week," I said into his chest. "You will be back for dinner, right?"

"Unless I get kidnapped again," he said, struggling to maintain a straight face.

I swatted him. "Don't even joke about that." I handed him my car keys. "Now, drive safely, and carry a clean hanky."

"Thanks, Em. See you later."

"I should hope so."

CHAPTER 27

The Romans wore rings set with stones on every finger and changed them with the seasons.

After yet another slow day, we closed up the shop at six. Nessa and Allison followed me upstairs, and while they gushed over the dogs, I ordered several assorted pizzas.

Cam was next to arrive.

"Did you sort everything out at work?" I asked. "Were they worried when you didn't show up?"

"Not really. It's a pretty informal group."

"Well, they're keeping you humble if they didn't even miss you. I've ordered pizza. Can you run out and get some beer and whatever anyone else wants to drink?"

"No problem. Allison, you want to come?"

"I do," she replied promptly, holding out her hand. Cam held it all the way to the door and probably would have kept on holding it except that it was a little difficult to go down the stairs that way.

They passed Frank on his way in. He looked pleased with himself and the world, but then, he usually did. He brightened noticeably when he saw Nessa. "Nessa, my dear, I wondered where you'd hidden yourself."

"I haven't gone far, Frank," she replied placidly.

"Frank, you want to stick around for dinner?" I asked. "Because I'm hoping we can pool the bits and pieces of information we have and see where we are."

"Delighted, and I may have a few nuggets of my own to share."

Matt appeared next, unannounced but somehow not unexpected. "Hi," I greeted him. "Pull up a chair. Dinner's on its way. Oh, before I offer you a beer, I should ask, is this business?"

"Sort of. Let me get business out of the way, and then I'll think about that beer. Is Cam here?"

"He was — he will be. I sent him out to get the aforesaid beer. Allison went along."

"How's he doing?" Matt asked.

"Seems fine to me. I think Allison agrees."

"Good. I've got some stuff I want him to look at."

Cam, Allison, and the pizza all arrived together, and we busied ourselves for a few minutes with distributing and ingesting food and drink. Once everyone had managed to consume a slice or two, I judged we were ready to get down to business.

"Okay, everybody," I began. "Looking at the brainpower around this table, we should be able to work out who drugged Cam and who killed Alex in no time, right? Matt, why don't you start? You said you wanted Cam to look at something?"

Matt carefully wiped the pizza grease off his hands with a paper napkin while I moved used plates and glasses out of the way. He picked up a large manila envelope he had brought with him and pulled out a stack of papers. "We had no problem with Alex's disk — it wasn't protected. And we didn't find much interesting stuff on it. Mostly property records, deeds, expense reports, that kind of thing. It's probably as innocent as it looks — Alex thought Denis should have a full copy of all the business information, all on one disk, but I don't think it was because he expected to die. So no great Sherlock Holmes surprise."

"What is it you want from me?" Cam asked. "I don't know much about the business side of what Alex and Denis were doing."

"It's not that. There are some pictures of rock formations that were included, and I thought I'd run them by you to see if they look like what you saw on the property where the RV was parked. I'd like to know if the RV was parked at the site the stones came from, or if they're from somewhere else. These were the only landscape shots on the disk, so Alex must have thought they were important. Frank, you can take a look too — you've been out there."

"Happy to help, Matt," Frank replied.

Cam held out a hand for the photos, and Matt passed them to him. "You know I'm not a geologist," he said absently as he studied each image.

"Did you walk the property?" Matt asked.

"Yes, a few times, mostly early in the morning. That RV could get a little claustrophobic, not to mention hot, even at this time of year, and I needed air now and then. It was kind of fun, trying to match up what I was seeing to the data I had. Not easy. Hang on . . ." Cam was staring at one of the photos. "Who's this?"

Matt peered at the picture. "I don't know. Do you recognize him?"

I leaned closer and saw a man standing off to one side in the picture. It looked as though he didn't realize he was being photographed, and only part of his face was visible.

Cam said hesitantly, "I think he's the one who picked me up at the RV."

"Do you recognize the rocks there?"

"I think so. It's a distinctive formation about a mile west of the RV, where I thought there's a good chance there are gems. See that sort of double hump?" He pointed to a rock formation.

"Frank, will you take a look?" Matt pushed the picture across the table toward him.

"Sure, mate." Frank reached for the picture and spun it around to look. "You've got a good eye, Cam. That formation looks right to me."

"Wait a minute," I interrupted, dragging the photo back to my side of the table. "Frank, isn't that the guy from the casino? And the Gem Show?"

Frank took the photo back. "Good on you too, Em — I think you're right."

Matt swiveled between us. "Fill me in. You know this guy?"

"No," I said, "but we've seen him twice now — once at the Gem Show, at a booth talking with the guys who run the reservation peridot business, and again at the casino near the reservation. I think he's a bartender at the casino."

"You wouldn't have a name, would you?" Matt asked us. He directed the same question to Cam, who shook his head ruefully.

"We didn't actually talk to him either time," I responded, "but you can find him easily enough, right?"

"Sure," Matt said absently. Then he straightened up. "But let's go with what we know, for the moment. I think we can assume that Alex knew the guy. This is part of a series of pictures, and they look like they were taken openly, carefully framed and all that, like he was documenting the rock formations. So as a working assumption, he could be Alex's behind-the-scenes buyer. I'll have to run the photo by Denis and see if he recognizes him."

"Well, that's progress," I said. "We've confirmed that there's somebody else involved, and we've got most of a face for Cam's kidnapper, and we know you can identify him and probably track him down." When Matt didn't volunteer any additional information, I addressed the rest of the group. "Anybody else have any ideas?"

Frank looked as though he had swallowed a particularly tasty canary. "I might." He paused until all eyes at the table turned to him. "A couple of things. First, I did some nosing around, talking to gem people I know, asking what the word on the street was and whether anybody was talking about something new coming along. Started with Miranda and Stewart, and they asked a friend, and so on. They came up with a name this morning, and then I had to find the guy. He admitted that he had a line on something new, but he thought it might not pan out 'cause he hadn't heard from the seller. He's headed back to Madagascar as soon as the show ends."

"You have his name, and where we can find him?" Matt asked.

"I do. He's got no problem with talking to you, as long as he makes his plane. He saw a business opportunity, but he's got a lot of irons in the fire and he won't be too upset if this particular deal falls through. And you may not want to hear it, but he's got himself a pretty good alibi. He was out taking a look at the desert and tangled with a tarantula — he was sick as a dog for a couple of days and has the medical bills to prove it."

"Where'd he find a tarantula at this time of year?" Even I knew they weren't active in February.

"Asked a friend to show him one. Anyway, it seems kind of unlikely that this bloke was running around threatening anybody, much less killing someone."

Damn — there went one of our favorite scenarios, the unknown buyer of the peridot as bad guy. "You said you had found out more than one thing, Frank?"

"Little thing, maybe. I've told you before about how peridot is mined, where you find it, and all that. But there's more. Only members of that particular Apache tribe, and a few individual families that are descendants, are allowed to mine on the reservation." Frank reached into his pocket and pulled out a folded piece of paper. "I got you a list of those people."

"Let me see if I understand this," I said. "The San Carlos Apaches have a pretty tight hold on the flow of peridot, right? That guy we talked to at the Gem Show said as much, although he put a positive spin on it. Are you thinking that one of the people or families on the list thought that maybe Alex and Denis could be a threat if they came up with a significant source of gems off reservation?"

"It's possible," Frank replied.

"Well, it is far-fetched, but it could be a motive, right, Matt? And oh . . ."

Matt sighed. "What, Em?"

"The use of mescaline would fit, wouldn't it?"

"Good thought, although I'd really rather not go there. But, yes, right here in our little home town there's the Peyote Way Church of God, which worships peyote, and one of the founders' father came from the San Carlos Reservation. So you could say there's a link, although there are plenty of non-Indians who use peyote, not quite legally." He slumped in his chair. "Oh hell — you know how complicated it would be to get at someone down on the reservation, much less arrest or prosecute him? Where do you want me to start?"

I broke in before he could launch into a lecture on the history of Arizona. "Matt, let's take the simplest case. Suppose someone from the reservation killed Alex to protect the Indian peridot industry and dumped his body in Pima County, and we have reasonable proof. What happens then?"

"Depends on how friendly the San Carlos Apache tribal police and court are feeling. Best case? The Pima County sheriff could arrest him and the case would end up in the federal court system, since murder or manslaughter is a major crime. But if the tribe wanted to protect the guy, they could close ranks and we'd have a heck of a time prying him loose."

We all fell silent, trying to work through

the twists and turns of this new information.

I was startled by the sound of Nessa's voice. Seated next to Frank, she had been scanning the list he had laid on the table. "Em, look at this." She pointed to one name.

I pulled the list toward me and looked. "What? Oh, I see. Oh hell."

"I don't want to ask," Matt groaned.

"Well, if you thought this was complicated before . . . There was a woman in the shop today. Nessa and I both thought she looked kind of nervous. In the end, she bought a bowl and left. She charged it, and I saw the name on the card — Beverly Harrison. Which is also on this list. Good catch, Nessa."

"Describe her," Cam said abruptly.

"Medium height, dark hair, nicely dressed but not fancy," I said. "Kind of twitchy. Why?"

"Could she have been Apache?" Matt asked.

I thought. "Maybe. I wouldn't say no."

"I can probably pull up her driver's license and run it by Cam. You said there was a woman involved, right?"

"Yes, I think so," Cam said slowly. "But I won't promise I'd recognize her, especially not from a DMV photo. If there were some way of meeting her face-to-face, maybe. But why would she come by the shop? That doesn't make sense."

"She did ask if it was Em's shop," Nessa said.

"She seemed pretty jumpy to me. Maybe she was just scoping me out. Or maybe she wanted to see if Cam had made it back all right?"

Matt stood up abruptly. "Let me make a couple of calls." He headed for the far end of the room for privacy, his cell phone at his ear.

"Thank you, Frank," I said quietly. "That helps."

I cleared away what was left of our meal while Cam leafed through the printouts from Alex's disk, with Allison leaning on his shoulder to see. I was startled when Matt came back quickly. "Your customer today, Beverly Harrison? Doesn't live on the reservation, and she works here in Tucson, at the Indian Center."

"Does that mean she's Apache?"

"Not necessarily, but it makes it more likely. I expect she'll be at the center in the morning. I can talk to her then. I think she'll hold that long, since she doesn't know we know who she is or why she was here.

342

Which, I might remind you, could have been completely innocent. You did say that she bought something."

"What about Cam and me? We can identify her, maybe connect her to some of this."

"Remember, she hasn't done anything wrong that we know of. I just want to ask her a few questions. You can come along if you promise to keep your mouths shut, after a yes or no on the ID. Got it?"

"Yes, sir," I said. Cam nodded in agreement.

Matt looked at me sternly. "Em, I mean it. One man is dead, and there's a lot going on here that we don't understand. I just want you to be safe, all right?"

While my independent side had some issues with his attitude, my romantic side was touched by his concern. I knew enough to quit while I was ahead. "Thank you. I'll try to stay out of your way."

Matt looked as though he wanted to say more, but we had an audience. "The Indian Center opens at eight. Why don't I come by and pick up you two about then?"

"Fine," I said.

Matt's departure triggered a general exodus, as Nessa and Allison gathered up their belongings and left — delayed only by Allison's lingering good-bye to Cam.

"I'll give you a ride, Allison," Cam offered, "if Em will let me use her car again."

"You needn't bother, Cam," Allison said. "You must be tired."

"I want to," he said firmly. Allison stopped protesting.

Finally Frank and I were left to ourselves.

"I'm guessing Tucson isn't quite what you expected, eh, Frank?"

Frank grinned. "More fun than I would have thought."

I sighed. "I just hope Matt and his buddies wrap this up so that I can get to work and settle down. Well, I'm going to bed. Uh, Frank? I hope you didn't have to sabotage any of your professional relationships to find out what you did."

"No worries. Gem traders can be a secretive bunch, but I've made my share of friends over the years, and I know who to trust and who trusts me. Nobody's the poorer for what they gave up, and now they'll figure I owe them one when the time comes. It's all good."

"Hang on." I waited for my brain to pop out something that had been niggling at me. "Matt didn't seem very interested in that Madagascar dealer you talked about, right?"

"Not very, no. I gave him the name."

"Do you think we can tell Denis? I mean,

he still has a chance to salvage something from this deal, maybe get some of the money he needs, if not all. I mean, this dealer guy has no reason to hang around after the show. And Denis said he has full rights to whatever the partnership produced, so the money's his, more or less, if the deal goes through. Let me give him a try."

I dialed his home phone but got no answer. I didn't want to just leave the name of the gem dealer, so I left a message for him to call me when he got in. I felt obscurely pleased with myself for having come up with one good deed — even though I didn't particularly like Denis, and I certainly didn't feel like I owed him anything. But if Alex had died for these stones, somebody should reap the benefits.

Frank and I had just finished tidying up and I was contemplating a last walk for the dogs when there was a brisk knock on my door. I looked through the peephole: Denis. Again. Only this time he was with his wife Elizabeth. I turned to Frank and mouthed "Denis" silently, then reluctantly opened the door.

Denis pushed past me quickly, pulling his wife behind him. "Sorry to barge in like this, Em, but I got your message and I thought it might be important."

"So you couldn't have called?" I stood, arms akimbo, blocking his progress.

"No, I was already out — I was picking up Elizabeth at the airport. You two have met, right?"

"Briefly." I nodded at her. "Hi, Elizabeth. I thought you were back east, visiting your parents?"

"I was, until I heard about Alex's death. I can't believe he's gone." Elizabeth's eyes were red — at least Alex had one person who mourned for him. "I had to come back. I assume there'll be a funeral?"

Why was she asking me? I had no idea. "Depends on how long the authorities need the body."

"I can't believe anyone would want to kill Alex!"

I finally relented and backed away to let everyone into my living area. The dogs kept an eye on the newcomers. "Can I get you something to drink? Tea, coffee?"

"Coffee would be fine," Elizabeth responded absently, sitting gingerly while trying to curl her feet under her, away from the dogs.

"It won't be long." I headed for my stove to boil water and was surprised when Denis followed me.

"I'm sorry, Em," he said in a low voice. "I

wasn't sure what you wanted to tell me, and it didn't seem right to call, but I thought it might be important. . . ."

"Denis, calm down. It's no big deal, and I don't see why you had to drag your wife along."

"I don't want to leave her alone until we figure out what's going on. Why did you call?"

"Frank tracked down the guy who wanted to buy your stones."

Denis's face lit up. "Really? That's terrific. Is he still interested?"

"Denis, you'll have to ask Frank, but I don't think he got down to details. But he can give you the name. He's already given it to Matt."

Some of the light went out of Denis's eyes. "Oh. I hope that doesn't put him off, if a cop comes around asking questions — I could really use the money, even part of it."

"That's what I figured. You can still give him a try."

"Thank you, Em. It's kind of you to do this, after I've made such a mess of things."

The water boiled and I busied myself making coffee. When it was ready, I carried mugs back to the main part of the room. Denis and Frank were talking about gems, so I sat down next to Elizabeth.

"So you're not a Tucson native?"

Her lip twitched with a barely concealed sneer. "No, I grew up on Long Island, but I came out here when Denis got the job at the university."

"He said something about you working in insurance?" I felt as if I were following some outdated manual for social etiquette. She wasn't making it easy.

"Yes. It was the best I could find out here." She made it sound as though this was a corner of Outer Mongolia.

"We must have arrived about the same time, but I've come to love it here."

"Lucky you," Elizabeth muttered. Then she must have realized how rude she sounded. "I'm sorry. I appreciate the help you've given Denis, but I wish he'd never gotten into this crazy scheme."

"The gems?"

"Oh, that, and this whole land deal. I think he honestly believed it would make him rich, but Denis isn't much of a businessman. Or a judge of character."

"You mean Alex?"

"I'm sure Alex would have come out of this just fine, but I don't know about Denis. He's just not lucky."

How much did Elizabeth know? I wondered. Had Denis told her that he'd gambled it all on one last harebrained scheme with the peridot? He had said something about wanting to surprise her. Whether or not she knew the facts, she had some intuition that things weren't going well. Poor Denis: I didn't want to be in his shoes when he had to admit to the whole mess.

Somehow Elizabeth had finished her coffee while I was trying to puzzle out what was going on behind the scenes in their marriage. She stood up abruptly. "Denis, we've disturbed these people long enough. We should go home."

Denis followed suit. "All right. Thanks for the information, Em, Frank. I'll look into it in the morning."

"Denis." Elizabeth's voice held a warning note now. "Thank you for the coffee, Em. I hope we won't need to bother you again." She turned on her heel and marched toward the door, Denis trailing behind. I had to scurry to let them out. When I heard them descend the stairs, I turned to Frank.

"What was that all about?"

"No clue, but I don't think I want to be in Denis's shoes. Not a happy woman, that."

"I agree. Well, let me walk Fred and Gloria, and then I plan to crash for the night."

As the dogs and I made our way through the half-lit streets, I had to wonder just why Denis had thought it was so important to come by this late. Or had it been Elizabeth's idea? Was he watching out for her, or was she keeping an eye on him? I had no idea.

CHAPTER 28

Due to its relative softness, peridot is difficult to polish to high brilliancy.

Cam and I were up and well stoked with caffeine by the time Matt knocked on the door just before eight. When we were settled in Matt's car, I said, "Denis came by last night — with his wife."

Matt nodded. "I know. He already called me on my cell this morning to ask if it was okay to talk to the gem dealer."

"What did you tell him?"

"I know of nothing illegal about the gem transaction. I mentioned he might need to take a look at his business agreement with Alex, but that's not my problem."

"So maybe Denis will sell his stones after all. Have you talked with the wife yet?"

"She's coming in later this morning."

"Ah," I responded intelligently.

As we approached Beverly's office building, Matt said, "Remember — you two keep your mouths shut and let me do the talking. This is still an official murder investigation."

"Yes, sir. Understood, sir."

"Em . . ." Matt's tone was exasperated.

"I'm sorry, I'll be good. I'm just excited to see all the pieces come together. This Beverly person knows something. Why else would she have turned up at the shop?"

"Because she wanted to buy something maybe?" Matt said wryly.

Cam sat glumly in the back seat and said nothing, staring out the window. I guessed he wasn't as excited as I was. But then, he was the one who had been kidnapped and drugged, so I supposed he had good reason to take this more seriously than I did.

The Tucson Indian Center was housed in a relatively new building that dominated the block. It was full of crisp angles, with rows of windows facing the street; an Indian Village Trading Post occupied the corner diagonally across from it, and I wondered irreverently if it was connected somehow. Matt found a convenient parking space and led the way, with Cam and me trailing like ducklings. He stopped at the desk and said, "We'd like to see Mrs. Beverly Harrison, please."

The very young receptionist looked

startled by the appearance of three people at once, so early in the morning, and even without a uniform and badge Matt exuded authority. "Is Ms. Harrison expecting you?"

"No. Will you call her, please?"

"Uh, what name should I tell her?"

"Police Chief Matthew Lundgren."

Matt's announcement flustered the poor young woman. She had to hit the phone extension buttons three times before she finally connected. "Beverly? There's a policeman here to see you." She listened for a moment before setting the receiver down. "She'll be right out."

Time seemed to stretch while we waited, although it couldn't have been more than thirty seconds before Beverly Harrison pushed through the double doors that led to the back of the building. I watched the woman's face as she approached and saw who was waiting: polite curiosity followed by a flicker of something else when she saw Cam and me, but she maintained her composure. She stopped five feet away from us and said, "Can I help you?"

Cam looked at Matt and shrugged helplessly. Matt looked at me: I nodded. Cam and I exchanged glances, and he looked apologetic. Then all eyes returned to Beverly, who turned to the receptionist and asked, "Is the conference room free?"

The receptionist scrabbled through piles of paper on her desk until she came up with a calendar and riffled through it to find the right month. "Yes, until noon." She looked up at Beverly, her eyes begging for an explanation.

She didn't get one. Beverly said to us, "Will you follow me, please? We can talk in the conference room." She turned on her heel and walked away, and we followed her to a small, windowless room dominated by a large, battered oval table surrounded by folding chairs. She turned to face us. "Can I get you anything? Coffee?" Was she stalling, maybe to get her story straight, or was she just being polite?

Matt spoke for us. "Nothing for us, Ms. Harrison. I have some questions to ask you. Please, sit down."

We arrayed ourselves around the table. Matt and Beverly sat facing each other across the table, with Cam and I flanking Matt. I almost pitied her: it felt as if we were ganging up on her, three to one.

"What do you want to know?" she said.

Matt pulled out a small notebook. "Ms. Harrison, do you confirm that you are Beverly Ann Harrison and you live at 555 La Cholla in Tucson?"

"Yes."

"Are you married?"

Her chin came up. "I was, but I'm divorced now. My ex-husband's name is William Montoya. I took my own name back."

"And where is he employed?"

"He works part-time at the Apache Gold Casino as a bartender."

"Are you a member of the San Carlos Apache Nation?"

"Yes, I am," she said with no expression.

"And your ex-husband?"

"Yes."

"Is your family one of those granted the right to mine peridot on the San Carlos Reservation?"

She almost smiled, as though she was enjoying watching Matt stalking the reason he was really here. "Yes. My brothers work a mining claim there and own the organization that markets the peridot for the reservation."

"Do you recognize the man to my right?"

She studied Cam gravely, again with little expression on her face. She hesitated before answering, "No, I don't think so."

"Cam, do you recognize this woman?"

Cam hesitated too, with a pained expression. "I can't say for sure." Was it my imagination, or did Beverly look relieved?

Matt pulled a copy of the photo we had all seen out of an envelope, and pushed it carefully across the table to Beverly. "Do you know the man in this photo?"

She glanced at it briefly. "Yes. That's my former husband." Then she looked directly at Matt. "Chief Lundgren, I know who you are. Can you tell me what this is about?"

"I'm investigating the murder of Alex Gutierrez and the kidnapping of Cameron Dowell. I have reason to believe that these two events are related. I also believe your ex-husband may have been involved in one or both events."

"What does that have to do with me? We're divorced. We don't live together. I have little knowledge of his activities."

She didn't know he'd been hanging out with her brothers? I interrupted, ignoring Matt's glare. "You came by the shop yesterday. Why?"

She turned her level gaze to me. "I had heard about your work, and I happened to be in the neighborhood." She didn't add anything else. Smart woman, I thought — it would be hard to disprove that.

Matt reasserted his authority by first clearing his throat — which I assumed meant he wanted me to shut up — and then asking, "Are you involved in your brothers' gem business?"

"Not directly. I see them from time to time, and we talk about it. But I do not live on the reservation, and I have a position here, as you can see. What is it you wish to know?"

Matt sat back in his chair and studied the woman, as if weighing his options. I knew enough to keep my mouth shut. Finally he said, "Ms. Harrison, we think that Mr. Gutierrez's death was related to a recent gem find he had made, that he asked Mr. Dowell to consult on. Do you know Denis Ryerson?"

She shook her head. "That name is not familiar to me."

"Ryerson was Gutierrez's partner in this venture. Based on that photograph, we think that your ex-husband knew Gutierrez and quite possibly knew about the gems. We're not sure where these gems were found, and we wonder if the reservation might be the source — illegally."

"Chief Lundgren, as I'm sure you know, members of the reservation sell stones all the time. I can't swear that residents would know if there were strangers at work there, but I can't imagine that they would remain undetected for long. And I am not involved in that trade, as I have told you."

"Tell us about your ex-husband."

Beverly had relaxed a bit, but I thought I saw her stiffen again. "I assume you want something more than his employment history and his taste in beer. I'll be blunt: Will has been known to ignore the law, if it suits him. That's one of the reasons we're no longer married. On occasion he has tried to involve my brothers in his dubious schemes, although they were usually smart enough to turn him down. It would not surprise me to learn that he was working on some kind of deal involving stones and that he had asked my brothers to participate. I'm sure they'd be willing to talk to you — they have no great love for Will." Beverly hesitated again before going on. "My ex-husband is a weak and foolish man, but I do not believe that he is a killer. Even if he were, it would be in the heat of the moment, and it would be personal — not for the sake of money."

I wondered whether any woman would admit to herself or anyone else that a man she had presumably once loved was capable of murder.

Matt continued. "Do you know if your ex-husband was acquainted with Alex Gutierrez?"

"I can't say. Will and I have been divorced for some time, and I really don't know what he's been doing since then, apart from what little my brothers tell me." She folded her hands calmly and fell silent. Stalemate. Beverly sounded credible, and it would be hard to prove any part of her story was a lie.

Matt's cell phone rang. He glanced at it, then stood up and said, "Excuse me," before leaving the room.

I couldn't keep still. "How did you and Will end up together in the first place? You seem like an intelligent, educated woman."

I wasn't sure if she would answer me. After all, she had no reason to share her personal life with me. In the end she smiled bleakly at me. "Intelligence had little to do with it. What can I say? I was young and stupid, and Will was pretty nice to look at, twenty years ago. Maybe I thought I could change him, persuade him that there was something more than making a quick buck now and then. I was wrong. So I got a good job and hung on to it, and saved as much of my paycheck as I could, and made sure he couldn't touch it. Will works when he feels like it. That job at the casino — he keeps it because it makes him feel like a big man."

"What made you split up, in the end?"

"I got tired of making excuses for him, to

myself, to others. He never did change, but I did."

Matt came in then, his expression grim. "Ms. Harrison, can you tell me where I can reach your brothers?"

"Of course."

"We have an address for your ex-husband." Matt rattled off a street address I had never heard of. "Can you tell me if that's current?"

Again, a tiny hesitation. "That's where he lives, most of the time. It's a place his family's had for years, outside the reservation but not far from it. It's pretty beat up, and I never wanted to live there. I would agree that it's the best place to start looking for him. Although he has a number of friends on the reservation."

She left unsaid the obvious implication: if he was holed up on the reservation, Matt couldn't touch him.

"Ms. Harrison, has Will been in trouble before? Has he ever been caught, as you say, 'ignoring the law'?"

She cocked her head at him. "Surely you've checked your criminal records?"

"Of course, but I also recognize that some issues are handled within the reservation, and we may not hear of them. Is he on good terms with the tribal elders?"

Beverly shrugged. "He's had his problems there but nothing serious. I think they'd take his side over yours."

Matt stood up abruptly. "Thank you for your cooperation, Ms. Harrison. If you'd give me those numbers and addresses for your brothers, I think we're done here for now."

"Certainly." Beverly wrote something on a pad, tore off the top sheet, and handed it to Matt. "I'm sure they will be glad to help. The peridot industry is important to the reservation, and they would not want to see any trouble there. May I see you out?"

She said nothing beyond the barest of formalities as she escorted us out of the building. Cam kept his eyes on her for most of the walk, until she had disappeared inside. "Damn. I can't say she's the one, but I can't say she isn't either. My memory's just too fuzzy."

"Matt, did our exit have something to do with that phone call?"

Matt glanced at me. "Denis is MIA. Apparently, when he called me this morning, he wasn't calling from home. His wife called the station a little while ago to report him missing. She said he dropped her off at home last night — after leaving your place, I assume — and then went somewhere and never came back. She has no idea where he is."

"Do you think he's hiding? And why now?"

"I don't know, and I'm not going to guess. But one thing I do know: I need to talk to Will Montoya — assuming we can find him."

"Then let's go."

"Em, I didn't mean you and Cam. Cam's already identified Montoya from the photo, and taking him along would only complicate things. Montoya may be armed, and I don't want Cam in harm's way. This is police business. I'll drop you back at your place."

I sneaked a glance at Cam. "You go ahead — we'll get home on our own."

Matt looked torn. He wanted to get on with tracking down Will Montoya and the Harrison brothers, but I'm not sure he trusted me. "Em, don't mess with this."

"Matt, I am happy to leave the police work to you. And I'm sure Cam is too." I looked at Cam — I knew he would take my side. He nodded.

Finally Matt said, "All right. Go home, go about your business. I'll call you when I can, if there's any news."

"Thank you. And take care."

CHAPTER 29

Peridot is the softest of all the precious stones.

Cam and I watched as Matt pulled away. Then he turned to me. "All right, Em, what are you doing?"

"I want to talk to Beverly again."

"Why? She said she doesn't know what her husband has been doing lately."

"Cam, are you sure she wasn't the woman who brought you home the other night?"

"Em," he said, his tone exasperated, "I told you I wasn't sure about any of it. She could have been, but she's not about to admit it."

"Not to Matt and the combined police forces of three counties. But maybe she'll talk to us."

"Em, Matt said to stay out of this. He can handle it."

"Cam, I trust him to handle the search

for Will, and now for Denis. I trust him to run background checks and do forensic stuff and make arrests. But I don't think he's the right guy to talk to a woman who's trying to protect someone."

"Who? Montoya? Her brothers? Herself?"

"Maybe all three. Let's find out." I turned back to the building and pushed open the door. The poor receptionist flinched at the sight of us. "Excuse me, there's something I forgot to ask Ms. Harrison. I'll just pop into her office for a moment, okay?"

I started moving, with Cam trailing along, as the receptionist was saying weakly, "End of the hall, on the right."

It wasn't hard to find, especially since Beverly was standing in the doorway, her arms crossed, her eyes cold. "What do you want?" she demanded.

"Can we take this inside? Look, this isn't official police business — but I need to talk to you."

She wavered for a moment, looking briefly at Cam, then gestured toward the office, closing the door behind us after we'd all entered. We found chairs and sat.

"All right, why are you here?"

"I wanted to thank you," I said quietly.

"For what?"

"For getting Cam out of whatever mess

Will got him into. For bringing him home safe to me. You see, I do understand about brothers and loyalty. Look, I don't want to get you into any trouble, but I need to know what happened."

Beverly was silent for a long time, and I was beginning to wonder if she'd just throw us out. Finally she sighed. "Before I begin, I have to apologize to you, Mr. Dowell. You were a victim of William's scheme, and I did what I could to protect you."

Cam studied her face. "So you *were* the one who brought me back to Em's that night, right?"

"I was. You didn't remember? I persuaded Will that you were so addled that no one would believe anything you said, and then I got you out before he could change his mind."

"You had that right. And thank you," Cam said.

"And you came by the next day to make sure he was all right?" I asked.

She nodded. "I suppose I wanted to be sure that your brother had arrived safely. It was foolish of me, because I couldn't exactly come right out and ask you about him. But I was concerned that he could have wandered off after I left him there and been hit by a truck or picked up by the police as a drunk, in his state. I'm afraid I'm not very good at planning this kind of thing, but I haven't had much practice. In any event, I assumed that since you were there and did not appear distressed, that all was well."

"Yes, thanks to you. So how did you get caught up in this mess, whatever it is?"

"I don't generally see much of my ex-husband, but my brothers had told me something that troubled me, about Will trying to broker a deal for some stones, and I went to his house to speak to him about it. They said they had turned him down, but I didn't want my brothers involved in his scheme, whatever it was, and I wanted Will to stop bothering them. When I went to his home, I discovered Mr. Dowell there. Will made some pathetic excuse that he was a tourist who wanted to experiment with mescaline, and Will was babysitting him through his trip, but I didn't believe him. But since Mr. Dowell didn't appear to be at any immediate risk, I took Will aside and confronted him with what my brothers had said. When he tried to explain, I told him he was a fool and that he should back out now before he got into any more trouble, much less drag my brothers into it, but then he said it was more complicated than that."

"Did he tell you that there was a murder

involved?" I asked.

Beverly looked down at her hands. "Eventually. He admitted that he had helped to dispose of a body. He claimed that the death was an accident and that he hadn't been responsible for the death. All he had done was leave the body in the desert."

"Did you know who the dead man was?"

"Will told me."

"Did he tell you who killed the man?"

"He didn't say. I didn't press him — it seemed safer not to know."

"And you didn't ask?" I said, incredulous. I was going to have to pull the story out of her bit by bit.

"Not then. I didn't want to be involved, and I wanted only to get Mr. Dowell out of there before Will made things worse. But he wanted to explain what had happened, and I let him — I thought it would calm him down."

"And?" I prompted.

"Will gave me the story about the gem transaction. He claims he met Mr. Gutierrez at the bar at the casino on a slow night, and they got to talking. Mr. Gutierrez returned a few times to gamble and drink, and eventually he started complaining that he was in a financial fix. You know the old story about people spilling their secrets to bartenders? It's true more often than you would think. Mr. Gutierrez told him all about his real estate investments and how they'd gone sour on him, and now he was in a real bind for money. And for once Will paid attention. He started asking questions, and no doubt gave Mr. Gutierrez a few free drinks, and eventually Mr. Gutierrez told him about this deposit of peridot that he'd found, that he hoped would be the solution to his problems. And of course, Will saw an opportunity, so Will offered Mr. Gutierrez a deal: Will would give him enough money to cover his most pressing debts *and* he would help Mr. Gutierrez sell the stones, for a share of the proceeds. Perhaps Mr. Gutierrez was overly optimistic about Will's connections, or maybe he was just desperate, but apparently he agreed."

"Did Will have the money?"

Beverly shrugged. "He has been working steadily, which hasn't always been the case, but that was when he came to my brothers, to ask them to chip in. They claim they didn't put up any money — they know Will and his schemes too well."

"We know that the dead man did manage to pay off some of his debts, so I assume that money came from your ex-husband. What did Will hope for?"

"Money, in time. But he also thought he would be doing my brothers a favor, because they could get the stones for very little since Mr. Gutierrez was so desperate, and get them off the market. And it would eliminate Mr. Gutierrez as a potential competitor, help maintain reservation control over the stones."

"But your brothers didn't go along?"

"No. As I said, they don't trust him. But then my brothers told me that this deal of Will's had gone wrong somehow — although they thought he had just screwed up, as he so often has in the past."

Since apparently I knew more than she did about what had gone on, I surmised that this was the point where Alex had gotten the bright idea that he could improve the stones and make more money that way, and gone off to cut his own deal. I wondered if Beverly's brothers had in fact forked over any money, and how upset they would have been if the deal evaporated. Would it have been worth it to them to kill Alex?

"Did you get any details?"

"My brothers told me that according to Will the seller had changed his mind. I think that was all they knew."

"Did you talk to Will about this?"

"I really didn't care about my ex-husband's business dealings — I just didn't want him involving my family. But then he told me that it was Mr. Gutierrez — Alex — who was dead, whose body he had gotten rid of."

"More or less — Alex was found within a day or two."

Beverly shrugged. "He didn't do a very good job, apparently, but that is typical of Will. He thought just dumping him in the desert would be enough — either he would never be found, or if he was, the authorities would believe he was just another illegal and wouldn't try very hard to identify him. Many people get lost in the desert, and too many are never identified."

I sorted through what she had told me. "Okay, so you're saying it went like this: Alex and Will cooked up a deal. Will went to your brothers for financing, but they turned him down. So Will was possibly out of pocket to Alex, and then Alex cut him out and found another buyer. Then Will claimed somebody killed Alex and asked him to take care of the body. Do you believe that? Are you sure it wasn't Will who killed Alex?"

Beverly looked me directly in the eye. "My ex-husband may be many things, not all of them good, but he is not a killer. He is weak and lazy and he likes to take shortcuts, but he would not murder anyone. Even at the casino, he relies on his size to intimidate people. He seldom uses violence. So, yes, I believe him."

Was that wishful thinking on her part? After all, she had been married to him. And then I realized that whoever had asked Will to take care of Alex's body had known about the gem deal, had known that Alex had a connection to Will. Which narrowed the field to a very few people: Beverly's brothers, possibly the Madagascar dealer, and Denis. Beverly's brothers might have had motive to get rid of Alex, for financial or tribal reasons. But why would Will not have told Beverly? To protect her feelings? It sounded as though there was little love lost between the brothers and Will. From everything Frank had said, the Madagascar dealer was an unlikely villain, and had little motive — the deal just wasn't that important to him. Which left Denis.

But why would Denis have killed Alex? They were friends and partners. He needed Alex's geology expertise to make this project work. He needed the money from the deal that Alex had set up. Alex had all the paperwork. Had Alex been cheating Denis? Did Denis benefit from Alex's death? He'd claimed that the partnership was deep in the red on the real estate, and Alex's death compounded that. So, why would he have killed him? It didn't add up.

"Em, you still with us?" Cam asked. I must have zoned out while I tried to think.

"Oh, sorry. I was trying to sort out the pieces. Beverly, you went to your ex-husband's place to talk about what your brothers had told you, and found Cam there. Obviously Will knew Cam was at Alex's RV. Why didn't he just get rid of Cam too? Or wait until he left?"

"He didn't say. He knew about the location from Alex. The killer must have told him that Cam was there and asked him to dispose of him. I assume Will was supposed to kill him and get rid of the body, but Will couldn't do it. So Will went out and collected Cam and then slipped him some peyote. I guess he thought he could find out how much Cam knew, how much of a threat he might be. Perhaps he intended to kill him, somewhere away from the RV, but lost his nerve." She stopped and swallowed, then went on. "Em, Will is not a good thinker or planner. He saw what he thought was a financial opportunity with Alex, and he jumped on it. And that might have worked out just fine. It was only when things went wrong that I happened to hear of it from my brothers. So I went to confront him and discovered he had more or less kidnapped Cam."

"Why didn't you go to the police?"

She looked away. "I was married to him once, and my brothers were involved. I may have concealed evidence, but Alex was already dead, and I couldn't change that. I believed Will's story. And Will had already taken Cam, but he didn't know what to do with him. He was keeping him high on peyote until he could figure out a plan. Perhaps if it had been anyone other than my idiot ex-husband, I would have let the authorities handle him. But he is Apache, and his misdeeds reflect upon us all. And, selfishly, I thought perhaps my brothers would be implicated, although they had nothing to do with the murder, as far as I know. So I chose to make sure that Cam was not harmed, and then I returned him to you — I found your name and address among his things, and he babbled something about a sister, so I made the right connection. And that is all I know. Em, I couldn't let your brother come to harm. He was an innocent, an outsider. And, to be honest, I didn't want to see Will commit a deliberate murder. Alex's death could well have been an accident, but it would have been something else if Will had killed your brother. I think he was relieved when I talked him out of it."

We all fell silent. Who was Will working with, or for? It seemed to me there were multiple crimes in there somewhere, but I had no idea who was guilty of what. The kidnapping was pretty straightforward. Beverly had concealed information. And somebody had killed Alex. I leaned toward believing Beverly when she said Will couldn't have done it, but I could be wrong.

"Do you think Will is still at his house?" I asked, breaking the silence. "You have to know that the police are on their way there now."

"Probably. He has no reason to think anyone is looking for him. He lives in a pretty isolated area, so no one was likely to have noticed Cam there. And had Cam identified him, someone would have been there already, so by now he would think he was in the clear."

As in fact he had been, until we'd talked to Beverly.

Denis. Matt had said he was missing — but where would he go? And why? He needed to close his gem deal if he hoped to realize any money to pay off his debts, so why would he leave town now while the dealer was still around? The timing didn't make sense.

Either Denis was the victim of Alex's killer, or he was hiding from him. If Will wasn't the killer, and the killer was still out there, what did he gain by eliminating Denis? Denis claimed not to know anything, so how could he identify the killer — unless he was lying? Something was not making sense here.

Denis's wife Elizabeth — she was still at home. I stood up abruptly. "Cam, we have to go."

He looked startled. "What?"

"I'll explain in a minute. Beverly, thank you for being honest with us."

"Will there be trouble, about what I said?"

"I hope not. I'll do my best to prevent it. I hope you're right about Will, that he's no killer. And thank you again for looking out for Cam — I will always be grateful for that."

"It was the right thing to do." Beverly stood up as if to walk us to the door, but then stopped. "Oh, wait a moment." She reached into a lower drawer of her desk and pulled out a small dusty backpack. "Cam, I almost forgot to give you this."

Cam's eyes lit up. "My laptop?"

"Yes. I didn't want to leave it with you before, in case you wandered off and forgot it, or someone took it from you. Will brought back whatever he found at the RV. I've got your clothes and the rest in the trunk of my car, but I didn't want to leave this there. I can drop off the rest of your things later, if you don't wish to take them now."

"Thank you! This means a lot to me."

"I thought it might," she said with a small smile.

Beverly led us out, past the bewildered receptionist, and once again Cam and I found ourselves standing on the sidewalk.

"Okay, Em, what's going on?" Cam demanded.

"Matt told me that Denis has gone missing again. I don't think he'd leave town without closing this deal, if he's so desperate for money. So there must be a good reason — either somebody grabbed him, or there's something we don't know. I want to talk to his wife."

"Em, wouldn't Matt or someone have done that already?"

"Of course. But maybe whoever talked with her wasn't asking the right questions. He blew it with Beverly." Well, that might be overstating it, but he hadn't gotten everything from her.

He let out a snort. "So you're going to wangle Elizabeth Ryerson's secrets from her with sisterly sympathy?"

I swatted his arm. Did I really seem that socially inept? "Cam, don't look so skeptical. I can be sympathetic if I try."

"I'm going with you."

"I don't think that's a good idea, if I'm going to play the sympathy card."

"Em, there's a killer out there somewhere."

"Cam, I know that. I just think Elizabeth might be more forthcoming if you weren't around."

"I guess," he said glumly. I suspected Cam secretly enjoyed the role of sensitive guy.

"Trust me on this. Let's go."

CHAPTER 30

Wearing peridot is supposed to bring success, peace, and good luck.

"Uh, Em? How're we getting home?"

Oh, right. I had forgotten that Matt had brought us here; my car was at home, Cam's still impounded. "We'll go get my car. I could use the exercise, and maybe the fresh air will clear my head." We set off at a fast clip and covered the half mile to the shop in ten minutes.

When we got there, I realized I needed to touch base with Nessa and Allison. "Cam, can you take the dogs out for a quick walk? I'll just tell Nessa where I'm going."

When I walked into the shop, both Nessa and Allison looked up eagerly. "What's going on?" Nessa said.

"You were right about Beverly — turns out the guy in the picture is her brother. Matt and his gang are headed out to his place. Beverly says that he's the one who kidnapped Cam from the RV. But don't tell Matt that part."

"Is he the killer?" breathed Allison.

"I can't say for sure, but his sister doesn't think so. Oh, and Denis has gone missing, or so Matt says. This just keeps getting more and more confusing. We figure out one piece, and something else pops up. I'm going over to Denis's house to talk with his wife."

"Does Matt know?" Nessa asked.

"Uh, not exactly. But we figure he's already talked to her, so I'm not trampling on his turf or anything. How's business been?"

Nessa and Allison looked around the shop, looked at each other, then burst into laughter. "I don't know if we can handle the crowds," Allison said.

"Things should be back to normal by next week, once the gem people leave. Not Frank, Nessa! He's welcome to stay as long as he wants."

Cam came in, the two dogs dancing around his feet and tangling their leashes, followed by Frank. Cam was carrying a newspaper. "Cam, we use plastic bags for dog poop here," I said.

"Em, look at this." He thrust the paper in front of me, folded to show the front-page article about Alex's death. "That's not Alex."

"What?" Three of us spoke in unison. Frank simply grinned, apparently enjoying the new turn of events.

"Of course it is," I said. "What are you talking about?"

"If that's Alex Gutierrez, he's not the man who took me out to the RV."

We all stared at him in stunned silence for several seconds. I was beginning to get a very bad feeling about this. At last, I said, "Describe the man."

"Mid height, maybe two, three inches shorter than me. Sandy hair, kind of thinning on top. Glasses. Twitchy."

Nessa, Allison, and I exchanged glances. "That sounds an awful lot like Denis," I said. They nodded in agreement. "Where did you rendezvous with him?"

"At Alex Gutierrez's house. Alex sent me directions by e-mail, when we firmed up the details. I told him I'd be there by noon. I arrived a little early, and the guy there said he was Alex — or at least, he didn't say he *wasn't* Alex when I introduced myself."

"Did you go into the house?"

"No. He seemed kind of in a hurry, and I wasn't in any mood to make polite chitchat, so we just headed out for the RV. He dropped me off, said he'd be back in a week. He'd warned me that phone reception was lousy out there, so we just set a time. And he left."

"And he had no trouble finding the place?"

"No. Why would he?" Cam looked puzzled.

"Because if it was Denis, Denis claimed he didn't know where the RV was. Hang on, I've got to think this through."

"Are you going to call Matt?"

"And tell him what? That we think Denis bamboozled Cam? And . . ." I stopped for a moment as ideas started bouncing through my head. "Denis probably engineered the kidnapping, because he knew Cam was out there."

"And he must know Will — something else he lied about," Cam added.

"And now he's disappeared. Things aren't looking good for Denis, are they? But I still don't get it — why would he want to kill Alex? Frank, can you find out if that Madagascar dealer is still around, and can you ask if they closed the deal for the stones?"

"Right." Frank fished his cell phone out of his pocket and retreated to a corner to make a call.

I turned back to the rest. "He said he had

no money, so how could he run unless he sold the stones?"

Frank returned quickly. "He's still at the show, and he hasn't seen Denis."

I thought a moment. "Okay, here's what we'll do. Matt is looking for Will, so that's covered. Frank, can you go over to the show and keep an eye on the dealer, see if Denis shows up?"

"No worries. What're you going to do?"

"I'm going to talk to Denis's wife. Maybe she knows something that she didn't want to share with the police."

"Woman's touch, eh?" Frank said. "Don't they have ladies on your police force, for the softer stuff?"

"Of course they do, but they don't always know what questions to ask. Cam, I can drop you at the police station so you can reclaim your car."

"Em, be careful, please," Allison said.

"Trust me, I will be. I should be back in an hour or two, anyway."

CHAPTER 31

An old process for working peridot to give it shine used vitriol, a caustic metal sulfate.

I dropped Cam off at the police impound lot and made my way toward Denis's home on the fringes of town. As I drove, I tried again to identify a motive for Denis to kill Alex. Okay, Denis had been under a lot of pressure. He'd seen his real estate investments tank, and he'd let Alex talk him into some harebrained scheme to pretty up peridot in order to recoup at least some of his losses. Did he blame Alex for the poor investments? But why kill him? The gem treatment seemed to be working, and there was a buyer lined up for the enhanced stones — why upset the applecart now?

I pulled into the driveway at the house, behind a car I hoped was Elizabeth's. I parked and approached the door to ring the doorbell. Elizabeth answered after about two minutes, and when she opened the door she looked even worse than she had the last time I had seen her. "What do you want?" Not the warmest of welcomes.

"I wanted to talk to you about Denis."

"The police have already been here. I told them I don't know where he is."

"Then how do you know he's missing?"

"He's not here. He's not at his office. Oh hell, come on in — it's stupid to stand here on the front step."

I followed her into the house. The stresses of the last few days had apparently affected her housekeeping standards, for the house was nowhere near as neat as the last time I had seen it. She must really be upset.

"You want something?" she said ungraciously. "Water, iced tea?"

"Water would be fine." I followed her into the kitchen. There were dirty glasses left in the sink and crumbs on the countertop.

Elizabeth put some ice cubes in a glass, added tap water, and thrust the glass toward me. "Here. Okay, we've done the social bit. What do you want to know?"

Right to the point. I answered in kind. "Who do you think killed Alex?"

To my surprise, her eyes filled with tears. "I don't know," she whispered.

Her reaction seemed kind of extreme, but

was it Alex's death or something else that was bothering her?

"You'd been friends for a long time, hadn't you?"

She had turned away and was staring out the window over the sink; there was a view of houses, stacked up like cards, with a glimpse of tawny mountains beyond. She didn't speak for a long time, but I had the feeling she had something she wanted to say. I waited.

Finally she turned back to me, and her cheeks were wet with tears. "How would you describe Denis?"

"I don't think I've seen him at his best. Nervous, mostly. Intelligent, focused. Obsessive maybe."

"Pretty close. Sure, he's smart — he's a college professor, isn't he? Me, I've got an associate degree from a two-year college that doesn't even exist anymore. Obsessive? Definitely. He likes everything just so, in its place. He hates anything he can't control. I can't imagine how he manages to teach classrooms full of eager young people who actually have minds of their own."

Hold on — Denis had accused Elizabeth of being compulsively neat. Which one of them was it?

Elizabeth was still rambling on. "We've

been married for fifteen years. I thought there would be kids, but that didn't happen. I hate this place. I hate my job. Do you know how goddamn boring insurance is?"

Was she coming to a point anywhere in here? There was a killer on the loose. "If you're so miserable, why don't you just leave?"

I watched the struggle on her face before she answered in a tight-throated whisper. "Alex."

Oh no. "You mean, you and Alex . . . ?"

She nodded. "Yes. For a couple of years now."

The next question seemed obvious, at least to me. "So why didn't you leave Denis and get together with Alex?"

She shook her head. "He didn't want that. I mean, I think he actually liked Denis, though I guess sleeping with your friend's wife is a pretty funny way of showing it. And they had this investment partnership going, and it would have been complicated to get out of that, and if they bailed out now they'd lose money." She swallowed a sob. "I guess they would have lost money anyway, right?"

There was a growing feeling of dread in the pit of my stomach. "Elizabeth, did Denis know? About you and Alex, I mean?"

She shook her head again, her hair hanging over her face. "I don't think so. I certainly didn't tell him, and I can't see why Alex would — he was happy with the way things were. Maybe Denis had some idea, but he never said anything. I mean, you've been together with somebody this long, you kind of sense things, you know?"

No, I didn't know, but I was willing to take her word for it. I picked my next question carefully. "Is Denis a violent man?"

Elizabeth snorted. "Denis? He's a professor, for God's sake. He has trouble killing a spider in the house. You don't think . . . ?"

I watched as she realized what I was really asking. If her emotions were always this obvious, Denis must have been clued in about the affair with Alex from the start.

"You think Denis killed Alex?" she whispered. "But how? I heard he was found out in the desert. Denis doesn't know squat about anything outside of city limits."

"Did he know where Alex's RV was?"

"Yes. I made him take me out there once, because I wanted to see the place. I thought maybe it would be a safe place for Alex and me to meet, but it was too far out."

What kind of idiot would visit her lover with her husband along? "So Denis knew where it was. He lied to the police about that."

"Is that where . . . ?"

"No. The police have gone over it, and they didn't find any evidence of murder. Did Alex keep the place neat?"

Elizabeth smiled, a small sad smile. "No, it was a mess. I mean, what do you expect, a guy roughing it? I liked it — I mean, Denis is such a nut about keeping things clean. With Alex I felt I could relax."

So Denis was the compulsive one — and Denis would have been the likely candidate to clean up the RV after Cam was gone from it. "Does Denis have any friends? I mean, apart from Alex?" If Alex was his best friend, Denis had pretty poor taste.

"Not really. We live pretty simply. He goes to work, I go to work. We don't see a lot of other people."

"If he had to find someone to help him with something, uh, kind of illegal, who would he ask?"

Elizabeth looked at me blankly. "I don't know. Besides, he never does anything like that. He doesn't even cheat on his income taxes. I mean, he takes every legitimate deduction he can find, but nothing dishonest."

"He keeps good records? He read all the

stuff Alex gave him?"

"Of course."

Another lie of Denis's. "Elizabeth, are you sure you have no idea where Denis would go? Did he say anything the last time you saw him?"

"I told the police everything I knew. When we got back from your place last night, he came in, checked his phone messages, and he left in a hurry — he said there was something he had to clean up. I didn't ask anything, because lately he's been biting my head off at almost anything I say."

That phone message might tell the police something, but it might take a while to track down who the caller was, and I had the feeling there wasn't much time. Matt and possibly some other law enforcement types were at this very moment headed out to question Will Montoya, and they didn't have all the facts.

"Elizabeth, did Denis ever mention a guy named William Montoya?"

"I don't think so. No, wait — I think there was a phone message one day from someone with a name like that. Why?"

"Will was the one who dumped Alex's body in the desert, but he said he didn't kill him. If he knew Denis . . ." I let the thought hang in the air between us. I wondered how long it would take Elizabeth to draw the logical conclusion that her husband was a murderer, and what she would do then.

"Oh God," she whispered. "It's my fault that Alex is dead."

"Nonsense. People have affairs all the time, and that doesn't mean that someone ends up dead. Maybe Denis just snapped. But that's his problem, what with everything else that's been going wrong. I've got to make a call, before somebody else gets hurt." If Denis had gone to "clean up" Will, thinking that the law hadn't figured out Will's role in all this, then Matt could be walking into a real mess that he wasn't prepared for. I had to talk to him. If Will ended up dead before we got his side of the story, then Denis would be the only one talking, and he seemed to be pretty good at spinning the facts. I needed to let Matt know.

Easier said than done. I tried calling his cell, but of course he had no reception out there — I knew that from my own experience. But I knew the desk sergeant at police headquarters, and I was pretty sure she'd have a way to connect me to Matt.

"Mariana? This is Em Dowell. Do you know where you can reach Matt right now?"

"He's out in Pinal County. Why?"

"Listen, I wouldn't ask if it wasn't important, but can you get through to him? There's something he needs to know about what he's walking into out there."

"Uh, let me see what I can do. Can you sit tight a couple of minutes? I'll ask him if he can call you."

"Cell phone reception sucks where he's going. Any way you can patch me through to his car?"

"Maybe. Let me find out."

She put me on hold. I stared blindly into space, imagining worst-case scenarios. Denis with an Uzi, blowing away the entire police force of two counties before fleeing across the Mexican border. Denis slitting Will's throat and then playing dumb and innocent, a role he knew well. Or maybe they were equal partners, and they would both come out with guns blazing. It all sounded absurd, but it was just within the far reaches of possibility. And if there was the slightest chance that somebody could get hurt or killed, then I had to tell someone. I could worry about looking foolish later, when this was all over.

Oh hell, Em — at least admit to yourself what you're thinking. I didn't want Matt to get killed or hurt. I wasn't sure when that feeling, that need to protect him, had happened, but there it was, and there wasn't a bleeping thing I could do about it now except try to warn him about what he was facing. If I could.

"Em?" Mariana's voice interrupted my maudlin fantasies.

"Yes?"

"Hang on, I've got you linked."

"What?" Matt barked abruptly.

I tried to figure out how to condense what I knew into the fewest words. "Matt, I think Denis was in this from the start, including Alex's death. He may have been working with Will all along. He lied to us."

Matt said something that was lost in static.

"Matt? Did you hear me? Denis may have gone to Will's to eliminate the last person who knows what he's done. He's playing us."

"Got it. Gotta go." His end of the line went dead.

I'd done all I could. Except to tell him to take care of himself, because I wanted him to come back in one piece.

Elizabeth was staring at me. "What happens now?"

"I have no idea."

CHAPTER 32

It has been claimed that peridot calms madness, increases wealth, and prevents sudden death.

I'm not very good at waiting. Especially when I can't control the situation.

I went home. I invited Elizabeth to come along, mostly because it seemed cruel to leave her there alone, wondering, but she declined. I didn't press her.

The rest of the gang was assembled at my place, as if they knew there was some sort of showdown coming. I gave them a brief outline of what I'd learned from Elizabeth, and what I had deduced, and the fact that I had tried to warn Matt.

"Em? Lunch." Cam thrust a sandwich in front of me.

Oh, right, food. I chewed without tasting. We'd finally accepted that no business was going to get done today, so Nessa and Allison had closed up the shop and were on hand too, and I noted with a pang that Cam and Allison were sticking to each other like glue, and even Nessa and Frank were sitting pretty close.

"I'm sure it will be fine," Nessa said. I didn't ask what "it" was. I hoped she was right. Maybe everything would be neatly wrapped up with bows on it just in time for the five o'clock news. Or maybe the sheriffs and Matt would still be arguing about whose turf they were on, while Denis and Will in their ignorance cackled about their success in getting away with it all. Which they might yet, the way things were going. Too bad Denis was much smarter than I had thought. He'd fooled me, and I'd written him off as a neurotic professor with money problems. Great judge of character I am.

"So you think it may have been Denis who was the mastermind all along?" Allison asked, her eyes wide.

I nodded. "Maybe. Although I get the feeling that some of the people involved were just improvising. But I did tell Matt not to trust Denis, assuming he finds him. One thing that worries me — if Denis manages to shut Will up, then we'll have only his story on how things happened. And he's already proved he's pretty smart, if he's kept us all in the dark this long. Damn, I hate being taken in like that. I really believed he was a clueless bumbler."

"It's far easier for a smart man to play at being stupid than the other way around. And you had no reason to doubt him," Allison said gently.

"Matt can handle himself, Em," Nessa added.

Her perception startled me. "I don't want anyone else to get hurt."

"Of course you don't," she went on. "Least of all Matt."

Exactly. Nessa could see right through me. I wish I could see through me more often. I had been sucked in by Denis's idea of treating stones. It had seemed harmless enough, and it meant a nice piece of change with little work attached. Who knew that it would lead to uncovering a murder and a kidnapping? Even though I had lived with the Gem Show for years now, I hadn't realized how strongly people felt about sparkly colored things. But I really didn't care about stones, so I hadn't paid attention. If I had, would I have questioned Denis's motives?

Time passed — one hour, then two. We talked, but each conversation petered out quickly. Cam had booted up his beloved laptop and was clicking away at it in a corner. After a while he reported, "I've been watching the local Internet news, but nobody's said anything about arrests or solving a murder. Maybe that's good news?"

"Or maybe Denis and/or Will has killed everyone," I said glumly. "If they'd brought them in, there should at least be a mention."

"Relax, Em," Cam responded. "They're probably arguing about who should do the paperwork."

I stood up, unable to sit still any longer. "I'll walk the dogs — I need the fresh air. You want to come, Cam?"

"Sure."

Fine group we made, with the infectious fidgets. The dogs didn't seem to mind, as long as they got attention. I handed Cam one leash, I took the other, and we each hoisted a dog and went down the stairs.

As we meandered down the block, I said, "You know, Cam, I don't think we've had time to talk since all this whole mess started. You okay with your job?"

"Yeah. I told them I'd start next week. I said I had a few personal matters to take care of. They were cool with that."

"How about finding a place to live?"

"I don't plan to crash with you forever, if that's what you're worried about."

"Hey, I'm happy to have you around, but things could get complicated." I decided to stop beating around the bush. "Are you and Allison going to move in together?"

We walked a few more paces before he answered. "I don't know. We've sort of talked about it, but you know she's old-school Irish Catholic, and she has problems with the idea of 'living in sin,' as she puts it. I didn't know anyone still thought like that, but I have to respect her position. I guess."

"There's one way to fix that, you know."

"You mean get married?"

"Well, that would take care of the 'sin' part. You have a problem with that? Or does she?"

"I've been reluctant to bring it up. I mean, we haven't been together that long, and then there was that whole Ireland mess. I haven't wanted to press."

I stopped to let Fred sniff a particularly interesting post. Gloria sat down to watch him. I turned to Cam. "Cam, you and I don't talk about serious stuff too much, you know? But I'd hate to see you mess up with Allison just because you didn't want to confront things. Life is short, and you never know what's going to happen."

"I know, Em. I know. But if we're being open here, what about you and Matt?"

It was a fair question, even if I didn't like it. "Right now we're taking it one day at a time. We like each other, and I think we're good together. But I also like my life the way it is, and I don't see how we can put our lives together. It's not like you and Allison."

"Are you sure? Is it enough for you to get together now and then, when it happens to fit your schedules? You're not getting any younger, Em. Do you want to be alone in ten, twenty years?"

I stared at him, and then I burst out laughing. "Listen to us. How did we come to this so late? We should have been having these discussions, oh, fifteen years ago." Then I sobered. "Cam, I don't think either one of us is qualified to give romantic advice, but we seem to be doing it anyway, so here it is. Allison loves you, you love Allison. That's a pretty simple equation. Get married, shack up, whatever suits the two of you, and get on with it. There are no guarantees that you'll be happy, but so what? You've got to try."

"I will if you will."

"It's not that simple."

"You just told me it was. You're chicken."

Maybe I was. Maybe I'd fought too long and hard to create the life I had, and I liked it, and I wasn't about to change it for another person. Even one I cared about. And I did care about Matt, but I'd seen my parents' empty marriage and I wasn't convinced I was cut out for marriage or anything like it. And I knew Matt had been burned once by a bad marriage. But, to be honest, I had no idea how he felt about where we were going, and I had never asked. Maybe Cam was right: Matt and I were old enough to know our own minds, and maybe it was time to clear the air.

Assuming he came back.

No, I couldn't think like that. He was a trained and experienced law officer, and he knew what he was doing. Plus he had help with him out there. "We should get back, in case there's some news. But think about what I said, will you?"

"If you'll think about what I said."

"We'll see," I said. Mistress of noncommitment, that was me.

When we arrived back at my place, we ran upstairs to deposit the dogs. There was no news.

CHAPTER 33

Peridot will cause a beam of light to separate into two.

More hours passed. Once darkness had fallen, I couldn't stand being cooped up in my apartment. "I'm going out for some air," I announced.

"You want company?" Cam volunteered.

"No!" I said, more sharply than I intended. "No," I said more softly this time. "I just want a little alone time, okay? I'll be right outside if anything . . . if anybody needs me." *Trying to breathe.*

Before anyone could protest, I slipped out the door, shutting it behind me, and sat at the top of the stairs, looking at the familiar streetscape, dimly lit by the shadowed streetlights. I took a deep breath, savoring the scent of mesquite in the air.

The streets were all but empty, and then less so, as a lone man turned the corner by the shop and headed in my direction. My first thought was that it was a mugger, but then the dark figure resolved itself into Matt.

I was down the stairs in seconds, just in time to throw myself into his arms at the bottom. His arms went around me and we simply stood there, silent. I couldn't think of anything to say, but it didn't matter. He was safe. I found myself patting him, making sure he was in one piece.

He noticed. "Looking for something?"

"Just making sure you're all there. No bullet holes."

"Nope. Everything accounted for."

He wasn't letting go, I noticed. Then he tilted my face up and kissed me. Some centuries later, we finally came up for air. "You were waiting for me?" he asked.

I nodded. "I was worried. I didn't know what you'd find out there. That's why I called you, to make sure you knew what you were walking into."

"It's kind of nice, knowing someone's worried about me. It's been a while."

"It scares me, Matt. Not because it's your job, but because it matters to me. Does that make sense?"

"I think so."

"Okay." I took a deep breath. "So tell me what happened. Just the outline — there are several people upstairs who want the whole story, or as much as you can share."

"First, no casualties. We found Will's house, and Denis was there. And you were right — Denis tried to convince us that Will had kidnapped him. I think there was a good chance he would have killed Will if we hadn't gotten there when we did."

"So you arrested them both? Or somebody did?"

"Yup. The sheriff took them back and split them up and we got their stories, bit by bit. Denis finally caved."

I let out a breath that I hadn't known I was holding. "Thank goodness. So it's over?"

"Looks like it, all but the paperwork. Denis killed Alex."

I swallowed. "That's what I figured." I waited a second before going on. "I talked to his wife, after you left. She said she and Alex had been having an affair. Did Denis know?"

"Wait 'til we get upstairs." He fell silent, but neither of us moved. It felt good to be here in his arms, all worries gone. Maybe independence wasn't all it was cracked up to be. Maybe Matt and I had some things to talk about.

Finally I said, "People are going to send

out a search party for me soon. We'd better go up."

"Can't have that. Let's go fill them in, shall we?"

I turned and headed up the stairs, and he followed. I opened the door, and we were greeted by hearty cheers — and barks. I took inventory: Frank, Nessa, Cam, Allison, and the pups. Yes, everyone was here, apparently waiting to hear whatever Matt had to say.

We made them wait as I scrounged up beer and chips and we all settled ourselves on sofa, chairs and floor. First Matt launched into his summary report.

"Denis killed Alex?" I prompted.

"Looks like it. I don't think Denis meant to kill him — it probably was an accident. But after that Denis kept trying to patch over things and they just kept getting worse."

"Did he tell you how it happened?"

"He found out Alex was sleeping with his wife. They got into a shoving match, sounds like, but Alex hit his head on the counter, and that was that."

This was news to everyone but me. "So it wasn't the gems?" Nessa asked.

"I think the financial problems forced Denis and Alex together more than usual recently, and Denis must have noticed something going on with Alex and his wife."

"Or maybe he knew all along and was afraid to say anything. His wife hasn't been happy with him for a long time," I added.

"When Denis told us that he had shipped her out of town for her own safety, he was lying. She'd planned the trip for a while, and he wasn't sure she was coming back."

"But she came back when she learned that Alex was dead?"

"She did. You'll have to ask her why."

Cam broke in. "When did Alex die?"

"The night before you met Denis at Alex's house. Denis went there the next morning to see if there was anything incriminating, and you surprised him. He knew you were coming, but he didn't know when. So when you conveniently assumed he was Alex, he thought he'd just shuttle you out to the RV, where he knew you couldn't communicate with anyone, and then try to figure out the next step. In the end he asked Will to take care of things."

"He'd been working with Will all along?"

Matt nodded. "Yes, both he and Alex."

"And Denis asked Will to dump Alex's body. But why was Will helping Denis at all?"

"Denis promised him a cut of the proceeds

from the sale of the stones, after he'd settled his debts. The original deal was with Will, and he laid out some money up front. But then Alex found a better deal and wanted to cut Will out."

"He probably figured he'd never see his money unless he helped Denis out." At Matt's look, I added, "I'll explain later. Anyway, Will couldn't bring himself to kill Cam, so he settled for scrambling his brains." I was glad that Beverly had been right. It would be hard to live with the knowledge that your brother was a cold-blooded murderer. Stupid was easier.

Matt turned to Cam. "Denis said Alex came by to drop off the new gem-sale contract while Elizabeth was at work, and that's when he confronted him about the affair. He'd had his suspicions for a while, but he didn't want a messy argument, and he wasn't sure how to get out of the business relationship."

I pictured the gleaming kitchen, with its trendy granite countertops. How well did granite hold blood evidence? "But how did he get rid of the body so fast? And what about Alex's car?"

"Denis called Will in a panic and asked him to meet him at Alex's house. Then he drove Alex's car back there and waited for

Will. When he showed up, he told Will to get rid of the body where nobody would find it. And Will did. It came pretty close to working. If I hadn't pushed the ME, he probably wouldn't have looked at the body for months. And then Denis went home and cleaned up. The police never did examine Denis's house, at least not as a crime scene."

"Do they need any evidence? Or is Denis's confession enough?"

"That's up to the lawyers. They'll go over his place more carefully now anyway," Matt said.

I mulled that over for a moment. "Denis showed up at my studio the next day. Why?"

"He needed to finish the stones to get the money from the gem sale, to pay off the loans — and Will."

"Did Denis clean up the RV too? I don't think Will could have managed that."

"Yes."

"Is Will okay? And what's he told you?"

"Denis was going to try and lay the murder and the kidnapping on him, and then fake his own kidnapping and kill Will to make it look convincing. When he heard that, Will was happy to tell us everything he knew."

We all digested this for a few moments. Finally I said, "I feel stupid, letting Denis fool me the way he did."

"You weren't the only one he fooled. You did see through him when it mattered. That call of yours put us on the alert, or else we might have fallen for Denis's story. And he hadn't worked up the courage to kill Will, so we have his story too. I don't think Denis is really a killer at heart — he just got caught up in a mess."

"What happens to the gem find? Who ends up with that?" Frank asked. Trust Frank to worry about that detail.

"We'd have to check the articles of incorporation and also see if Alex left a will. I'd guess Elizabeth. Why does it matter?"

"She might be able to follow up on the technique, sell the stones, if she's interested."

With all the details now dissected and discussed, none of us had much else to say. We sat quietly, exhausted by all that had happened. It had been a hell of a week, but at least everyone had emerged more or less intact. I looked around me: at Matt, tired but satisfied; at Cam and Allison, their hands entwined; at Frank and Nessa, sitting companionably side by side on the couch. Safe home, every one.

At last, Matt stood up. "I should be going. It's been a long day."

"Wait, Matt," I said. He turned toward me. I looked around the room at the happy couples. "It's getting kind of crowded here."

"It is," he agreed amiably.

Damn the man, he was going to make me come out and say it. "Can we go to your place?"

"I'd like that," he replied, watching my face.

"I would too." I made a point of not meeting anyone's eye as I gathered up a few things. At the door where Matt waited, I turned to the group. "Will somebody walk Fred and Gloria, please? Allison, Nessa — you'll be in tomorrow?"

Nessa smiled. "Of course, dear."

Maybe now life would get back to normal, as soon as the Gem Show ended in a couple of days. Although normal might not be what it had been.

"See you in the morning." Before anyone could say anything else, I turned and fled with Matt.

At the foot of the stairs I stopped, turned to him, and said, "Matt, I promise I won't run out on you in the middle of the night this time. I think . . ." I couldn't finish, because I didn't know what I was trying to say.

He put his arms around me. "I know. We'll

worry about that later."

At least there would be a later. I leaned against him, and enjoyed the moment before saying, "Matt, there's a lot we haven't talked about — about us, I mean."

"I know."

"About where we're going."

"Yes?"

He really was going to let me do all the work here. *Damn you, Cam — why did I let you push me into this?* "I think maybe we need to." I held my breath waiting for his answer.

"Whenever you're ready, Em."

I relaxed into his arms. "Maybe tomorrow, after . . ."

Smart man, Matt — I didn't need to explain.

SOURCES

If you want to know more:

Colored stones have fascinated people since their earliest discovery, and gems have been assigned various mystical properties from the beginning. Some of the more entertaining reference books were written in the nineteenth century, and include:

Antique Gems: Their Origin, Uses, and Value, C. W. King, 1866.

The Curious Lore of Precious Stones, George Frederick Kunz, 1915 (a classic, and still in print).

Gems, Helen Bartlett Bridgman, 1916.

A Text-Book of Precious Stones for Jewelers and the Gem-Loving Public, Frank B. Wade, 1918.

Other more recent writers such as Deanna J. Conway in *Crystal Enchantments* (1999) have perpetuated the fascination with stones, and there are many websites that provide additional information.

The employees of Thorndike Press hope you have enjoyed this Large Print book. All our Thorndike, Wheeler, and Kennebec Large Print titles are designed for easy reading, and all our books are made to last. Other Thorndike Press Large Print books are available at your library, through selected bookstores, or directly from us.

For information about titles, please call:
 (800) 223-1244

or visit our Web site at:
 http://gale.cengage.com/thorndike

To share your comments, please write:
 Publisher
 Thorndike Press
 295 Kennedy Memorial Drive
 Waterville, ME 04901